澄清聲明

親愛的讀者：

倍斯特出版事業有限公司鄭重聲明，大陸<u>中國紡織出版社</u>與本社無業務往來。

近來發現本社之公司Logo，出現於<u>中國紡織出版社</u>之貝斯特英語系列書籍，該出版社自 2012年11月1日起之所有出版品與本社並無任何關係；鑑於此事件，懷疑有人利用本社之商業信譽，藉此誤導大眾，本社予以高度關注。特此聲明，以正視聽。

倍斯特出版事業有限公司 敬啟

跟著偶像劇學英語會話

Let's Talk in Love

番外篇

伍羚芝◎中文寫作
倍斯特編輯部◎著

愛像是氧氣，
把我們輕輕托起，
是我們全部的需要！
<<紅磨坊>>

心靈不在它生活的地方，
但在它所愛的地方。
在所愛的地方
用英文慢慢地品嚐愛情吧！

愛情裡難免會 *suspicious*...
但只要能一起就會 *satisfy*.....
沒了愛情宛如失去 *gravity*....
希望挽著你手裡拿著 *bouquet*...

70個
愛情偶像劇情境
陪你用英文走過
愛情的憂傷與甜蜜。

作者序
Preface

感謝所有支持前作《跟著偶像劇的腳步學生活英語會話》與購買本書的讀者，是你們讓筆者對美好愛情的想望得以幻化成鉛字，透過文字交織出一幕幕你我都曾經歷過或期望過的情路百態。其中每位性格各異、或受人喜愛、或令人恨的牙癢癢的男女主角也因此有了再度活躍於紙上偶像劇場的機會。

本書創作方向與前作一致，可說是擁有相同血脈卻又各自獨立的雙胞胎姊妹。兩書相同之處在於理念，皆希望讀者在投入欣賞每場動人戀愛情節的同時，能夠學到生活化且實用的英語會話及單字。兩書不同之處則在於偶像劇本的編寫與人物關係，不但加入了全新的出場人物，角色間所碰撞出的火花更是一幕比一幕精彩！最重要的莫過於，還能學到與前作毫不重複的英文單字與會話。

誠心邀請你一起來閱讀浪漫的、有趣的、揪心的紙上偶像劇，一起來代入自己在情路上的點滴經歷隨之又哭又笑吧！讓我們學會如何用英語表達想告訴對方的委屈、不安、感動和思念後，一起成長。

伍羚芝

Vivianna Wu

編者序

你曾隨著偶像劇的劇情聲淚俱下久久不能自己嗎？或是跟著偶像劇的景點四處旅行呢？或許你已經發現，偶像劇的元素滲透生活，無處不在；沒有國界之別，不受語言侷限。

而那如夢似幻的場景，似曾相識的情節，為英語會話提供了最實用、最豐富的情境。因此倍斯特編輯部繼《跟著偶像劇的腳步學生活英語會話》後，另籌備《跟著偶像劇番外篇學英文會話》，以回應讀者期待與需求。

本書收錄 70 個最實用的「情境對話」，讓你在熟悉的場景與對白中，自然地吸收單字與文法；每單元並附「30 秒對話教室」，讓你掌握說話訣竅，不吃螺絲不漏氣，放感情講台詞，真功夫當主角。

共同的感動打破語言的藩籬，語言學習的普及強化了這份感動。無論是不是偶像，不管身在劇裡劇外，我們每天努力生活，努力讓自己變得更好；就算再坎坷難行，再曲折糾結，我們用心寫自己的劇本，做自己的主角。

倍斯特編輯部

命運般的邂逅

好事必定多磨

Part 3

情路上的阻礙

兩人世界BYE BYE

讓夢想的種子萌芽

命運般的邂逅

情境 1 這是誰的筆記本？

會話訓練班

Louis 結束了大學裡上午的課程，準備到學校餐廳吃午餐。就在此時他在校舍外的草皮上發現了一本小巧的筆記本，他左看右看，並沒有發現這本筆記本的主人，於是他拿出手機撥打了寫在筆記本封面的電話……

After finishing the morning course, Louis goes to school's **cafeteria**. In the meantime, he finds a natty **notebook** outside the greensward of the dorm. He looks around and doesn't find notebook's **owner**. Thus, he dials the phone numbers, written on the **cover** of the notebook.

Louis Hello, is this Eliza Jones? This is Louis Thompson, junior of Program Design Department.

Eliza This is Eliza. What can I do for you?

Louis Did you lose a brown notebook with golden lace?

Eliza Oh yes, my notebook! I couldn't find it during the **Psychology** course.

Louis I saw there are your name and number in the notebook, so I boldly called over; no offence!

喂，妳好。請問是 Eliza Jones 嗎？我是程式設計系三年級的 Louis Thompson.

是的，我是。請問有何貴幹？

請問妳是否有遺失一本棕色外皮和金色花邊的筆記本？

喔對，我的筆記本！剛剛上心理學課時就一直找不到。

我看到筆記本上寫有妳的名字和電話，就冒昧打了過來，真是不好意思！

Eliza That is all right, thank you for your **help**, Louis! In addition to the class' notes, there are my **schedule** and the **outlines** of the final report. I just worried about what if I couldn't find it?

沒關係的，真是謝謝你的幫忙，Louis！裡面除了上課的筆記之外，還有我的行事曆和期末報告的大綱，我正在擔心如果找不到該怎麼辦？

Louis Fortunately, you wrote your **contact details** you on your notebook's cover. I shall make an appointment with you to return your notebook.

還好妳在筆記本封面寫上連絡方式，我跟妳約個方便的時間將筆記本還給妳吧。

Eliza I was just off the class, and nothing has to deal with. I can come over to you right away.

我剛下課，待會也沒事，可以馬上過去找你。

Louis I'm going to the cafeteria now, so let's meet there. You can look for a handsome guy wearing the blue-plaid shirt at the entrance. Even without seeing the good-looking boy you want, you can still **identify** the notebook from the one I hold.

我現在正好要去學校餐廳吃飯，就約在那裏見吧。妳可以在入口處尋找一位穿藍格子襯衫的帥哥，就算沒看到妳所想的帥哥，也可以認我手中的筆記本。

Eliza It seems not hard to find, see you later, Louis.

那應該不難找，待會見囉，Louis。

必會單字一手抓

❶ cafeteria n. 學生餐廳

The food of our cafeteria is cheap and delicious.

我們學校的學生餐廳便宜又好吃。

❷ notebook n. 筆記本 字彙連結站 jotter

This notebook is full of English vocabularies.

這本筆記本寫滿了英文單字。

❸ Psychology n. 心理學

Psychology is a very interesting subject.

心理學是一門有趣的學問。

❹ owner n. 物主、所有人

The owner of the house decides to sell it cheaply.

這棟房子的所有者決定將它便宜售出。

❺ cover n. 封面

The fashion magazine's cover girl of this issue is a hot model.

這期時尚雜誌的封面女郎是一位當紅的女模特兒。

❻ help v. 幫忙

I will do all what I can to help you.

我會竭盡所能去幫你。

❼ schedule n. 行事曆 字彙連結站 to-do list 要做的事的清單

She has a full schedule with study, work, and family responsibilities.

她的日程表排滿了學習，工作，和家庭的責任。

❽ outline n. 大綱

It took me one week to think the outlines of the final report.

光是思考期末報告的大綱就花了我一個禮拜的時間。

❾ contact details **n.** 聯絡方式

Please write down with contact details in this grid.

請在這張表上寫下你的聯絡方式。

❿ identify **v.** 辨認 字彙連結站 recognize

She identified him as the person who found her purse.

她認出他就是那位撿到她的錢包的人。

30 秒會話教室

在電話中報上自己的名字要用 This is Louis Thompson speaking. 或是 Louis Thompson speaking. 而不是像日常對話中使用 I'm Louis Thompson. 的說法

情境2 沒關係，讓我來

會話訓練班

Austine 到大學圖書館裡借書，在層層書架之間，他看到一位嬌小的女生努力伸手想拿取放在上層的書，卻怎麼也搆不到。於是他走了上前小聲地說……

Austine bought some books in the university **library**. He saw a small cutie trying to get the book on the top of the **bookshelf**, but couldn't **reach** it. So he stepped forward and **whispered**...

Austine	May I give you a **hand**?	請問妳需要幫忙嗎？
Jocelyn	Oh, thank you. Could you please help me to get that **German dictionary** on the top?	喔，謝謝。可以請你幫我拿放在最上層的那一本德文字典嗎？
Austine	No problem. Is that the dark brown one?	沒問題。是這一本深褐色的嗎？
Jocelyn	No. It is the third one counted from the dark brown book's left side.	不是。是從那一本左邊數來的第三本。
Austine	Oh, the **thicker** one! Here you are.	喔，是比較厚的這一本啊！來，給妳。
Jocelyn	Thank you, I haven't asked your name yet.	謝謝你，我還沒有請問你的大名。

Austine	I am Austine Newman; a senior in the **History** department. And you?	我是歷史系四年級的 Austine Newman，妳呢？
Jocelyn	I am Jocelyn Wagner in the German department. I am about to do the report of German **history**, could you please give me some **advice**?	我是德文系的 Jocelyn Wagner。我正好要做一份與德國歷史有關的報告，不知道你能不能給我一些建議呢？
Austine	I would love to, but we can't speak loudly in the library. We had better go to other places to discuss.	我非常樂意，不過在圖書館內無法大聲交談，我們還是另外找個地方討論吧。
Jocelyn	Then I go to the counter to proceed borrowing this dictionary, see you outsides later.	那我先到櫃檯去辦理這本字典的借書手續，我們待會外面見。

必會單字一手抓

❶ **hand** n. 手

Could you give me a hand?

你可以幫我一個忙嗎？

❷ **library** n. 圖書館

Everyone could borrow five books from the library.

每個人可以從這圖書館借五本書。

❸ bookshelf **n.** 書架

Remember to put the books back to the bookshelf.

看完書記得把書放回書架上。

❹ reach **v.** 觸及

Do not put the dangerous stuff up to where the children can reach.

不要把危險物品放在孩童伸手可及的地方。

❺ whisper **v.** 低語

Daisy and Lily whisper to each other during the class.

Daisy 和 Lily 在上課中互相低語交談。

❻ German **adj.** 德語的 **n.** 德語

When I find out I could understand the German I hear accidentally, it's so wonderful! -Mark Twain

當我發現我偶然聽到的德文是我聽得懂的，這是件多開心的事啊！——馬克・吐溫

❼ dictionary **n.** 字典

Please look up the dictionary while you have the words that you don't know.

有不會的單字請查字典。

❽ thick..**adj.** 厚

He wore a glasses with the thick rim.

他戴了一副粗框眼鏡。

❾ history **n.** 歷史

He has a great interest in Chinese history.

他對中國歷史非常有興趣。

❿ advice **n.** 建議

He took his teacher's advice to join the singing contest on TV.

他接受他老師的建議去參加電視歌唱比賽。

30 秒會話教室

問對方是否需要幫忙可說 May I give you a hand? 若是等不到別人幫忙，可以主動出聲詢問 Can you give me a hand? 或是 Can you help me, please? 若想進一步協助拜託您的人，則可進一步詢問 Sure. What do you need?

名人怎麼說？

We're all a little weird. And life is a little weird. And when we find someone whose weirdness is compatible with ours, we join up with them and fall into mutually satisfying weirdness—and call it love—true love. —Robert Fulghum

我們都有點怪怪的。而生命也是有點怪。當我們找到一些人而他們奇怪的地方剛好跟我們一樣，我們跟他們在一起也在彼此相同的地方得到滿足—我們稱之為愛—真愛。—作家

My feelings will not be repressed. You must allow me to tell you how ardently I admire and love you.—Jane Austen

我的心意沒辦法再壓抑了。你一定要讓我告訴你我多麼熱切地欣賞你與愛你。
—珍・奧斯汀

情境 3 鬼屋試膽大會

會話訓練班

Louis 邀 Eliza 一起去參加由學生會舉辦的一年一度鬼屋試膽大會。他們在被當成鬼屋舞台的廢棄校舍外面排隊，等著兩人一組進入鬼屋探險。鬼屋內不時傳出探險者的一陣陣尖叫聲，讓周遭瀰漫著一股詭異的氣氛……

Louis invites Eliza to join the **annual haunted** house guts-testing conference held by the student **association** together. They line up outsides the **abandoned** school dorm where was used as a haunted house' stage, and wait for entering the haunted room to **explore** as the double teams. Screams from the exploreres are heard from time to time, which makes the surroundings filled with a **weird** atmosphere.

Louis	It's our turn, let's go! Lady first.	輪到我們了，走吧！女士優先。
Eliza	No, it is so scary, you go first.	不要，好可怕，你先走。
Louis	Don't be nervous! This was just furnished by the members of the student association.	別緊張啦！這些都是學生會的成員佈置出來的。
Eliza	But this is held in the old and abandoned school dorm; don't you feel that it is very weird?	可是辦在廢棄的舊校舍裡，你不覺得氣氛很詭異嗎？

Louis	You watch too many **horror movies**! There was none of any murders happened in our school.	妳恐怖片看太多了啦！我們學校裡又沒有發生過命案。
Eliza	Oh my god! Something is touching my hips!	我的天啊！有東西在摸我的屁股！
Louis	Don't be afraid! Hold my hands, I will take you all the way to the **exit**.	不要怕！牽著我的手，我帶妳一路跑向出口。
Eliza	Wait! It's my cellphone's vibrating! Sorry to bother you in a non-existing scare.	等等，原來是我的手機在震動啦，不好意思虛驚一場。
Louis	I have told you there is no ghost at all! But if you are **frightened**, you could still hold my hands, I will protect you.	我早就跟妳說這裡根本就沒有鬼吧！不過妳害怕的話還是可以牽著我，我會保護妳的。
Eliza	Thank you, you are so nice.	謝謝你，你真好。

必會單字一手抓

❶ association **n.** 協會、社團

Who is eligible to apply for membership of the association?

誰有資格申請參加這個協會？

❷ annual **adj.** 一年一次的
We have held the annual class reunion for over 30 years.
我們已經舉辦每年一次的同學會超過三十年了。

❸ haunted **adj.** 鬧鬼的
No one dares to go to that haunted house in town.
鎮上那棟鬧鬼的房子沒人敢去。

❹ abandon **v.** 遺棄
She didn't want to abandon her toys she played in her childhood.
她不想遺棄她童年的玩具。

❺ explore **v.** 探索
We must explore all the possibilities.
我們必須探索出所有的可能性。

❻ scream **v.** 尖叫聲
If you don't leave ASAP, I will scream!
你不馬上離開，我就要喊了！

❼ weird **adj.** 神秘的、怪誕的
There is a mysterious packet in front of our house gate.
我家大門口放著一個神祕的包裹。

❽ horror movies 恐怖片
We should not let our children watch horror movies.
我們不該讓小孩在睡前看恐怖片。

❾ exit **n.** 出口
We have to know where the emergency exit is.
我們必須要知道緊急出口在哪裡。

❿ frightened **adj.** 害怕 字彙連結站 fear、scared、frightened

She is frightened that her ex-boyfriend will know where she lives now.

她害怕她的前男友知道她現在住在哪裡。

30 秒會話教室

在日常生活中經常會遇到需要表達紳士風範的時候，這時男士可以說 Lady first. 讓女士優先，或是以 After you. 表達您先請、我隨後跟上的君子風度。

關鍵字搜尋

鬼~~~屋~~~hauted house，光聽就會頭皮發麻了。以下是一個有趣的加菲貓Garfield遊戲，讓你在鬼屋裡尋寶。遊戲裡只要讓加菲貓嚇破膽就輸囉！

加菲貓的任務：在鬼屋找到七種甜甜圈Donut和瑪芬

assorted Donuts	綜合甜甜圈
Chocolate Covered Donuts	巧克力甜甜圈
Sour Cream Donuts	酸奶油甜甜圈
Mini Powdered Suger Donuts	迷你糖粉甜甜圈
Mini Cinnamon Donuts	迷你肉桂甜甜圈
Blueberry Muffins	藍莓英式瑪芬
Chcolate Chips Muffins	巧克力碎英式瑪芬

快來玩玩看吧！

http://www.searchamateur.com/Play-Free-Online-Games/Garfield-Scary-Scavenger-Hunt.htm

情境 4 原來你也喜歡同一支球隊

會話訓練班

Brian 買了這個周末的籃球比賽門票，準備到球場去看他最喜歡的籃隊比賽。比賽到了就快分出勝負的時候，當他正要為喜愛的球隊加油時，身後不時傳來比他更大聲的女性加油聲……

Brain buys the basketball game **ticket** on this **weekend**, and gets ready to the **basketball** court to watch his **favorite team** in the campaign. While the winner and the lost comes out to know sooner or later in the campaign, and Brian is about to cheer for his favorite team, the louder the women's **cheers** goes spread out from his back.

Phoebe	Watch out! He is going to shoot! Hurry up to block him! Yeah! Now pass the shooting guard quickly....Mm, excuse me, do I speak too loudly?	小心！他要投籃了！快點蓋他火鍋！耶！現在快點傳球給得分後衛……嗯，不好意思，請問我太大聲了嗎？
Brian	Yes, a little bit.	是有一點。
Phoebe	Excuse me, I'm too **excited** because this campaign would turn out which team could **win** the **final championship**. I will keep my voice low.	對不起，我太激動了，因為這場比賽將會決定哪一隊可以獲得總冠軍，我會小聲一點的。

Brian	That's OK; it's quite charming actually. I've never met a girl who likes basketball, especially likes the same team as I do.	沒關係，其實這樣挺迷人的。我從來沒有遇過喜歡籃球的女孩子，尤其是跟我喜歡同一隊。
Phoebe	Your **favorite** team is also Los Angeles Lakers? Wow, that's a coincidence.	你也喜歡洛杉磯湖人隊（Los Angeles Lakers）嗎？喔，那真是太巧了。
Brian	Yeah, though their opponent Boston Celtics is also great.	是啊，雖然對手波士頓塞爾提克隊（Boston Celtics）也不錯。
Phoebe	Wait, you look! The three-point shot shoots in....Yeah! We win the annually Final Championship!	等等，你看！三分球（threepoint shot）進了……耶！我們贏得年度總冠軍了！
Brian	It's a pity that I only eyed on talking to you, and didn't watch the excellent shooting picture.	可惜我顧著跟妳說話，沒看到精采的進球畫面。
Phoebe	Let's go to the nearby sport bar to watch the replay, and drink a bear to **celebrate** in passing!	我們到附近的運動酒吧裡去看重播，順便喝杯啤酒慶功吧！
Brian	OK! Let's go. Treat on me.	好啊！我們走。我請客。

必會單字一手抓

❶ weekend n. 周末
He insists on spending the weekend with me.
他硬是要跟我過周末。

❷ basketball n. 籃球
He looks so gorgeous when he plays basketball.
他打籃球的時候好帥！

❸ final n. 決賽
They were defeated by Korea team at the final.
他們在決賽中輸給了韓國隊。

❹ ticket n. 門票
Excuse me, how much does it cost to have the entrance ticket?
請問一下，入場門票多少錢？

❺ favorite adj. 特別喜愛的
Grapes are my favorite fruit.
葡萄是我最喜歡的水果。

❻ win v. 贏
We'll try to win this competition.
我們會設法贏得這場比賽。

❼ champion n. 冠軍
He wants to be the Olympic champion of weight-lifting.
他希望能成為奧運的舉重的冠軍。

❽ excite v. 興奮；激動
Don't be too excited, Keep calm.
不要太興奮，冷靜一點！

❾ celebrate v. 慶祝
They celebrated their victory cheerily.
他們興高采烈地慶祝勝利。

❿ cheer v. 歡呼、喝采
Everyone cheered when the national holiday firework show started.
當國慶煙火秀開始時，人群發出了熱烈的歡呼聲。

30 秒會話教室

描述激動的情緒時可以用 excited + about + V-ing 或是 excited + to-v 的形式。例如：我聽到這個消息時非常興奮。
I'm very excited about learning this news. 或者 I'm very excited to learn this news.

情境 5 誰來救救我！？

會話訓練班

精心打扮過的 Victoria 準備前往餐廳與朋友聚會，在熙來攘往的大街上卻遇到一位陌生男子過來搭訕，對方的態度死纏爛打讓她無法脫身……

Victoria **dresses up** to go to a **restaurant** to meet her friends. On the big **street** of **hustle and bustle**, a male **stranger** comes over and starts a conversation. The stranger **harasses** her repeatedly and makes her hard to get rid of...

Stranger	Hey! Girl, you are so gorgeous, do you want to drink a cup of coffee with me?	嗨！女孩，妳好漂亮，要不要跟我去喝杯咖啡？
Victoria	Sorry, I'm really in a rush.	不好意思，我真的在趕時間。
Stranger	Just making a new friend, do you have a boyfriend now?	交個朋友又沒關係，妳現在有男朋友嗎？
Victoria	I	我……
Harvey	Dear, I have been waiting for you for a while in the front. Are you okay? Does that guy harass you?	親愛的，我在前面等妳好久了。妳沒事吧？妳被這個人騷擾了嗎？

Stranger	N....no, I got to go! Sorry!	沒……沒有，我先閃了！抱歉！
Victoria	Thanks for the help, I didn't know what should I do. May I have your name, please?	謝謝你救了我，我正不知該如何是好呢。請問先生的尊姓大名是？
Harvey	I am Harvey Ross. Wait, that man is still looking around far at the distance! Where are you going? Let me walk with you for a while.	我叫 Harvey Ross。等等，那個人還在遠處觀望呢！妳要去哪裡，我先陪妳走一段路吧。
Victoria	That is so great, I will go to the restaurant to have a lunch with my friends three blocks away. If you don't mind, please join us to have lunch!	那真是太好了，我要到三街區外的餐廳跟朋友聚餐。不嫌棄的話請跟我們一起吃頓午餐吧！
Harvey	If your friends don't **mind**, we could share this **experience** with them, instead.	如果妳的朋友不介意的話，我們倒是可以把這段經驗分享給她們聽。

必會單字一手抓

❶ dress up 打扮

She dressed up for the prom.

她為了畢業舞會盛裝打扮。

❷ restaurant n. 餐廳
The French restaurant is recruiting the waiters now.
這間法國餐廳正在招募外場服務生。

❸ hustle and bustle 熙熙攘攘
I like the hustle and bustle of the night market.
我喜歡夜市裡熙來攘往的景象。

❹ street n. 街道
Both sides of the street to the station are planted full of trees.
通往車站的街道兩旁種滿了路樹。

❺ stranger n. 陌生人
Don't talk with strangers especially in the complicated big city.
不要跟陌生人講話尤其是在人心複雜的大都市。

❻ conversation n. 談話
He tried to make conversation with the stunning girl.
他試著和這位大美人聊天。

❼ harass v. 騷擾
Two women claimed that they had been sexually harassed by a male manager.
兩位女性聲稱曾被男性主管性騷擾過。

❽ experience n. 經驗
Studying abroad could learn many valuable experiences.
出國留學可以學到寶貴的經驗。

❾ mind v. 介意
I don't mind what you order, really.
你們點什麼吃我都不介意，真的。

30 秒會話教室

在生活中我們總是會顧慮他人的想法，因此在行動前可以先徵詢對方是否介意某事，如 Do you mind if I close the window? 和 Would you mind closing the window? 你介意我把窗戶關上嗎？

關鍵字搜尋

搭訕是一種藝術，如何有禮貌但又帶一點侵略性才是搭訕的要領。以下分享一些經典有趣的搭訕句子，有遇到心儀的女士男士可以大膽用喔！

Can I buy you a drink?〈我可以請你喝一杯嗎？〉→這句在酒吧餐廳可以用喔！

You're so beautiful that you made me forget my pickup line.〈妳好美，妳讓我忘了怎麼搭訕。〉→真的忘了嗎？

Did it hurt when you fell from heaven?〈你從天堂掉到人間痛不痛呀？〉→寶貝你是美若天仙的天使。

Somebody better call God, because he is missing an angel.〈有人最好打電話給上帝，因為他掉了一個天使。〉→又是天使！！

Do you have a map?〈你有地圖嗎？〉→因為我在你眼裡迷路了。

Can I have directions?〈你知道怎麼走嗎？〉→怎麼去你的心裡。

Are your legs tired?〈你腳不酸嗎？〉→因為你一直在我心裡跑上跑下。

情境 6 拾金不昧

會話訓練班

Fiona 在上班途中的電車上撿到一個錢包，裡面除了現金、信用卡之外，還有許多證件。她覺得失主一定會感到很不方便，於是立刻送交最近的警察局……
Fiona finds a purse on her way to work in the train, with some **cash**, credit cards and some credentials. She thinks that the owner must be very **inconvenient**. Therefore, she **delivers** it to the nearest **police** station.

Fiona	Hi, I am Fiona Price, I got this purse in the train. I would like to put on record.	你好，我叫 Fiona Price，我在電車上撿到這個錢包，我想要備案。
Police officer	Okay. Could you please **describe** how you found the purse?	好的。可以簡述一下妳撿到錢包的經過嗎？
Fiona	Hmmmm I took the train to work from Banqiao to Taipei at 7:50. When I just got in the train, I saw the purse under the seat.	嗯……我像平常一樣從板橋搭 7:50 分的電車要到台北上班。一上車就看到這個錢包在某個坐位底下。
Police officer	Did you open the purse to check inside?	請問妳有打開錢包看過裡面嗎？

Fiona	I just took a **glance**, and I didn't move anything in the purse. Because of that, I was late for work.	我只打開看了一眼，甚麼也沒動就直接交過來了。我甚至已經上班遲到了。
Police officer	Got it. We will use the **identity card** in the purse to contact the owner. Please leave your information.	瞭解。我們馬上用錢包裡面的身份證聯絡看看失主，請在這裡留下妳的基本資料。
Fiona	OK.	好的。
Police officer	Miss, We have connected with the owner. He is on the phone right now, and he wants to talk to you.	小姐，我們已經連絡上失主了，他正在電話線上，想親自跟妳說幾句話。
Derek	Hello Miss Price, this is Derek Murray. I just heard from the police officer that you found my purse and was late for work. I do appreciate! Please take out a business card from my purse. If there's anything, I can be use of, please let me know.	小姐妳好，我是 Derek Murray，聽警察先生說妳撿到了我的錢包，還為此上班遲到，真是太感謝妳了！請妳拿一張我錢包裡的名片，如果有任何我可以為你做的，請讓我知道。

Fiona You really don't have to do this. But if you **insist**, maybe you can call my boss You just **prove** the **reason** why I was late.

其實不用這麼客氣，但如果你堅持的話，或許今天你就會接到我老闆的電話，要你證明我今天遲到這麼久的原因。

必會單字一手抓

❶ cash **n.** 現金

I didn't have any cash today, could I use the credit card to check?

我今天身上沒帶現金，可以用信用卡結帳嗎？

❷ identity card **n.** 身分證

The police asked him to show his identity card.

員警請他出示他的身分證。

❸ inconvenient **adj.** 不方便的

I am inconvenient to meet you today.

我今天不方便跟妳見面。

❹ police **n.** 警察

We need to call the police when the car accidence happens on the roads.

在路上發生車禍必須通知警方。

❺ describe **v.** 描述

The little girl describes her dream last night in detail.

小女孩詳細地描述了自己昨晚所做的夢。

❻ glance **v.** 一瞥
He glanced at the audience down the stage, and found out all his family came to cheer him up for his singing contest.
他瞥了一眼台下的觀眾，發現全家人都來為他的歌唱比賽加油。

❼ insist **v.** 堅持
My grandmother insisted me on keeping this red envelope.
祖母堅持要我收下這個紅包。

❽ prove **v.** 證明
Can you prove that gravity works on earth?
你能證明地球有地心引力嗎？

❾ reason **n.** 原因
The reason why she was late for school must be her staying up to read novels last night.
她上課遲到的原因一定是因為前一晚又熬夜看小說了。

❿ deliver **v.** 送交
Her gifts from her boyfriend will be delivered on Saturday.
她男朋友寄給她的禮物會在星期六寄到。

30 秒會話教室

在日常生活中我們可能會遇到有人堅持請客、主人熱情留你吃飯等等，無法推託對方的好意與熱情的狀況，例如 A: It's my treat today. 今天我請客。R:Well, if you insist. 嗯，如果你堅持的話。在表達「恭敬不如從命」的感覺時非常好用。

情境 7 小姐，請拿出妳的駕照

會話訓練班

剛考取駕照的 Irene 興奮地開著剛買的新車上路。順暢地在高速公路上行駛的她，後方卻突然出現一輛警車示意她靠邊停，於是她只好緩緩減速，將車停在路邊……

Irene **drives** the new car excitedly after she got the driver's license. She is driving smoothly on the **highway**. Suddenly, there is a **patrol** car behind her, and the policeman signals her to **pull over**. She slows down, and pulled the car over by the roadside.

Fred	Good afternoon, Miss. I am Fred Morrison, could you please **roll** the window down?	午安，小姐。我是 Fred Morrison，可以請妳搖下車窗嗎？
Irene	Good afternoon, police officer. Did I drive **against** traffic regulations?	午安，Morrison 警官。請問我違規了嗎？
Fred	You didn't **turn off** your **headlights**.	妳的大燈沒有關。
Irene	Oh, sorry, I will turn it off right now.	喔，抱歉，我馬上關。
Fred	Could I see your driver's license?	可以看一下妳的駕照嗎？
Irene	Did I get a traffic ticket for not turning off the headlights?	請問大燈沒有關也會被開罰單嗎？

Fred	Actually, you did not only keep your headlights on but also didn't use the **turn signals** when you switch to another lane. It is dangerous.	其實妳不只大燈沒有關，一路上切換車道也都沒有打方向燈，這樣很危險。
Irene	I just had the driver's license recently. Could you please let me off the hook. I will be watchful from now on.	我才剛考到駕照還不熟悉，能不能請你放我一馬，我從現在開始一定會注意的。
Fred	I didn't **intend** to give you a ticket originally. I just wanted to make sure of your name and age.	我本來就沒有打算開妳罰單，只是想看一下妳的全名和年紀。
Irene	God! I'm all at sixes and sevens!	天啊！你害我心裡七上八下的！

必會單字一手抓

❶ highway **n.** 高速公路

The ambulance was stuck on the highway and it couldn't get moved.

救護車塞在高速公路上動彈不得。

❷ drive v. 駕駛
My dad drives me to school every morning.
爸爸每天清晨開車送我上學。

❸ patrol v. 巡邏
The police have to patrol every day.
警察每天都要四處巡邏。

❹ pull over 把…開到路邊
Pull over by the roadside right now! I'm feeling carsick!
快把車停到路邊！我暈車了！

❺ roll v. 捲、轉動
Mom rolled up the sleeves and was ready to clean the room.
媽媽捲起袖子準備打掃房間。

❻ headlight n. 大燈
A headlight of that car was broken.
那輛汽車的大燈壞了一個。

❼ turn signal 方向燈
When you make a turn, you must use the turn signals.
開車轉彎一定要打方向燈。

❽ intend v. 想要、打算
Susan intends to study abroad next year.
Susan 打算明年出國留學。

❾ against prep. 違反
The use of certain drugs is against the law.
使用某些藥物是違反法律的。

❿ turn off 關掉
Could you please turn off the music?
可以把音樂關掉嗎？

30 秒會話教室

檢舉違規是執法人員的責任，但若遇上情節較輕的違規，多半會網開一面，因此若滿懷誠意與歉疚地說 Q: Could you let me off the hook? 你可以放我一馬嗎？或許可以得到以下的回答喔 A: I'll let you off the hook with a warning. 我可以放過你，但是下次要注意。

名人怎麼說？

Gravitation is not responsible for people falling in love. —Albert Einstein
萬有引力對墜入愛河的人不成立。—愛因斯坦

Who, being loved, is poor? —Oscar Wilde
誰，在愛中，是窮的？—王爾德

Time is too slow for those who wait, too swift for those who fear, too long for those who grieve, too short for those who rejoice, but for those who love, time is eternity.
—Henry Van Dyke
時間對於等待的人太緩慢，對於恐懼的人太快速，對於悲傷的人太漫長，對於愉快的人太短暫，但對於相愛的兩人，時間是永恆的。，—作家

情境 8 狗狗幫主人送作堆

會話訓練班

假日午後 Albert 牽著他所養的拉不拉多出門遛狗，到了公園時，有一位同樣牽著狗的女生迎面而來。當兩人正要擦肩而過時，他的拉不拉多停在那位女生所牽的狗身邊……

Albert **walks** his **Labrador** in the afternoon on the weekend. When he arrives at the park, the girl with the dog just walks oncoming. When the two almost **brush** past, his Labrador stops by the side of the dog that the girl walks ...

Albert	Excuse me....Seems they are interested in each other.	不好意思……牠們看起來似乎對彼此很有興趣。
Marjorie	That's okay, dogs just like humans need **social** interaction.	沒關係的，狗狗也像人類一樣需要社交。
Albert	Your dog is so cute, what is its name?	妳養的狗好可愛，請問牠叫甚麼名字？
Marjore	Dolly, it is a female **Poodle**. Yours is a Labrador, I guess. What is its name?	Dolly，牠是隻母的貴賓狗。你養的是拉不拉多吧？牠的名字呢？
Albert	Oh, it is Hero, a **purebred** Labrador. Isn't Dolly scared of big dogs?	喔，牠叫 Hero，是純種的拉不拉多。Dolly 不害怕大型狗嗎？

Marjorie	Usually it does, I'm surprised that it doesn't this time. Maybe they really like each other?	平常牠是會怕的，看到牠這樣我也很驚訝，或許牠們真的很喜歡彼此吧？
Albert	Oops, Just without attention, their **leashes** make us **twisted** around tightly.	喔，真是糟糕，一不注意，牠們的狗繩把我們兩個越纏越緊了。
Marjorie	It is a little bit **embarrassed** though, what should we do?	這就真的有點尷尬，我們現在該怎麼辦呢？
Albert	I think they want us to have a cup of coffee.	我想牠們是希望我們能一起去喝杯咖啡。
Marjorie	But we have to **unwind** the leashes first.	那也得先把纏繞在一起的狗繩解開吧？

必會單字一手抓

❶ Poodle **n.** 貴賓狗

Amy's dad gave her a cute Poodle as a gift on the day of her tenth birthday.

Amy 的爸爸在她十歲生日這天送她一隻可愛的貴賓狗。

❷ Labrador (Lab) **n.** 拉不拉多獵犬

The Labrador is a very friendly dog.

拉不拉多是一種很友善的狗。

❸ walk v. 遛（狗）
Walking dogs is not only exercise, but could also develop the relationship between owners and pets.
遛狗不但可以運動，還能增進與寵物之間的感情。

❹ brush v. 擦過、掠過
The wind blew lightly, brushing through the little girl's hair.
微風輕佛小女孩的頭髮。

❺ social adj. 喜歡交際的、社交的
Her social life is active and fantastic.
她的社交生活多采多姿。

❻ purebred adj. 純種的
Purebred pets are expensive, not everyone could afford them.
純種的寵物要價昂貴，不是一般人負擔的起的。

❼ leash n. （牽狗等的）繩索、皮帶
Put a leash on your pets before you enter the restaurant.
要進入這間餐廳的寵物都必須繫上牽繩。

❽ twist v. 交纏
She twisted her handkerchief into a knot.
她將她的手帕打成一個結。

❾ embarrassed adj. 尷尬的
Breaking wind in the public is very embarrassed.
在大庭廣眾下放屁是一件非常尷尬的事情。

❿ unwind v. 解開 字彙連結站 untie、unfasten、unloose
The doctor helps him unwind the bandage on his arms.
醫生幫他解開纏在手臂上的繃帶。

30 秒會話教室

當你遇到措手不及的狀況，不知該如何是好時，可以詢問對方 What should we do? 我們該怎麼辦？或是 What's your suggestion? 你有甚麼建議？以及 What's your plan? 你有甚麼計畫？來集思廣益解決眼前的難題。

名人怎麼說？

The only creatures that are evolved enough to convey pure love are dogs and infants.— Johnny Depp
發展成能表達純潔的愛的生物只有狗和嬰兒。—強尼・戴普

The dog is a gentleman; I hope to go to his heaven not man's. — Mark Twain
狗兒是紳士，我希望我可以去他們的天堂而不是人類的。—馬克・吐溫

情境9 在機場拿錯行李

會話訓練班

Patrick 剛從英國出差回來，從機場拿完行李後就急忙趕回公司彙報。到了公司打開行李，Patrick 才發現裡面的東西根本不是他的，他打電話到機場詢問，目前並沒有人找不到行李，一定是對方錯拿到他的了。於是他只好開始翻找眼前這個行李箱，看裡面有沒有可以連絡上對方的資訊……

Patrick just came back from a business trip in the England. After he gets his **baggage** from the **airport**, then he leaves for the company to give a report. When he **arrives** at the company, he opens the baggage and finds out the **stuff** is not his. He calls the airport to ask, and every passengers get their baggage. It must be someone mistaking his stuff. So he starts to **rummage** around this baggage and see whether there is some information about the owner.

Patrick	Hello. Is this Celia Murphy?	喂，請問是……Celia Murphy 小姐嗎？
Celia	This is me. And you are...?	我是。請問你是……？
Patirck	This is Patrick Larsson. We seems to get wrong baggage in the airport.	我是 Patrick Larsson，我們好像在機場錯拿彼此的行李了。
Celia	Really? I just arrived home. I haven't opened the baggage yet.	真的嗎？我才剛到家，還沒有打開行李來看。

Patrick	Our baggages are **exactly** the same, but there is a laptop and some documents inside my baggage. Could you please check the one you got?	我們的行李箱長的一模一樣，但是我的裡面有筆記型電腦和一些文件，可以麻煩妳幫我確認一下是不是妳拿到的那個嗎？
Celia	Sure, I am opening the baggage... It's true! Besides those stuff you mentioned, there are several clothes and a simple **sponge bag**. By the way, how did you know my information?	當然沒問題，我正在開行李……真的耶！行李裡面除了你講的東西，還有幾套衣服和簡單的盥洗用具。對了，你是怎麼知道我的資料的？
Patrick	Very sorry... I have no choice but to rummage your **personal** belongings. I found a piece of paper, written with "I am Celia Murphy, from the US. I'd like to make friends with you. My phone number and address are..."	很抱歉……我不得不翻找妳的一些私人物品，我發現了一張寫著「我叫 Celia Murphy，來自美國，想跟你做個朋友，我的電話和地址是……」的紙條。
Celia	Oh, god, I am so embarrassed! And I remember I put this inside my unwashed dirty clothes....I wrote this for a handsome guy I met in England! But I didn't have enough courage to **hand over**.	喔，天啊，真丟臉！而且我記得那張紙條還是塞在沒洗的髒衣服裡面…那是我在英國遇到一位帥哥的時候寫的啦！但我最後還是沒有勇氣把那張紙條交給他。

Patrick It takes only 30 minutes away by car from your home to my company. If you could take a taxi from now and **exchange** our baggage, I will be very grateful!

Celia Ok, I will be there soon, but you pay the taxi fare!

看妳家地址離我公司大約只要 30 分鐘的車程，如果妳願意現在坐計程車過來跟我交換行李的話，我會非常感激的。

好，我馬上去。不過計程車錢你出！

必會單字一手抓

❶ airport n. 機場

I'll meet my boyfriend at the airport now.

我要去機場接我男朋友。

❷ baggage n. 行李 字彙連結站 luggage

We just go to visit grandma. Why you bring so much baggage?

只是要去探望外婆，何必帶這麼多行李？

❸ sponge bag n. 盥洗用品袋 字彙連結站 toilet articles

Mom, did you see my pink sponge bag?

媽，妳有看到我的粉紅色的盥洗用品袋嗎？

❹ personal adj. 私人的

These are personal belongings of the boss, and he doesn't like others to touch them.

這些東西都是老闆的私人物品，他不喜歡別人亂碰。

❺ stuff **n.** 物品、東西
The stuff that young people are interested in nowadays doesn't make sense to me.
現在年輕人感興趣的東西我都無法理解。

❻ rummage **v.** 翻找、仔細搜查
Marianne went to rummage in the refrigerator.
瑪麗安娜在冰箱裡翻了翻。

❼ exactly **adv.** 完全地、正好地
I knew exactly how you felt.
我完全能體會你的感覺。

❽ arrive **v.** 抵達
Our vacation just was starting when the airplane arrived at the destination.
當飛機抵達目的地，我們的假期才正要開始。

❾ hand over 遞交
The teacher asks the little boy to hand over the toy he just played under the table.
老師要小男孩把剛剛在桌子底下偷玩的玩具交出來。

❿ exchange **v.** 交換　字彙連結站　interchange、swap
Joy has been to Japan as an exchange student for two years
Joy 曾到日本當過 2 年的交換學生。

30 秒會話教室

人在江湖，身不由己。要表達像這樣的「不得已」有以下幾種說法：I have no choice but to face the truth. 我不得不接受事實。I have to face the truth. 我必須接受事實。I cannot help but face the truth. 我不得不接受事實。

情境 10 行車小擦撞

會話訓練班

Irene 開車出門兜風，她在一個十字路口前停紅綠燈，當綠燈亮起，她要在十字路口右轉的時候不小心跟後方來車發生了小擦撞，她跟那位駕駛都趕緊下車察看……

Irene goes for a ride, and she stops in the **crossroad** in front of the red-green lights. When the light turns green, she is about to turn right in the crossroad but have a **fender-bender** with the rear car carelessly. She and the car's driver hurriedly get off their cars to check...

Kenneth	Miss, why didn't you use the turn signals when you turn right?	小姐，妳要右轉怎麼沒有打方向燈啊？
Irene	Oh, really? I'm very sorry.	咦，是這樣嗎？真的耶，真是不好意思。
Kenneth	Let's me see...your car looks okay, but there are some **dents** on my car.	我來看看……妳的車子看起來沒事，不過我這邊有些凹陷。
Irene	It's my **fault**. I was **warned** by the policeman that I should use the turn signals on the freeway last month. But I still forgot it.	都怪我不好，我上個月才在高速公路上被交通警察提醒沒有打方向燈，我剛剛好像又忘了。

Irene	Do we need to call the police or **insurance** company?	我們有需要叫警察或是保險公司來嗎？
Kenneth	If they come, you will be **inquired** into **liability**, and it would take a lot of time for you to be made a report by the police.	如果叫他們來的話，妳就要被追究責任了耶，還要花許多時間做筆錄。
Irene	But if we let it be this may, I will feel really sorry; please let me pay the fixing cost.	可是就這樣算了，對你感到很過意不去，請務必讓我賠償你修車的錢。
Kenneth	Just some tiny dents, it doesn't cost much money, and my car is not new. Why don't we move the car first and you treat me a meal?	一點點小凹痕而已，不用花多少錢的，而且我的車也不是甚麼新車，不如我們趕快把車移好，妳請我吃個飯吧。
Irene	No problem. I just turned right for the spaghetti restaurant. Let's go! I will take you there.	沒問題，我剛剛就是要右轉去前面的一家義大利麵店，走，我帶你去。

必會單字一手抓

❶ crossroad n. 十字路口

Drive safely in the crossroads.

在十字路口要小心駕駛。

❷ fender-bender n. 小車禍、擦撞

Most of the accidents are fender-bender.

大部分的車禍都是些小擦撞。

❸ dent n. 凹痕

Mark's car was pelted by hail and had many tiny dents.

Mark 的車被冰雹打出了一個個的小凹痕。

❹ fault n. 錯誤、責任

Every man has his faults.

人無完人。

❺ insurance n. 保險

Her first job is selling insurance.

她的第一份工作是去推銷保險。

❻ warn v. 警告、告誡

The doctor warns him not to smoke anymore or he would have lung cancer.

他被醫生警告他不要再抽菸，可能會得肺癌。

❼ liability n. 責任、義務

I think many people should have liability for the stray animals.

我認為有許多人都應該為流浪動物的問題負責(liability for)。

❽ inquire v. 訊問、調查

You can inquire of your new classmate where the dorm is.

你可以讓你的新同學詢問宿舍在哪裡？

❾ question **v.** 詢問、審問
Don't question her about her family.
不要問她家裡的事。

30 秒會話教室

人非聖賢，孰能無過。能承認自己的錯誤並道歉是一件很偉大的事情，想表達歉意有以下幾種說法：I feel terrible. 我覺得很過意不去。
I really feel sorry about that. 對那件事情我感到很抱歉。I don't know what to say. 真不知道該說甚麼好。

名人怎麼說？

Everything is clearer when you're in love. —John Lennon
所有事物變得更清晰，當你戀愛時。—約翰藍儂

One is loved because one is loved. No reason is needed for loving. —Paulo Coelho
被愛就是被愛。相愛不需要理由。—保羅・科爾賀

We love because it's the only true adventure.—Nikki Giovanni
我們愛因這是一場真正的冒險。—作家

情境 11 浪漫燭光晚餐

會話訓練班

Harvey 跟 Victoria 到一家高級餐廳約會，到 Victoria 到了現場才發現原來 Harvey 為她精心準備了一頓燭光晚餐……

Harvey and Victoria have a **date** at the **exclusive** restaurant. After they arrive at the restaurant, Victoria finally **realizes** that Harvey prepares an **elaborate candlelight** dinner for her.

Victoria	Wow...candles and flowers, so romantic.	哇……桌上擺著蠟燭跟鮮花，好浪漫喔。
Harvey	I **especially** asked the restaurant to prepare these. Come, Lady, please have a seat. I will **serve** you tonight.	這是我特地請餐廳準備的喔。來，女士，請坐。今晚由我來為妳服務。
Victoria	Anything worth celebrating?	有甚麼值得慶祝的事情嗎？
Harvey	To meet you and be with you, does that **count**?	跟妳相識、相戀算嗎？
Victoria	Oh, darling. You are so sweet.	喔，親愛的，你嘴巴真甜。
Harvey	Is it strange? Should I do it on the proposal?	很奇怪嗎？我是不是該等到要求婚的時候再這麼做？

Victoria Not at all, I am really happy. Thanks for what you did for me.

Harvey Only if I could see your smile at this moment. It is **worthy**.

Victoria Oh...Harvey, I was so glad to meet you.

Harvey Me too. You are **starving**, aren't you? Let's get something to eat!

不會啊，我真的很高興，謝謝你為我做的一切。

只要能看到像妳現在這樣的笑容，一切就值得了。

喔……Harvey，我真高興當時遇見的是你。

我也是。妳應該餓壞了吧？我們來點餐吧！

必會單字一手抓

❶ exclusive **adj.** 高級的、時髦的

She knew some celebrities in an exclusive club.

她在一家高級的俱樂部認識了幾位名流。

❷ date **v.** **n.** 約會

My supervisor wants to date with me, should I?

我的上司找我去約會，我該答應他嗎？

❸ realize **v.** 領悟、瞭解

It is too late that he realized how much he loves her.

等到他終於領悟自己愛她有多麼深時，一切已經來不及了。

❹ elaborate adj. 精心製作的
She had prepared a very elaborate meal for her husband.
她精心準備的飯菜給他先生吃。

❺ candlelight n. 燭光
Before the electric light invented, every one read books under the candlelight.
在還沒有發明電燈的時代，大家都是在燭光底下看書。

❻ Especially adv. 特別、特地
I pick up this gift that is special for you, please take it.
這個禮物是我特別為你挑選的，請你收下。

❼ serve v. 服務
The waitress serves me a cup of coffee and a plate of French toast.
女服務生為我端上一杯咖啡和一盤法式吐司。

❽ worthy adj. 值得的
Is it worthy to overwork and lose your health?
超時工作賠上健康值得嗎？

❾ count v. 將…計算在內
There are over 50 people in the wedding, not counting the relatives of bride and groom.
有超過 50 人參加婚禮，不包括新娘與新郎的親人。

❿ starve v. 挨餓、（口）非常餓
Lots of people are starving in Africa every day, and they need everyone's help.
在非洲仍有許多人每天都在挨餓，急需外界的幫助。

30 秒會話教室

當肚子餓的時候除了可以用 I'm hungry. 我餓了。以外，還可以用 starve（餓壞了）這個單字來加強肚子餓的急迫性，例如：I'm starving, Let's get something to eat. 我餓壞了，我們吃點東西吧。

關鍵字搜尋

A romantic dinner

1.First you must choose where the dinner is to take place. Make sure you two can be alone.
第一步驟先選擇晚餐在哪裡舉辦，確保兩人能獨處。

2.Set the table with red roses with a couple of candles on each side of the roses. Get your food prepared and set the mood with some love songs to play.
桌子放玫瑰花與蠟燭，在輕柔的音樂下準備食物。

3.Toss rose petals gently on the floor making a path from the door to the table, so that when your loved one arrives they can follow the rose petal. Have dinner on the table when they arrive so that you can spend the time with them.
把玫瑰花瓣輕輕的撒落在地板形成路徑，當你的愛人回家時可以依循著花瓣從大門走到餐桌。將菜擺好和愛人一起享受用餐時光。

4.Some people think that feeding each other is romantic. After dinner, have another place to go so that you are not staring in each other with the eyes over a mess on the table.
很多人覺得互相餵食很浪漫。吃完飯後，找一個可以去走走的地方，這樣兩人就不用在亂亂的餐桌上互看彼此。

情境 12 湖邊小屋渡假

會話訓練班

Brian 帶剛交往的女朋友 Phoebe 到叔叔的湖邊小屋渡假。他們開車行駛在風光明媚的鄉間，遠離都市的壓力。當車子抵達湖邊小屋，Phoebe 不自覺驚嘆了起來……

Brian takes his new girlfriend Phoebe to his uncle's **log cabin** to take a vacation. They drive through the beautiful countryside and fly away the worries of city life. When they arrive at the log cabin, Phoebe marvels at the beauty of the scenery view....

Phoebe	Wow, that is your uncle's log cabin. It is better than I thought.	哇，這就是你叔叔的渡假小屋，比我想像中的還要漂亮耶。
Brian	Of course, the cabin was built by the whole log, just like the forest.	當然囉，這棟小屋全都是用整根原木搭建而成的，很有原始森林的感覺。
Phoebe	No wonder your family will take a vacation here every summer.	難怪你說你們家族每年暑天都會到這裡來渡假。
Brian	Yap, we have many memories here. Let's go, I will show you around.	對啊，這裡可是充滿許多回憶呢。走吧，我帶妳到裡面瞧瞧。

Phoebe	Wow, there is not only a **fireplace** inside, but also a **specimen** of deer on the wall, out of my surprise. Besides, the bearskin **rug** is put on the floor. Are these all from **hunting**?	哇，裡面不但有壁爐，牆上竟然掛著鹿頭標本耶，還有地上鋪著的熊皮地毯，這些都是打獵得來的嗎？
Brian	These are just decoration. Although we have rifles, we don't hunt animals in the forest.	這些都是裝飾品而已啦，這裡雖然有來福槍，但是我們不會去獵殺森林裡的動物。
Phoebe	What **activities** do you do here?	那你們在這裡都在做些甚麼活動？
Brian	We can go **fishing**, swimming, and **rowing** a boat at Crystal lake. There are many places to explore and have fun.	可以到水晶湖釣魚、游泳、划船，森林裡還有許多地方可以探險，這裡有很多樂子。
Phoebe	Wow, sounds great! That is absolutely awesome. I can't wait.	哇，聽起來真棒，我已經等不及了。
Brian	Let me take you to your room first. After you get ready, then we go fishing for the dinner by the lake.	那我先帶妳到妳的房間裡，等妳安頓好我們再到湖邊去釣晚餐要吃的魚吧。

必會單字一手抓

❶ cabin n. 小屋

That cabin was abandoned for decades, and no one dares to come in.

那棟小屋已經荒廢十幾年了，現在沒有人敢進去。

❷ log n. 原木、圓木

The price of log was soaring these days, so the price of paper is getting more costly.

原木價格飆漲，紙張的價錢也越來越貴了。

❸ fireplace n. 壁爐

When the weather gets cold, we will sit around the heating fireplace to keep warm..

天氣冷的時候我們會圍坐在生了火的壁爐前取暖。

❹ specimen n. 標本

There are many specimens in biology teacher's office.

生物老師的辦公室裡有許多動物的標本。

❺ rug n. 毛皮地毯

A beautiful Persian rug covered the hardwood floors.

美麗的波斯地毯鋪在硬木的地板上。

❻ hunt v. 打獵

My father taught me hunting and fishing since I was young.

從小爸爸就有教我打獵與捕魚。

❼ forest n. 森林

Forest is just like the lungs of the earth, without it human can't breathe.

森林就像是地球的肺部，少了它人類就無法呼吸。

❽ fishing **n.** 釣魚、捕魚
My dad likes fishing, but we don't know what's so fun in it at all.
爸爸非常喜歡釣魚，但是我們一點都不懂其中的樂趣所在。

❾ activities **n.** 帶消遣性的活動
What activities do you do every weekend?
妳每到假日都做些甚麼消遣活動呢？

❿ row **v.** 划（船）
The old grandpa rowed the boat to the center of the lake in order to get bigger fish.
老爺爺把船划到湖中央以便釣到更大的魚。

30 秒會話教室

覺得對方的提議很棒、正合我意時，可以用以下幾種口語方式表達，如:Sounds great, I can't wait. 聽起來很棒，我等不及了。 That's absolutely awesome. 真是棒透了。

關鍵字搜尋

Log Cabin Puzzle
原木的小屋充滿木頭的香氣與渡假的閒適讓人彷彿置身在北緯國家。
網站：http://www.dailyjigsawpuzzles.net/landscape-jigsaws/log-cabin_513.html
此網站提供各種圖案的拼圖遊戲，各難度皆有，快來挑戰看看！

好事必定多磨

情境 13 與搬家的青梅竹馬重逢

會話訓練班

Miles 在上班的午休時間到外面用餐。他在一家餐廳裡聽到一個熟悉的聲音，他的眼睛下意識地尋找著聲音的主人，不久 Miles 就認出那是他的青梅竹馬 Doris，於是他立刻上前⋯⋯

Miles is having his lunch break outside. He hears a **familiar voice** in the restaurant, and he searches for the owner of the voice subconsciously. Shortly, he recognizes that was his **childhood** sweetheart—Doris, so he stepped forward...

Miles Excuse me, are you Doris Watson?

Doris You are...Miles, god, it has been a long time. You look **almost** the same since last time I saw you.

Miles You also look the same as high school time. I can recognize you just by your voice. Do you work nearby?

Doris Yes, I was just **transferred** to the branch. The idea crossed my mind that I might run into you somewhere in the city, so I accepted this transfer. Dreams come true now.

請問妳是 Doris Watson 嗎？
你是⋯⋯Miles，天啊，好久不見了，你幾乎跟我最後一次見到你一樣沒甚麼變。
妳也是跟高中的時候一樣，我一聽聲音就認出妳了，妳也在這附近上班嗎？
嗯，剛被派到這裡的分公司來，心想說不定會在這個城市裡遇到你，我就答應了這個調動，願望果然成真了。

Miles	If you want to meet me, just call my home number.	妳想見我的話，只要打個電話到我家給我就可以了啊？
Doris	But, **Since** you moved to New York, I have called you so many times. That was not **available**.	咦，可是自從你搬到紐約後，我打過好多次電話給你，不過都是空號。
Mile	How come, I still use the number, 845-7258368.	怎麼可能，那支電話我到現在還在使用耶，電話號碼 845-7258368 沒錯呀。
Doris	The note you wrote to me is 845-72583 "0" 8, no **wonder** I couldn't get through.	可是你寫給我的紙條上是寫 845-72583「0」8，難怪我怎麼打都打不通。
Mile	I am sorry about that, my handwriting is too **illegible**. I thought you didn't miss me at all after I moved.	真是抱歉，我的字太潦草了，我還以為我搬家後妳一點都不想念我。
Doris	I thought you are on **purpose** to give me the wrong number! You have to **make it up** to me for loneliness I bore these years.	我才以為你故意給我錯的電話呢！你要好好補償我這幾年的。

必會單字一手抓

⓫ familiar adj. 熟悉

That man looks familiar; isn't he my teacher at the elementary school?

那位先生看起來很面熟，不知道是不是我的國小老師。

❶ voice n. 聲音、嗓子

Can the student who sits at the end of the back hear my voice?

坐在最後面的同學聽的到我的聲音嗎？

❷ childhood n. 童年時期

Many children from low-income families do not have happy childhood.

許多在貧困家庭中成長的孩子都沒有快樂的童年。

❸ almost adv. 幾乎

Alex and his girlfriend had been in love for almost three years.

Alex 和他女朋友相戀快要三年了。

❹ since adv. 自從

He has started doing house chores since his wife was dead.

自從妻子過世後，他才開始學著自己料理家務。

❺ transfer v. 轉換、調動

The manager of my department was transferred to head office for his outstanding work.

我們部門的主管因為表現良好而被轉調到總公司去了。

❻ available adj. 有效的

Your passport is not available; please replace it as fast as possible.

您的護照已經不再有效了，請盡速辦理換發。

❼ illegible **adj.** 潦草的
Her signature on the contract was illegible.
她在合約的簽名很潦草

❽ purpose **n.** 目的、意圖
The purpose of the meeting is to decide the new product.
開這個會的目的是為了決定新的產品。

❾ wonder **v.** 覺得奇怪
You have just eaten some snacks; no wonder you are not hungry.
原來你剛剛已經吃過零食了，難怪你一點也不餓。

30 秒會話教室

「好久不見」有幾種表達方式，最標準的就是：It has been a long time. 或 It has been a while. 至於 Long time no see 這個用法雖然有點像中式英文，但是只要對方聽的懂，倒是無傷大雅。

名人怎麼說？

Tis better to have loved and lost
than never to have loved at all. —Alfred Tennyson
寧願愛過但失去了，也不要從來沒有愛過。—阿佛烈・丁尼生

情境 14 愛慕者送的不識相禮物

會話訓練班

某天下班回家後，Irene 在自家門廊前看到了一個包裝精美的禮物盒，上頭還附了一封信，信封上註明「Irene Jenkins 收」而信裡面則是寫著「我是上次臨檢妳的警察，Fred Morrison，希望妳會喜歡這個禮物，我的電話是……」於是她將禮物拿進屋裡，小心翼翼地拆開……

One day after work, Irene found a beautifully wrapped gift box in front of her porch, with an envelope attached. The attached envelope was addressed to "Irene Jenkins" and inside the **envelope** is a letter that says, "I am Fred Morrison, the police officer pulling over your car last time. I hope you like this present. My number is ..." So she took the present inside the house, and opened it **carefully**...

Irene　Mr.Morrison, I have got your present.

Fred　Oh, glad to hear that. I was wondering whether you would call me by the number in the letter?

Irene　Is that a **joke**? I just don't understand what you thought!

Fred　What...? I just want you to be happy!

Mr. Morrison，我收到你的禮物了。

喔，很高興妳收到了，我還在擔心妳不知道會不會打信裡內所寫的電話給我呢！

請問這是某種玩笑嗎？我不懂你究竟是甚麼居心！

什……甚麼？我只是希望妳開心啊！

Irene	Want me to be happy!? Why you gave me a black **mush** crawled with lots of ants, which was awfully **stinking**, **disgusting**. That just freaked me out!	希望我開心！？請問你送一個爬滿螞蟻的黑色糊狀物體給我是甚麼意思？又臭又噁心，把我嚇了一大跳！
Fred	I gave you a chocolate cake from a famous bakery, and I lined up for so long to buy it.	我送的明明是知名蛋糕店的巧克力蛋糕啊，我排隊了好久才買到的。
Irene	So... why so many **ants** crawling full on it? When did you bring this here?	那……怎麼會爬滿螞蟻？請問你是甚麼時候送過來的啊？
Fred	I delivered it to your porch by myself at 7 o'clock in the morning. I thought you would get it before you went to work.	我早上七點親自送過去放在門廊上的，想說妳在出門上班前就會收到。
Irene	Oh, god, I stayed at my girlfriend's home last night, so I came home until now. No wonder the cake would be **decayed** with ants' crawling.	喔，老天，我昨晚在女性朋友家過夜，現在才回到家，難怪蛋糕會腐壞了而且爬滿螞蟻。
Fred	Sorry, I made a **rash** decision to give you a present. Sorry to bother you.	對不起，都是我太輕率地要送妳禮物，給妳添麻煩了。

必會單字一手抓

❶ porch **n.** 門廊、入口處
Standing at the porch, mom chatted with the neighbors.
媽媽站在門廊跟鄰居聊天。

❷ envelope **n.** 信封
Address an envelope and put the letter in it.
在信封上寫好地址後把信放進去。

❸ carefully **adv.** 小心謹慎地
Move this box carefully, because there are some fragile glasses inside.
搬這個箱子的時候要小心一點，裡面裝滿了易碎的玻璃杯。

❹ joke **n.** 玩笑
The joke you made is too much, please say sorry to her.
你開的玩笑太過份了，請向她道歉。

❺ mush **n.** 軟糊狀的東西
The vegetables had been boiled to a mush, and were quite uneatable.
蔬菜煮爛了，有點不太能吃了。

❻ stinking **adj.** 發惡臭的
Most of the foreign tourists don't like the smell of stinking tofu.
大部份的外國遊客不喜歡臭豆腐的味道。

❼ disgusting **adj.** 令人作嘔的
You are really disgusting!
你真令人作噁！

❽ ant **n.** 螞蟻

The tiny ant can boost a burden, 50 times its weight.

小小的螞蟻可以抬起 50 倍重的東西。

❾ decayed **adj.** 爛了的，腐敗的

The fruit of this basket was decayed, please throw it away now.

這籃水果已經腐敗了，請現在拿去丟掉。

❿ rash **adj.** 輕率的

We can't rush to make a decision in business.

商場上的生意不可輕率地就做決定。

30 秒會話教室

當不確定對方的行為是否出於惡意或是無心，心情卻又已經被激怒的時候，可以先用這句話做最後的試探：Is this some kind of joke? 這是某種玩笑嗎？或是 Are you kidding me? 你在開玩笑嗎？

情境 15 原來你喜歡的是我姊姊

會話訓練班

Patrick 跟上次拿錯彼此行李的 Celia 成了朋友。一天，Patrick 照例跟 Celia 在電話中聊天，Patrick 突然提起了某個話題……

Patrick and Celia became friends after the baggage mistaking events. One day, Patrick **chatted** with Celia on the phone as usual. Patrick suddenly **referred** to a certain **topic**...

Patrick	Do you remember that I rummage around your baggage?	妳還記得我拿到妳的行李的時候，有翻找裡面的東西嗎？
Celia	Of course, I do remember. My **privacy** is gone.	當然記得啊，我的隱私都被你看光了。
Patrick	There is a photo of you and another girl at St Paul's Cathedral. You **mentioned** that she is your sister, Heather, didn't you?	裡面有一張妳跟另一位女生在聖保羅大教堂前的合照，妳曾說過她是妳姊姊 Heather 對嗎？
Celia	Yes, we took the photo in England by Polaroid.	對啊，那是我們去英國玩的時候用拍立得拍的。
Patrick	Your sister is as beautiful as you are, does she have a boyfriend now?	妳姊姊跟妳一樣長的很漂亮，她現在有男朋友嗎？

Celia She was busy finding a job after graduation, she didn't mention that but I **supposed** not.

她最近剛畢業忙著找工作，沒聽她提起，應該是沒有吧。

Patrick I see. Do you think she would mind having a new friend like me, if I invite you two to go out together?

這樣啊，那如果下次我想約妳們兩個一起出來，妳覺得她會介意認識我這個新朋友嗎？

Celia You tried to win the **affection** of my sister after you saw her picture? I thought you want to be my friend honestly.

原來你從看到那張照片的時候就在打我姊姊的主意啊？我還以為你是誠心想跟我交朋友。

Patrick Of course I did. But you just like my little younger sister, and your sister's age is closer to me, so...

當然是啊，但是妳就像我的小妹妹一樣，我跟妳姊姊的年齡比較接近，所以……

Celia Ok, I got it. I will ask her for you next time. You have to be nice to me or I will speak **ill** of you to my sister!

好啦，我知道了，我下次幫你約看看。你不對我好一點的話我就要跟姊姊說你的壞話！

必會單字一手抓

❶ chat v. 閒談、聊天

The girls mostly chat together during the break, and boys play basketball at the playground, instead.

女同學們下課時大多聚在一起聊天，而男同學則是跑到操場上打球。

❷ refer v. 談到、提及

Mom referred to several typhoons that are heading to the north, and ask me to be more careful.

媽媽在電話中提到好幾次最近正朝北部而來的颱風，要我多加小心。

❸ topic n. 話題、題目

I don't have too much interest on this topic, could we talk about others'?

我對這個話題沒甚麼興趣，可以聊些別的嗎？

❹ mention n. 提及、說起

Why didn't you mention your car being stolen? I could look for it with you.

你怎麼沒有跟我說你的車被偷了，我可以陪你一起找啊。

❺ suppose v. 猜想、以為

I supposed that dad was so angry for mom throwing his books.

我猜爸爸那麼生氣一定是因為媽媽把他的書都丟了。

❻ affection n. 愛慕、感情

Abby has affection for her P.E. teacher.

Abby 對她的體育老師充滿愛慕之情。

❼ ill adj. 壞的、不健康的

I am feeling ill today, so I want to stay at home.

我今天不舒服，所以我想留在家裡。

❽ privacy **n.** 私事、隱私
Please respect my privacy, knock the door before you come.
請尊重我的隱私，進房之前先敲門好嗎？

30 秒會話教室

想委婉地對對方表達反對意見時，可以用：I supposed not. 我想應該沒有。或是 I don't think so. 我不這麼覺得。最後再加上自己的觀點給對方做參考。

名人怎麼說？

You know you're in love when you can't fall asleep because reality is finally better than your dreams. — Dr. Seuss
你知道你戀愛了，當你發現晚上睡不著是因為現實比夢境還要更美好。
這句話出自蘇斯博士，也就是著名童書The cat in the hat.《戴帽子的貓》的作者。

情境 16 暗戀對象有男友？

會話訓練班

Fred 繼上次送一個災難般的禮物給 Irene 後，這次為了賠罪，也因為想繼續討 Irene 的歡心，因此又動了再送一次禮物的念頭。但這次他學乖了，先打電話做確認……

After the last time Fred gives a **disaster** present to Irene, he wants to **apologize** and also **please** Irene. So he has a **thought** of giving her a present again. However, this time he is smarter. He calls her in advance to make sure....

Fred Is this Irene? It's me, Fred. I'm so sorry for Last chocolate cake **incident**.

Irene Oh, that is okay. My friend and I just **cleaned** it, so **smell** and **culicid** was gone.

Fred That is great. By the way, I want to buy some puffs for you from a famous bakery, will you at home these days?

Irene Hmm...Fred, I really **appreciate** your **kindness**, but you really don't have to give me anything.

Irene 嗎？是我，Fred。上次的巧克力蛋糕事件真是不好意思。
喔，沒關係啦，我已經找朋友來幫我打掃過一番了，異味和蚊蟲都不見了。
那真是太好了。對了，我想再買一份知名蛋糕店的泡芙給妳吃，請問妳這幾天都會在家收件嗎？
嗯……Fred，我很感謝你的好意，但你真的可以不用再送我東西了。

Fred	Why? This time it will not smell, or you don't like puffs, I could buy other things for you.	為什麼？這次不會再發臭了啦！還是妳不喜歡吃泡芙，我可以換送別的東西給妳。
Irene	I couldn't receive your present, because I already have a boyfriend.	你的禮物不管是甚麼我都不能收，因為……其實我已經有男朋友了。
Fred	It explains the matter....Sorry, I just thought you were single.	原來是這樣啊……。抱歉，我一直以為妳是單身。
Irene	I have mentioned that the friend who helped me to clean up is my boyfriend. He already knew what's going on, and he doesn't mind if you be my friend. As long as you are willing to, we can still be friends.	我剛才說有朋友來幫我打掃，就是指我男朋友，他也知道事情的來龍去脈了，不過他並不介意我跟你做朋友，所以只要你也願意，我們還是可以當朋友的。
Fred	I know. If you have any trouble afterwards, You can call me anytime.	我知道了，以後如果妳遇上任何麻煩，隨時都可以找我。
Irene	I will. Please don't buy any present to me. It costs money. Really!	我會的。不過別再破費送我任何禮物了。真的！

必會單字一手抓

❶ **disaster** n. 災難

The whole cake is just a disaster.

那一整個蛋糕簡直就是一個災難。

❷ **apologize** v. 道歉

The President apologized for disregarding people's rights and interests.

總統因為罔顧人民的權益而當眾道歉。

❸ **please** v. 使高興

The little boy tried so hard to please his sick mother in the bed.

小男孩很努力地想讓臥病在床的母親高興。

❹ **thought** n. 思維、想法

She has a thought to have a concert.

她有個開演唱會的想法。

❺ **incident** n. 事件、插曲

He referred to an incident that occurred in 2013.

他提到了 2013 年發生的一件事。

❻ **clean** v. 打掃

My mom asks me to clean the room once a week.

媽媽規定我每周要打掃房間一次。

❼ **smell** n. 氣味

What smell is that? Like someone hasn't showered for three days.

這是甚麼味道？聞起來好像有人三天沒洗澡了。

❽ culicid **n.** 蚊蟲

Aunt is obsessed with cleanliness. Every time she sees culicid at home, she becomes hysterical.

阿姨有嚴重的潔癖，只要看到家裡出現任何蚊蟲都會歇斯底里。

❾ appreciate **v.** 感激

I do appreciate your speaking for me in the meeting just now; otherwise, I really don't know what kind of difficult task the manager would pass to me.

我很感激你剛剛在會議中為我說話，不然真不知道主管還要派甚麼樣的難題給我。

❿ kindness **n.** 好意、友好的行為

I will always remember your kindness.

我會永遠記得你的好意。

30 秒會話教室

當你非常感謝對方的某些行為時，可以用 I appreciate your help. 我很感謝你的幫忙。appreciate 一詞若是加了 be 動詞，如：I'm appreciated. 是表示「自己被感激了」的意思，千萬要注意喔。

情境 17 好友橫刀奪愛

會話訓練班

本來跟 Austine 走得很近的大學同校同學 Jocelyn 最近都故意避不見面，也不接他的電話。Austine 在心急之下，終於在學校裡等到了剛下課的 Jocelyn，於是他小心翼翼地上前詢問……

Austine originally was close with Jocelyn, his classmate at the college. Recently, Jocelyn **avoids** him on purpose, and doesn't answer his phone call. Austine is anxious for it. Finally, he sees Jocelyn just off the class, so he moves forward to ask....

Austine	Hi, Jocelyn, long time no see.	嗨 Jocelyn，好久不見了。
Jocelyn	Oh, hey.	喔，嗨。
Austine	Do you have things to deal with later on? Could I talk with you?	妳等一下有事嗎？可以跟妳談談嗎？
Jocelyn	We have nothing to talk about. I have my next course, please step **aside**.	我們沒甚麼好談的，我還要去上下一節課，請你讓一讓。
Austin	Wait a moment. I just want to ask you what happened recently? Why you treated me so **coldly** all of a sudden? Did I do something wrong?	等一下，我就是想問妳最近發生甚麼事情了，怎麼突然對我這麼冷淡？我做錯了甚麼事情嗎？

Jocelyn	You asked **while** knowing the answer. Last time, I introduced my friend Kimberly to you. As a result, she told me that just after you two exchanged numbers in front of me, you privately asked her out to the pub, and **bad-mouthing** me behind my back!	你還明知故問，我上次介紹我的朋友 Kimberly 給你，結果她說你們在我面前交換電話後，私底下馬上約她去夜店，還跟她說了我好多壞話！
Austine	Kimberly? You mean the girl who thinks she is **charming**? She invited me to the pub, but I **refused**. She was so **pissed off** on the phone! And she even said, “ You will regret it!”	Kimberly？喔，妳說那個覺得自己是萬人迷的女生嗎？是她約我去夜店的，可是我婉拒了，她在電話中生氣到不行呢！還放話說:「你一定會後悔的！」
Jocelyn	That is really her **style**...but I can't totally trust what you said!	這的確有點像她的作風……但我還是無法完全相信你說的話！
Austin	What I said is true! I texted her to tell her that I have had someone in my heart already, you see.	我說的都是真的！我還傳訊息告訴她，我已經有喜歡的人了，不信妳看。
Jocelyn	So Kimberly liked you, but in vain, then she made **rumors** to let me dislike you. She almost achieves her purpose, not way too far.	所以是 Kimberly 喜歡你不成，才造謠想讓我討厭你囉。她差一點就得逞了呢！

必會單字一手抓

❶ avoid v. 避開、避免

He is very careful in order to avoid offences.

他非常小心謹慎，以避免冒犯。

❷ aside adv. 到旁邊

She put the newspaper aside and picked up the English dictionary.

她把報紙放在一旁然後拿起英文字典。

❸ coldly adv. 冷淡地

I treat the people whom I am not acquainted with coldly.

我對不認識的人總是很冷淡。

❹ while adv. 當…的時候

While she was sleeping, her husband came home.

當她正在睡覺時，她先生才回家。

❺ bad-mouth v. 苛刻批評

Don't always bad-mouth us behind our back.

不要總是在我後面說我們的壞話。

❻ charming adj. 迷人的、有魅力的

All the colleges agree that the new sales manager is very charming.

辦公室裡的同仁一致認為新來的業務經理非常有魅力。

❼ refuse v. 拒絕

The counter's female clerk of the hotel refuses to admit my putting the baggage, which makes me feel very inconvenient.

飯店的櫃檯小姐拒絕讓我借放行李，讓我感到非常不方便。

❽ pissed off 惹惱
Mom was pissed off at my brother for using her lipstick to paint.
弟弟把媽媽的口紅拿來畫畫，讓媽媽氣炸了。

❾ rumor n. 謠言
Alice was disturbed about the rumor she dates with the teacher.
Alice 為她跟老師約會的謠言所困擾。

❿ style n. 風格、作風
He won't ask a woman out-it is not his style.
他不會邀女生約會一那不是他的風格。

30 秒會話教室

Get out of the way. 讓開。Please step aside. 請站到旁邊。Please make way for a fire-engine 請讓路給消防車。Please stand aside and let us through. 請站開讓我們通過。

情境 18 女友是朋友花錢請來的？

會話訓練班

Brian 跟女友 Phoebe 交往半年，一次 Brian 帶女友去參加朋友間的聚會，在席間他發現 Phoebe 跟自己的男性朋友 Howard 好像早就認識，而且 Howard 還偷偷塞錢給 Phoebe，這讓 Brian 非常懷疑，回家後馬上質問 Phoebe……

Brian dates with Phoebe for half a year. One day, Brain takes her to friend's meeting. During the meeting, he finds out Phoebe seemed **already** knew his friend, Howard. Moreover, Howard gives money to Phoebe furtively. It made Brian very **suspicious** of her.

Brian	Darling, I want to ask you something...Have you already known Howard?	親愛的，我有一件事情問……妳跟 Howard 是不是早就認識了？
Phoebe	Hmm...nope... Why did you think that?	嗯……沒……沒有啊，你為什麼會這麼想呢？
Brian	I just saw you two have eye contact, there is something suspicious!	剛剛我看你們兩個一直眉來眼去的，一定有甚麼曖昧！
Phoebe	You misunderstood it, there are many people at the meeting. It is **normal** we have eye **contact**.	你看錯了啦，聚會裡有那麼多人，兩個人彼此眼神相對很正常啊。

Brian Don't lie to me. I saw Howard give you money with my own eyes. It **broke** my heart! Tell me the truth, did you do the exchange that I think of in privacy?

妳別再撒謊了，我親眼看到 Howard 塞錢給妳，我傷心的快要崩潰了！老實告訴我，妳是不是私底下有在做我所想的那種交易？

Phoebe It was not what you thought! In fact...we met each other at the court was arranged by Howard. He was a **frequenter** of our flower shop. He thought I would suit your type so he wanted us to be friends.

我跟 Howard 真的不是你所想的那樣！其實……當初我們在球場上相識全都是 Howard 的安排，他是我們花店的常客，覺得我會是你喜歡的類型，因此希望我能跟你認識一下，交個朋友。

Brian No wonder he asked me which seat I had in order to buy your ticket behind me? Then why he didn't just introduce you directly?

難怪他當初會問我球賽的座位是買哪個位置，就是為了幫妳買我正後方的票囉？那他為什麼不直接介紹你給我認識？

Phoebe He said you didn't like him introducing girls to you, because you like to meet someone you like by yourself. He also said if I didn't like you, I didn't need to **lie** to myself. The **truth** is, I do like you, please believe me.

他說每次想要介紹女生給你，你都不願意，說想要自己認識喜歡的對象。他也說如果我不喜歡你，可以不用勉強欺騙自己的心，所以我是真心喜歡你的，請你相信我。

Brian	And why he handed over money to you?	那他塞錢給妳是怎麼回事？
Phoebe	He said he couldn't show up at your birthday party next week, so he wanted me to buy gifts for you to surprise you. But I turned down this for you, and thanked him.	他說你下個禮拜的慶生會他有事無法到場，要拿錢託我幫你買些禮物給你驚喜，不過我代替你婉拒了，並謝謝他這個好朋友。

必會單字一手抓

❶ suspicious **adj.** 猜疑的、可疑的

The strange man was very suspicious outside the classroom.

那個陌生男子在教室外面鬼鬼祟祟的模樣非常可疑。

❷ already **adv.** 已經、先前

I have already handed over my final report to the professor.

我已經把期末報告交給教授了。

❸ contact **v.** 接觸

If you have any problem, please contact me immediately.

如果有任何疑問請馬上跟我聯絡。

❹ normal **adj.** 正常的

It is very normal that a baseball player practices 8 hours a day.

棒球選手一天練習個 8 個小時是很正常的事情。

❺ frequenter **n.** 常客
Don't forget to reverse the frequenter's favorite coffee.
別忘了幫那位常客留一杯她最愛的咖啡。

❻ break **v.** 打破、弄壞
The firefighter broke the glass in order to save the children.
消防隊員為了救困在房子裡面的小孩，不得不打破玻璃。

❼ lie **v.** 說謊
I know she was lying because she looked strange.
我知道她在騙我因為她看起來怪怪的。

❽ truth **n.** 實情
The truth is that your score is not enough for entering our school.
實情是，你的測驗成績不足以進入我們學校。

30 秒會話教室

被某人傷透了心，可以向對方泣訴：You break my heart. 你傷了我的心。My heart is broken. 我的心都碎了。I'm a broken-hearted girl. 我是個傷心的女孩。

名人怎麼說？

We are all travelers in the wilderness of this world, and the best we can find in our travels is an honest friend. — Robert Louis Stevenson
我們都是荒漠的旅行者，我們能在旅途中找到最棒的就是真摯的友誼。
這句話出自於羅伯特・路易斯・史蒂文森，為金銀島與化身博士的作者。

情境 19 可疑小三原來是男方表妹

會話訓練班

Victoria 的鄰居打電話向她通風報信說，看到她的男友 Harvey 帶著一個年輕辣妹回家。於是 Victoria 馬上結束了服飾店的生意，趕回家看看到底是怎麼一回事……

Victoria's neighbor calls her and says she saw his boyfriend take a hottie home. Therefore, Victoria **immediately closes** her clothes shop and goes home to see what's going on...

Victoria	Harvey, I am back, where are you?	Harvey，我回來了，你在哪裡？
Harvey	Darling, why you closed shop so early today? Is the sales not good?	親愛的，妳今天怎麼這麼早就打烊了？生意不好嗎？
Victoria	How could it be? Why I can't come home earlier to see you? Or this makes you **displeased**?	怎麼了？我就不能早點回家來看看你嗎？還是早點回來使你不開心呢？
Harvey	Why...? Wait a moment! Don't go to the **bedroom** now, Sandra is changing her clothes.	怎麼會呢……等一下！妳先不要進臥室，Sandra 正在裡面換衣服。
Victoria	What the neighbor said is true! You took a woman to our home without **artifice**, and in our bedroom....	鄰居說的果然是真的！你竟然光明正大地帶女人回來我們家，還在我們的臥室……

Harvey	No, you **misunderstood**! Sandra is my cousin. She suddenly called me and said that she needed to **stay** here for one night at our home after joining the **costume** party, I wouldn't be able to talk to you yet……	不是的，妳誤會了！Sandra 是我的表妹，她剛剛突然打電話給我，說是參加完一場附近的萬聖節變裝派對，想在我們這裡借住一晚再回去，我還沒來的及跟妳說……
Sandra	Harvery, I took a shower and changed my clothes...Hello, I am Sandran, you **must** be Victoria! I heard about you many times from Harvey. You are such a beauty.	Harvey，我洗好澡換好衣服了……妳好，我是 Sandra，想必妳就是 Victoria 吧！我經常聽 Harvey 提起妳，妳果然是位大美人。
Victoria	You...are Harvery's cousin?	妳……妳是 Harvey 的表妹？
Sandra	That's right. Sorry to **disturb** you, it was late after the party, so I just thought I could stay at Harvey's home for one night. It is very sorry to make you misunderstand.	對啊，不好意思突然過來打擾，派對結束之後已經很晚了，所以想說來 Harvey 家借住一晚，讓妳誤會了真的很抱歉。
Harvey	Why not go out for a late-night snacks after resolving the misunderstanding?	既然誤會解開了，不如我們三個人去吃個宵夜吧？

必會單字一手抓

❶ close v. 關（店）、打烊

The bakery shortly opened for one month then closed.

那家麵包店才開幕短短一個月就關門大吉了。

❷ immediately adv. 馬上、立刻

Please give me the financial statement of last month immediately.

請馬上把上個月的財務報告給我。

❸ disturb v. 打擾

Sorry to disturb you so late.

不好意思這麼晚還來打擾妳。

❹ displease v. 使不高興

The children shouted outside which made granny very displeased.

孩子們在窗外大吼大叫，使老奶奶很不高興。

❺ bedroom n. 臥室

After the argument, Cindy spent an hour sobbing in the bedroom.

大吵完後 Cindy 在臥室大哭了一小時。

❻ artifice n. 詭計、欺騙

That woman cheated them with an artifice.

那女人用詭計欺騙了他們。

❼ misunderstand v. 誤會

The colleges' kindness was misunderstood to be a non-goodness' sarcacism.

同事的好意被她誤解成是不懷好意的嘲諷。

❽ costume n. 服裝、裝束
Do you know where I could rent the characters' costume of Disney?
妳知道要到哪裡才能租到迪士尼卡通人物的服裝嗎？

❾ stay v. 待在
Jessica stays at the hotel near Central Park.
Jessica 待在離中央公園附近的旅館。

❿ must aux. 一定是、八成
He must have a traffic jam on the way.
他一定是在路上遇到塞車了。

30 秒會話教室

以下幾種都是詢問「發生了甚麼事？」的用法，如：What's going on? What happened? What's happening? What's wrong?

名人怎麼說？

Between men and women there is no friendship possible. There is passion, enmity, worship, love, but no friendship. —Oscar Wilde
在男女之間是不可能有友情的。有激情、怨懟、尊敬、愛意，沒有友情。
—王爾德

情境 20 在女方家樓下看到影子以為是小王

會話訓練班

某個晚上 Ivan 跟女友 Jessica 約好在家中見面。當 Ivan 來到女友家樓下時，卻看到關著窗簾的窗戶背後，Jessica 正做著非常煽情的舉動……

One night, Ivan and Jessica plan to meet at home. When Ivan is downstairs, he sees her doing something very **steamy behind** the window **curtains**.

Ivan	Jessica, open the door now.	Jessica，快開門。
Jessica	Coming, Ivan, why are you in such a **hurry**?	來了，Ivan，甚麼事情這麼著急啊？
Ivan	Is there a man in your room?	妳房間裡是不是有其他男人？
Jessica	No! Why did you say so?	沒有啊！你為什麼會這麼說？
Ivan	I just saw you dancing steamily and then **jumping** into a man.	我剛剛在樓下看妳在窗邊一下跳艷舞、後來又撲到一個男人身上。
Jessica	How come? I knew you were coming, so I just **wore** my jeans by the windows.	怎麼可能？因為我知道你快要到了，所以剛才我只不過是在窗邊穿上牛仔褲而已啊！

Ivan	Wearing jeans?	穿牛仔褲？
Jessica	Yes! I could show you, because this **skinny jeans** are too **tight**, so it took me some efforts to wear it.	對啊！我示範給你看，因為這件緊身牛仔褲太緊了，我總是要花一番工夫才能穿上它。
Ivan	I saw you jumping to a man, what was that?	那我還看到妳撲向一個男人，那是怎麼回事？
Jessica	Where is a man? I was unsteady so I fell into a **hat-stand**!	哪裡有甚麼男人？那是因為我重心不穩，跌到衣帽架上了啦！

必會單字一手抓

❶ curtain **n.** 簾幕

I can see a glimmer of light through the curtain.

我可以透過窗簾看到一絲微光。

❷ behind **prep.** 在…後面

There is a bank behind the library.

在那棟銀行的後面有一座圖書館。

❸ steamy **adj.** 煽情的、狂熱的

The movie has some steamy scenes, so don't let the young children watch it.

這部電影裡有一些煽情的鏡頭，所以不要讓年幼的孩子觀看。

❹ hurry **n.** 匆忙

I had to wash and dress in a hurry, because I didn't have much time.

我必須匆忙的洗澡和換衣，因為我沒有太多時間。

❺ jump **v.** 撲向

It is a very powerful image that a lion jumps to the antelope.

獅子撲向羚羊的畫面非常具有震撼力。

❻ wear **v.** 穿

Why don't you wear the pink dress your mom bought you.

妳怎麼不穿上媽媽送妳的那件粉紅色洋裝呢？

❼ jeans **n.** 牛仔褲

Do my shirt and jeans go together?

我的襯衫和牛仔褲配嗎？

❽ tight **adj.** 緊的

My sister complained that the shoes I bought her were too tight.

妹妹抱怨我送她的那雙鞋子太緊了。

❾ hat-stand **n.** 立式衣帽架

Dad forgot his coat on the hat-stand at home and left.

爸爸忘了自己的大衣還放在家裡的衣帽架上就離開了。

❿ skinny **adj.** 極瘦的

She is skinny enough without going on a diet.

她不必節食就已經很瘦了。

30 秒會話教室

當你想完全否定某種可能性時，可以說:That's impossible. 那是不可能的。It's out of the question. 這是完全不必考慮的。It's never gonna happen. 這是不可能發生的。

關鍵字搜尋

牛仔褲Jeans

Skinny Jeans - It is a tight jeans that fit closely around the leg. You'll look chic if you have a slim figure, especially even better with longer legs.
窄管牛仔褲—褲子緊貼者腿。適合身材纖細者特別是腿長者。

Straight Jeans - Straight jeans is a kind of jeans which the leg opening is almost exactly the same from the knee down to the ankle.
直筒牛仔褲—這種牛仔褲從膝蓋到腳踝都是一樣的寬。

Flare Cut Jeans - The flared cut jeans is narrow at the thigh and knee, and then widens at the calf. It is great for making your legs look long. High heels are other most befitting footwear.
喇叭牛仔褲—在大腿與膝蓋比較窄而在小腿部分變寬，這類型的牛仔褲讓你的腳看起來更長。適合搭配高跟鞋。

Bell Bottom - It is loosed from the knee downwards while flaring from the thigh. You can wear with heels to lengthen your legs for the best effect. It is good for all body styles and great for hiding not-so-perfect legs.
大喇叭褲—在膝蓋以下變很寬，從大腿部分開始變寬，你可以穿高跟鞋以達到最強視覺效果，適合各種身材，特別適合把不完美的腿遮起來。

情境 21 西裝上有唇印

會話訓練班

Albert 再度約認識許久的 Marjorie 出去喝咖啡，但他發現平常開朗健談的 Marjorie 今天卻一反常態，看起來愛理不理的樣子……

Albert invites Marjorie whom he knows for a long time to have a coffee again. She used to be a **conversational** person, but today she looks indifferent...

Albert	Marjorie, what's happening? You didn't talk today, are you uncomfortable?	Marjorie，妳怎麼了？今天出來都不說話，身體不舒服嗎？
Marjorie	No, I am feeling well.	沒有啊，我身體好得很。
Albert	Or you are in the bad mood? What obstacles do you meet at work?	還是心情不好，或是工作上遇到甚麼問題了呢？
Marjorie	Albert, if you have a girlfriend, why you keep asking me out? This is not respectful!	Albert，如果你有了女朋友，為什麼還要一直約我出來呢？這樣很不尊重人耶！
Albert	I don't have a girlfriend.	我沒有女朋友啊。
Marjorie	Why you have **lipstick prints** on your shirt? If not your girlfriend, that would be a **one-night-stand** person?	那你的襯衫怎麼會有唇印？不是女朋友，那就是一夜情的對象囉？

Albert Oh, you mean this. That is a special design! I thought that was **funny**, so I brought it at the store right away.

喔，妳說這個啊！這是特別設計的圖案啦！我在店裡看到覺得很有趣，馬上就買下來了。

Marjorie Really? I thought you dated with other women, then asked me out later on. That was very **dirty**!

真的嗎？我還以為你先跟別的女人見面，馬上又約我出來，真下流！

Albert Of course not! Especially, nowadays girls don't use **lipstick**, but using lip **gloss**. So you are jealous of this and don't talk with me.

當然沒有囉！況且現在的女生不是都不擦口紅、而改用唇蜜了嗎？原來妳是為了這個在吃醋而不說話的啊？

Marjorie Hum, don't **flatter** yourself!

哼，你少臭美了！

必會單字一手抓

❶ conversational **adj.** 健談的

He met a customer who is very conversational.

他遇到了一位非常健談的客戶。

❷ print **n.** 印記

The time leaves its prints on all of us

時光在我們所有人身上留下印記。

❸ funny adj. 有趣
The cartoon is very funny that even adult would like it.
這部卡通很有趣就連大人都會喜歡。

❹ one-night stand n. 一夜情
I was hoping for a lasting love, not just a one-night stand.
我希望的是長存的愛情，而不是短暫的一夜情。

❺ dirty adj. 猥褻的、下流的
Three drunk men sat at the door telling dirty jokes.
有三個醉漢坐在門口一邊喝酒一邊說著黃色笑話。

❻ lipstick n. 口紅
Most of men think women wearing lipstick is sexy.
男性普遍認為女人塗口紅的模樣非常性感。

❼ gloss n. 光澤
Her hair has lovely gloss.
她的頭髮美麗又有光澤。

❽ jealous adj. 吃醋的、忌妒的
She was jealous of her beauty.
她忌妒她的美貌。

❾ flatter v. 諂媚、奉承
At the office, there always will have someone who likes to flatter boss.
辦公室裡總是有些喜歡奉承老闆的人。

30 秒會話教室

Don't flatter yourself. 少臭美了、少往臉上貼金了、少自以為是了。這句話非常好用喔！

關鍵字搜尋

Get Pink Lips.

1. Eat fruits and vegetables that are red in color. For example, you can eat more Tomatoes and Strawberries.
   多吃紅色蔬果。如：番茄，草莓。

2. Decreasing your tea and coffee intake might result in pink lips.
   減少茶與咖啡的攝取可以使唇色粉嫩。

3. Exposure to the sun might cause Lips be darken. Use a balm with SPF 15. Make sure to wear lip protection when going outdoors.
   唇色會變深是由於太陽的曝曬。要使用SPF15的護唇膏。確保外出時有做唇部防曬。

4. Avoid licking your lips. Wetting them with saliva might lead to dryness and darkening of the lips.
   避免用舌頭舔嘴唇，口水會使嘴唇弄得濕濕的又會使唇色加深。

情境 22 誰留下的女性內衣？

會話訓練班

Doris 幾乎每周都會到男友家約會，順便幫在外租屋的男友打掃房間。但這天她卻在男友的衣櫃裡發現一套女性內衣……

Doris has a date at her boyfriend's house almost every week, and helps him to clean the room he rented. One day, she finds out a piece of bras and panty in his **wardrobe**...

Doris	You had better **explain** these, a piece of **female bras** and panty?	你最好解釋一下這是甚麼，一套女性內衣褲！？
Miles	You...Why you touch my stuff?	妳……妳怎麼亂動我的東西啊！
Doris	Usually you are **pleased** to let me clean your room; could it be possible that you take a woman home?	平常你都很樂於讓我整理房間的啊，難不成你帶了其他女人回來？
Miles	No, I don't. Please trust me.	我沒有，請妳相信我。
Doris	So you are a **transvestism**？	那就是你有變裝癖囉？
Miles	I don't have such a strange hobby!	我沒有那種奇怪的嗜好啦！
Doris	Then tell me now, what is going on? Don't say that your mom left these.	那你快點說啊，這到底是怎麼回事？別跟我說這是你媽留下來的喔。

Miles Actually, my female co-workers have a group **purchase** of bras and panties, and they need some people to make it. I thought that was fun, so I bought it as a gift for you. See, the price **tag** is still there.

其實是我們辦公室的女同事在團購內衣，剛好還缺幾個人，所以我覺得好玩也買了一套，想說日後可以送給妳當禮物也不錯，妳看，上面的吊牌還沒拆呢。

Doris I won't wear such **revealing** underwear!

我才不會穿款式這麼暴露的內衣呢！

Miles Then I **keep** and admire them by myself.

那我就自己留著欣賞囉！

必會單字一手抓

❶ wardrobe n. 衣櫃

All the shirts and dresses hang together in the same wardrobe.

所有的襯衫洋裝都掛在同一個衣櫃裡。

❷ bra n. 內衣

She likes to buy expensive bras.

她喜歡買昂貴的內衣。

❸ explain v. 解釋

If she were here, I could explain myself to her.

如果她在的話，我可以當面和她解釋。

❹ pleased adj. 高興的、滿意的
I was pleased to get up in the early morning.
我很高興早點起床。

❺ transvestism n. 異性裝扮癖
He has been a transvestism since he was young; he doesn't care how others look at him.
他從小就是有異性裝扮癖；他不在乎外在的眼光。

❻ purchase v. 購買
You can purchase an airplane ticket online.
你可以在線上買機票。

❼ tag n. 標籤
The clerk attached a price tag to each item.
店員給每個商品貼標籤。

❽ revealing adj. 坦露身體的
She wears revealing and alluring dress.
她穿著很暴露又誘人的洋裝。

❾ keep v. 保留、保存
In morden times, people keep food in a refrigerator to preserve.
在現代，人們將食物放在冰箱以保存。

❿ female adj. 女性的
Being a nurse is regarded as a female career.
護士普遍被認為是女性的職業。

30 秒會話教室

You had better listen to your teacher. 你最好聽你老師的話。此處的「最好」帶有命令的口吻，適用於上對下的時候，如果是要禮貌地請求別人則是 It might be better for you to listen to your teacher. 你還是聽老師的話比較好。

關鍵字搜尋

Bra Designs

1. Adhesive Bra：也就是台灣說的Nu Bra隱形胸罩。Adhesive (adj.) 黏著的。
2. Built-in Bra：近年流行的有罩杯的細肩帶款式。
3. Push-up Bra：集中拉高打造事業線的Bra就是這個字。
4. Sport Bra：現在越來越多人有跑步的習慣，當然也有給運動時候穿的Bra囉！
5. Nursing Bra：專門給媽咪哺乳用的Bra。

情境 23 跟蹤你，去哪裡？

會話訓練班

暨上次 Harvey 帶表妹回家後，Victoria 便開始對男友不太放心。星期六，她像平常一樣跟 Harvey 說要到服飾店裡去顧生意，其實是故意在公寓樓下等著看 Harvey 平常假日都去了哪……

After Harvey takes his cousin home last time, Victoria starts being suspicious of him. On Saturday, she tells Harvey that she is going to work at her clothes store as usual. But in fact, she deliberately waits downstairs and investigates where he goes every weekend...

Victoria	You are **caught red-handed**! What are you doing here?	被我人贓俱獲了吧！你在這裡做什麼？
Harvey	Darling, why are you here? You don't have business at the clothes store?	親愛的，妳怎麼會在這裡？服飾店的生意不用做了嗎？
Victoria	I have already asked a **part-timer** to look after it for me. I want to make sure where you go around every weekend. As it turns out, you go to this store named "Small **wildcat**"?	我已經請工讀生幫我顧店了，就是要來看你平常假日都跑到哪裡去了。原來都是跑到這種「小野貓」店來啊？
Harvery	Are you following me all the way?	妳一路跟蹤我到這裡來嗎？

Victoria	yes, or how could I **nail** a lie? You always said that you go jogging every weekend!	對啊，不然我怎麼有辦法拆穿你一直以來的謊言？你都跟我說假日是去慢跑！
Harvey	I did go jogging for sure. I little by little have interest in the store since the day I saw it **accidentally**. I didn't intend to lie to you.	我的確是出來慢跑沒錯，自從某次偶然看到這家店，才慢慢開始產生興趣的，並不是有意要騙妳的。
Victoria	You said you only give your love to me in your entire life. It could be so **cheap**, even the girls here could get it?	你說這輩子只會獻給我一個人的愛，原來這麼廉價，連這裡的小姐也能得到？
Harvey	Girls? It is the **pound** for **stray** cats.	甚麼小姐？這裡是流浪貓收容中心。
Victoria	Stray cats pound?	流……流浪貓收容中心？
Harvey	Yes, every time I pass by, I would go inside and see the cute cats. How about adopting one?	對啊，我現在跑步經過這裡，都會進去看看可愛的小貓咪。我們養一隻怎麼樣？

必會單字一手抓

❶ red-handed **adj.** 現行犯的

Harry was caught red-handed stealing a car.

Harry 被當場抓到偷車。

❷ catch **v.** 抓住、捕獲

The police caught a criminal in one day.

警方一天之內逮捕到犯人。

❸ part-timer **n.** 兼職工作者

Some students would choose to be a part-timer during the school years.

有些學生會選擇在就學的時候當兼職工作者。

❹ wildcat **n.** 野貓、山貓

There are many wildcats in the forest.

那片森林裡有許多野貓。

❺ nail **v.** 揭露、揭穿

The teacher nailed Peter for the lie of not doing homework in front to the whole class.

老師在全班同學面前揭穿了 Peter 因為沒有寫功課而撒的謊言。

❻ cheap **v.** 便宜、廉價

The raw ham of that store is cheap and tasteful.

那家肉店所賣的生火腿便宜又好吃。

❼ stray **adj.** 流浪的、迷路的

In Taiwan, the problem of stray cats and dogs is very serious.

在台灣，流浪貓狗的問題非常嚴重。

❽ pound **n.** 動物收容所.
Monica found her cat at the pound.
Monica 在動物收容所找到她的貓。

❾ accidentally **adv.** 偶然的、意外的
We met accidentally in Taipei.
我們偶然地在台北相遇。

30 秒會話教室

當某人在意想不到的時間和地點出現時，可以用以下兩句來表達你的驚訝：What are you doing here? 你在這裡做甚麼？或是：Why are you here? 你怎麼會在這裡？

名人怎麼說？

Let us always meet each other with smile, for the smile is the beginning of love.
— Mother Teresa
讓我們見面時一直對彼此微笑，因為微笑是愛的開始。—德蕾莎修女

Love is composed of a single soul inhabiting two bodies. —Aristotle
愛是同一個靈魂住在兩個不同的身體。—亞里斯多德

情境 24 小三送的定情物？

會話訓練班

Kenneth 跟 Irene 這對情侶因為不住在同一個城市裡，所以聚少離多。這天 Kenneth 終於連放了幾天假可以到 Irene 家相聚，然而他卻在 Irene 家的廚房發現了一個東西……

Kenneth and Irene don't live in the same city, so they can't meet each other often. **Finally**, Kenneth has a few days off so he could meet her. Nonetheless, he finds something at Irene's kitchen...

Kenneth　Honey, when did you buy another new cellphone?

親愛的，妳甚麼時候又買了一支新手機呀？

Irene　What cellphone? Oh, you mean that one! Do you remember the policeman who gave me a cake full of the ants? He gave that to me.

甚麼手機？喔，你說那個啊！妳還記得有位男警察送我長滿螞蟻的蛋糕嗎？那也是他送的。

Kenneth　You said it was nothing **between** you and him? Why he gave you a present?

妳不是說跟他之間沒甚麼嗎？他為什麼還要送妳禮物？

Irene　Wait, he wanted to make up for making my kitchen a whole messy.

等一下，他是為了彌補把我的廚房弄的一團糟才送的。

Kenneth	Don't you know that it will make him have an **expectation** of you? You just used him to **fill** your **loneliness** because we couldn't meet each other regularly.	妳知不知道這樣會讓對方對妳有所期待？我看妳是因為跟我聚少離多，才拿他來填補寂寞吧？
Irene	Kenneth, you are away too far! I am always very **faithful**, and didn't betray you.	Kenneth，你這樣說就太過分了！我一直對你很忠貞，沒有做不出對不起你的事情。
Kenneth	Why he still gave you an expensive cell phone? Isn't that for the convenience of him to call you?	那他為什麼還要送妳這麼昂貴的手機，難道不是為了隨時方便聯絡嗎？
Irene	What cellphone? That is just a mobile phone style's **deodorant** spray.	甚麼手機？那只是手機造型的空氣清淨劑啦！
Kenneth	What? Hum...I couldn't tell it unless I pick it up and look carefully.	甚麼？嗯……不拿起來仔細看完全看不出來耶。
Irene	He hoped that even I had a boyfriend, but I still could ask him for help. We knew that was just being **polite**, so he gave me a **creative** gift.	他是希望即使我有男友，只要有事還是可以隨時找他幫忙，但我倆都知道這只是客套話，所以他就送了這個有創意的禮物。

必會單字一手抓

❶ finally adv. 最終

I finally finished this thick novel.

這本很厚的小說終於看完了。

❷ between prep. 在…之間

The tension between them has eased a little.

他們之間的緊張關係有比較緩和。

❸ expectation n. 期待

Profits are above our expectations.

利益超過了我們的預期。

❹ fill v. 填滿

Please fill out the form in English.

請你用英文填完表格。

❺ loneliness n. 孤獨

With many friends, he still has a fear of loneliness.

有很多朋友，但他還是很害怕孤獨。

❻ faithful adj. 忠貞的、忠誠的

Dogs are the faithful friends of human.

狗狗是人類最忠誠的朋友。

❼ deodorant n. 防臭劑、防臭的

She applies deodorant to her armpits after she takes a shower.

沐浴後，她在腋下塗上防臭劑。

❽ polite adj. 有禮貌的、客氣的

The young mom had a very polite child.

那位年輕媽媽有一位非常有禮貌的小孩。

❾ creative **adj.** 有創造力的、有想像力的
Students are encouraged to be creative at the American school.
美國的學校都鼓勵學童要有充沛的想像力。

30 秒會話教室

當對方說出某些口不擇言的話，或是做出很嚴重的行為，可以用以下說法來表達強烈的指責：You're away too far. 你太過分了。You've gone too far. 你這麼做實在是太過份了。

名人怎麼說？

Being deeply loved by someone gives you strength, while loving someone deeply gives you courage. —Lao Tzu
被人深深愛著給你力量，深深愛著某人給你勇氣。—老子

Choose your love, Love your choice. —Thomas S. Monson
擇你所愛，愛你所擇。

情境 25 忘了你是誰

會話訓練班

某天晚上 Derek 跟女友 Fiona 甜蜜地手牽著手走在人行道上散步，此時卻有一輛大卡車疑似司機酒後駕車，失控撞上了他們。兩人馬上被附近民眾送到醫院，急救撿回了一命，但醫生卻宣告 Fiona 可能失憶⋯⋯

One night, Derek and his girlfriend Fiona walk down the **sidewalk holding** hands. Suddenly, a truck driver seems to drive while being **intoxicated** and crush into them. They ard taken to the hospital by the people near by. They both save their lives. However, the doctor **declares** that Fiona might lose her memory...

Derek Fiona, it's me, Derek, do you remember me?

Fiona，是我，Derek，妳還記得我嗎？

Fiona Derek...who are you? My **head** hurts, where am I?

Derek⋯⋯你是誰？我的頭好痛，我在哪裡？

Derek Here is a hospital, don't be scared. Doctors and nurses will take care of you.

這裡是醫院，不要害怕，這裡的醫生和護士都會好好照顧妳的。

Fiona Why am I in the hospital?

我為什麼會在醫院裡？

Derek	That's my fault. I didn't protect you, and let you walk on the outer side, that's dangerous. When the accident happened, we walked on the sidewalk hand in hand. We were **hit** by a car. I have a minor injury, but you were in a **coma** for a whole day.	說起來這都是我的錯，是我沒有好好保護妳，讓妳走在比較危險的外側。事發當時我們手牽著手走在人行道上，被車輛給撞上，我的傷勢比較輕，但妳昏迷了一天。
Fiona	hand in hand...what kind of relationship are we?	牽手……我們是甚麼關係呢？
Derek	We are a couple of lovers in dating maybe you couldn't remember, but I really love you. Although the doctor says you might lose your memory, I still feel the pangs of heart when I see you can't remember me.	我們是交往中的情侶，或許妳不記得了，但是我很愛妳。雖然醫生說妳有失憶的可能性，但真的看到妳不記得我的樣子，我還是好心痛。
Fiona	Sorry....	對不起……。
Derek	This is not your fault. You don't have to apologize. You just need to take a **rest**. I will stay beside you and help you to **recall** the memories. As the last resort, we can always fall in love again.	這不是妳的錯，妳不需要道歉。妳只要好好休養就可以了，我會陪在妳身邊幫助妳喚回所有的記憶，大不了我們重新再相愛一次。

Fiona Haha. Darling, I am fine! It is very rare to see you have such deep feeling so I pretend I lost my memory deliberately.

呵呵，親愛的，我沒事啦！只是難得看到你這麼深情的模樣，所以故意假裝想逗你玩的。

必會單字一手抓

❶ hold v. 握住

We hold different views.

我們有不同的觀點 。

❷ sidewalk n. 人行道

The sidewalk is very uneven, so be careful.

人行道很凹凸不平所以請小心。

❸ intoxicate v. 使喝醉

The colleague only drank a glass and was intoxicated.

那位女同事只喝了一杯酒就醉了。

❹ declare v. 宣告、宣稱

His wife declared that she had the evidence of his love affair.

他的妻子宣稱已經掌握了他外遇的證據。

❺ head n. 頭部

To hold a new-born baby, you must protect his head.

抱起剛出生的小嬰兒時一定要保護好頭部。

❻ hit **v.** 打擊、碰撞

A big rock hit the car passed by.

一顆巨大的落石擊中了剛好經過的車輛。

❼ injury **n.** 傷害、損害

He survived from a car accident without injury at all.

他在一起車禍意外存活並毫髮無傷。

❽ coma **n.** 昏睡、昏迷

The patient rallied from the coma.

病人從昏迷中甦醒過來。

❾ rest **n.** 休息、休養

We need to get some rest after running 10km.

我們在跑完十公里後需要休息一下。

❿ recall **v.** 回憶、使想起

I can't recall where the key is.

我想不起來鑰匙在哪裡。

30 秒會話教室

As the last resort 有「做為最後一招」的意思，如：As the last resort we can always walk home. 大不了我們用走的回家就可以了。

情境 26 我們都後悔了

會話訓練班

Brian 自從得知 Phoebe 一開始是朋友雇來與他認識的之後，就開始對 Phoebe 的感情存疑。一天 Phoebe 在忍無可忍之下決定分手，並買了機票準備飛回洛杉磯……

Since Brain knows that Phoebe is hired by his friend to be his lover, he feels suspicious of their love. One day, Phoebe decides to break up because that is just **beyond bearing**. Not only that, she buys a ticket to L.A....

Brian	Excuse me, was Phoebe Jackson **boarding** on this **plane**?	請問一位叫 Phoebe Jackson 的小姐已經搭上這班飛機了嗎？
The ground staff	Just a moment, I will **check** it right now... Sir, we do not have this lady's **record** in our computer.	請稍等，我馬上為您查詢……。先生，我們的電腦裡面沒有這位小姐的登機記錄喔。
Brian	How comes...Wait a **moment**, my phone rings. Hello?	怎麼會這樣……等一下，我接一下電話。喂？
Phoebe	Hey, is this Brian? Where are you? Why aren't you at home?	喂，是 Brian 嗎？你跑去哪裡了？怎麼不在家？

Brian	I want to ask you the same question! Didn't you take the plane to L. A.?	我才想問妳一樣的問題呢！妳不是要搭飛機回洛杉磯嗎？
Phoebe	Yes, but... I couldn't let go this relationship, so I changed my mind, and took a taxi to your home. You are not there.	對啊，可是…我還是放不下這段感情，於是我轉變心意了，馬上搭計程車回家找你，你卻不在。
Brian	Actually, I came to the **airport** to have you back. I am sorry, and now I **regret** for treating you badly. If I didn't catch your phone call, maybe we will miss each other forever.	其實我也跑到機場來想要挽回妳，對不起。我很遺憾我對你不好。要是沒接到妳的這通電話，我們可能就錯過了彼此呢！
Phoebe	When I arrived home, and didn't see you. I thought you didn't care at all.	當我回到家卻沒看到你的身影，我以為你一點都不在意。
Brian	How come I don't care? You stay at home and wait for me. I will drive home right now. Let's have a talk about our future.	我怎麼可能會不在意，妳在家裡等我，我馬上就開車回去，讓我們好好討論我們的未來。

Phoebe	Hmm, moreover, thank you for **reconsidering** the relationship between us.	嗯，還有，謝謝你，願意重新考慮我們之間的感情。

必會單字一手抓

❶ bear **v.** 忍耐、忍受
Please do not leave me. I couldn't bear it.
請不要離開我，我沒有辦法忍受。

❷ beyond **adv.** 超出
The world is so big beyond our imagination.
這個世界的廣大程度超乎我們的想像。

❸ plane **n.** 飛機 字彙連結站 airplane
I saw a movie on a plane.
我在飛機上看了一個電影。

❹ board **v.** 登上（飛機等）
The girl boarded the plan to China today.
那女孩今天搭機要前往中國。

❺ record **n.** 紀錄
This month has been the hottest one in the record.
這個月是史上最熱的一個月。

❻ regret v. 後悔
Don't do anything that you will regret.
不要做任何會讓你後悔的事。

❼ airport n. 機場
They landed at Taiwan Taoyuan International Airport.
他們在台灣桃園機場降落。

❽ reconsider v. 重新考慮
You should reconsider before you make a decision.
你應該在你做決定之前重新考慮。

❾ check v. 查驗、核對
Let me check whether the steak is burned or not.
讓我檢查一下牛排有沒有燒焦。

❿ moment n. 瞬間、片刻
At that moment, everyone stopped eating.
在那瞬間，大家停止吃飯。

30 秒會話教室

服務業經常需要禮貌性地請對方稍待片刻，此時可以用以下兩種說法：Just a moment, please. One moment, please. 請稍等一下。

情境 27 父母反對

會話訓練班

Louis 和 Eliza 這對就讀同一所大學的情侶非常相愛，但隨著畢業的日子一天天逼近，Louis 的煩惱似乎也越來越加深……

Louis and Eliza is a couple of lovers, studying at the same college. They love each other very much. Though the **graduation** is getting **closer**, Louis becomes more and more worried...

Louis Eliza, didn't you say that after we graduate, you would introduce me to your parents, and then request them to agree with our living together plan?

Eliza，妳不是說等到我們兩人畢業後，就帶我回家介紹給妳的父母，然後請求他們讓我們在外面同居嗎？

Eliza Yes.

是啊。

Louis But you said your father **dislikes** man studying design, didn't you? He thinks man should like sports, or being a lawyer or doctor.

可是妳不是也說過，妳的父親非常討厭學設計的男生嗎？他覺得男生就應該要喜歡運動，或是當個律師或醫生。

Eliza Yes, he also dislikes the one who uses the computer all the time.

對啊，而且他也不喜歡一直用電腦的人。

Louis Then your parents would not like me. Maybe they will make me feel embarrassed in person.

那這樣妳的父母不會喜歡我？說不定還會當面給我難堪。

Eliza But he surely will keep asking you which team you like?

但他一定會一直問你喜歡哪支球隊？

Louis I don't want to see them **force** you to break up with me. We'd better separate now.

我不想看到他們逼妳跟我分手，那還不如，我們現在就分開吧。

Eliza What are you talking about? Even though my Dad doesn't like a man like that, it is just my father's **principles** about making friends. Do as you would be **done** by. He won't **impose** his thoughts on others. He is a **liberal** father.

你在說甚麼啊？我的父親雖然不喜歡那樣的人，但他是指他自己的交友原則啦。己所不欲，勿施於人，他不會硬要把自己的觀念強加在別人身上的，他是個很開明的父親。

Louis Really?

真的嗎？

Eliza Yes! He said everyone has **rights** to own one's **likes** and **dislikes**. I just tell you his, but it doesn't mean he would ask my boyfriend in demand, so don't worry.

沒錯！他說每個人都有權利擁有自己的喜好，我只是告訴你他的喜好，並不代表他會這樣要求我的男朋友，你別擔心。

必會單字一手抓

❶ close **adj.** 近的、接近的

Her house is close to the school.

她家離那間學校非常近。

❷ graduation **v.** 畢業

After graduation, Joe moves to Singapore and have a high paying job.

大學畢業後，Joe 搬去新加坡並有著一個高薪的工作。

❸ dislike **n.** 不喜愛、厭惡

Everyone has likes and dislikes of their own, so we should respect each other.

每個人都有自己的喜好，應該互相尊重。

❹ force **v.** 強迫、迫使

In spite of being forced to learn playing the piano in the beginning, John had the interest in it at last.

儘管一開始 John 是被強迫去學鋼琴的，他最後還是對鋼琴產生了興趣。

❺ principle **n.** 原則

The most fundamental management principle is to understand your staff.

最基本的管理原則就是要了解你的下屬。

❻ liberal **adj.** 心胸開闊的、開明的

He is lucky to have such liberal parents.

他很幸運能擁有那麼開明的父母。

❼ right **n.** 權利

Voting is the basic right of the people.

投票是人民的基本權利。

❽ done adj. 完成了的
This project is almost done.
這個計畫幾乎要完成了。

❾ impose v. 把…強加於
You could ask them to stay, but you can't impose on them.
你可以要求他們留下，但是不可以強逼他們。

30 秒會話教室

had better 的意思為「最好」，可簡寫為 'd better ，如:We'd better go now. 我們最好現在離開。You'd better go to school. 你最好去學校。

情境 28 在婚禮上悔婚

會話訓練班

Albert 跟 Marjorie 交往三個月就決定閃電結婚。但是隨著婚禮即將進行到走紅毯的最高潮前，Marjorie 突然開始產生了不確定感，甚至萌生了想要悔婚的念頭……

Albert and Marjorie decide to have a **flash marriage** after they start dating three months. Before the **climax** to walk the red **carpet** of the ongoing wedding, Marjorie suddenly starts to have a sense of being **unsure**, and even the idea of backing down the wedding...

Marjorie	Albert, I need to talk to you for a second.	Albert，我有事要跟你談一談。
Albert	Marjorie, you look so beautiful in that wedding dress, but what is it so urgent? Don't you know we cannot see each other before walking down the aisle?	Marjorie，妳穿婚紗的樣子好美，可是有甚麼事這麼緊急？妳不知道在走紅毯前我們是不能見面的嗎？
Marjorie	I know. I'm sorry, but I suddenly don't want to get married.	我知道，可是很抱歉，我突然不想結婚了。
Albert	You don't want to get married? Why? Didn't you happily say yes to my proposal?	不想結婚？為什麼？妳不是很開心地答應了我的求婚了嗎？

Marjorie I'm sorry. I was happy when you asked me to marry you. You see, I am an **introverted** person, and your **personality** is active and positive, which sometimes makes me feel under pressure. Just now there are so many guests waiting outside that I feel I can't **breathe**.

對不起，你向我求婚的時候我的確很高興，但是我是個內向的人，而你的個性卻主動又積極，這有時候會讓我感到很有壓力。光是現在有許多賓客在外面等，就快讓我喘不過氣了。

Albert Please take it easy. I know you have more constrained personality, but when two people are together, they are **complementary** to each other. Don't you think that each of us has grown up after being together?

妳別緊張，我知道妳的個性比較壓抑，但兩個人在一起是需要互補的，妳不覺得我們在一起之後，彼此都有成長了嗎？

Marjorie After being with you, I do become more positive and cheerful, but I still feel uneasy with getting married. I am really worried about whether I can play the **role** well of being a wife.

跟你在一起讓我變得比較積極開朗，但我對結婚這件事還是會感到不安，我在擔心自己能否真的能扮演好一個妻子的角色。

Albert That's what you are worried about. At least it is something I feel good about it because it's not like you don't want to marry me. If you really don't want to do this, then I will go tell everyone the wedding is off. You don't need to worry about the things later.

原來妳只是在擔心這個，而不是因為不想嫁給我，至少這是值得開心的事情。如果妳真的不願意，那我現在就去告訴大家婚禮取消了，妳就別擔心後續的事情了。

Marjorie Wait, Albert, thank you for your understanding. I decided to be brave for love once again. Let's get married!

等等，Albert，謝謝你的體諒。我決定為了愛勇敢一次，我們還是結婚吧！

Albert Really? That's great!

真的嗎？那真是太好了！

必會單字一手抓

❶ flash adj. 一下子的

Ten years seemed just flash by.

十年一晃而過。

❷ marriage n. 婚姻

That celebrity couple's marriage is very admirable.

那對銀色夫妻的婚姻非常令人稱羨。

❸ climax n. 最高點、高潮

The climax of the awards ceremony is the performance of a legendary singer.

頒獎典禮的最高潮是一位傳奇歌手所帶來的表演。

❹ carpet n. 地毯

The living room carpet was bitten a hole by the dog.

客廳的地毯被小狗咬破了一個洞。

❺ unsure **adj.** 缺乏信心的
The boy's lack of confidence in his unsure performance makes his parents very worried.
那個男孩缺乏信心的表現讓父母看了非常擔心。

❻ personality **n.** 個性
The girl's unique personality has attracted the attention of many admirers.
那個女孩獨特的個性吸引了眾多愛慕者的目光。

❼ breathe **v.** 呼吸
The bride is so nervous at the wedding that she cannot breathe.
新娘在婚禮上緊張到無法呼吸。

❽ complementary **adj.** 互補的、相配的
The couple's personalities are complementary to each other, so they can get along.
那對夫妻的個性互補，相處起來非常融洽。

❾ role **n.** 角色
My sister plays the role of a fairy in the school's drama play.
妹妹在學校的話劇演出中飾演仙女的角色。

❿ introverted **adj.** 內向的
My brother is an introverted person that he is embarrassed to say hello to the relatives.
我的哥哥是一個內向的人，連看到親戚都不好意思打招呼。

30 秒會話教室

向心愛的另一半求婚該怎麼說呢？把以下兩種用法學起來吧！
如：Let's get married! 我們結婚吧！Would / will you marry me? 你願意嫁（娶）我嗎？

Part 3

情路上的阻礙

情境 29 隨時都在玩手機

會話訓練班

Patrick 在 Celia 的牽線下，跟 Celia 的姊姊 Heather 第一次見面，兩人約在一家頗有情調的餐廳用餐，但席間 Patrick 卻不停地使用手機……

Through Celia's introduction, Patrick is meeting her sister Heather the first time. They are having meals at a romantic restaurant, but Patrick has been constantly checking his **cell phone**...

Heather	Mr. Larsson, I've heard a lot about you from Celia...	Mr. Larsson，我從 Celia 那裡聽說了不少關於你的事情……
Patrick	Just call me Patrick.	叫我 Patrick 就可以了。
Heather	Patrick, I think you're a nice guy, but when you are doing a thing like keeping checking your cell phone, that makes me feel **offended**.	Patrick，我覺得你是一個很好的人，但像你這樣不時查看手機，讓我覺得很不受到尊重。
Patrick	Oh, excuse me for doing that. My client has some **emergency** situations that need me to take care of. I don't want to go answering my phone all the time when I'm seeing you, so I ask them to send me emails that I can check on my cell phone.	喔，不好意思，我的客戶有緊急的事情要我處理，但我不想在與妳見面的時間一直跑去接電話，因此我請他們傳 email 給我，我在手機上查看。

Heather	I think by doing so; you neither take care of your work well, nor talk to me seriously. Why don't you **concentrate** on one thing only?	但你這樣不但沒有把工作處理好，同時也沒有認真地在與我談話，倒不如一次專心做一件事？
Patrick	I'm really sorry about that. You're right. People nowadays **depend** on the **high technology** products way too much. Since the launching of the **smart phones**, now I can't take some good rest on my days off because the clients can always find me, even though they bring so much convenience to life.	真的很對不起，妳說的對。現代人就是太依賴這些高科技產品了，自從智慧型手機問世之後，雖然為生活上帶來許多方便，卻也因為客戶隨時都找的到你，所以連假日都無法好好休息。
Heather	You bet. You know you can still put your work aside and take some rest on your days off if you do your jobs well on the weekdays.	對呀，其實只要平日有盡責地將工作處理好，假日的時候是可以暫時拋開工作休息一下的。
Patrick	As a matter of fact, The emergency situations the client has aren't that serious anyway. I've already sent him the steps of the solutions. Now I can really talk to you nicely.	其實這位客戶的事情也不是多嚴重，我已經將解決問題的步驟傳送給他了，接下來我會好好地陪妳聊天的。
Heather	Great!	好啊！
Patrick	Speaking of cell phones, there are so many new **functions** you really couldn't imagine before. Check out this fun **application**!	不過說到手機，還真的有許多以前無法想像的新功能呢！妳看這個有趣的 APP 軟體！

必會單字一手抓

❶ cell phone **n.** 手機

Almost everyone nowadays has a cell phone.

現代人幾乎人人都有手機。

❷ offend **v.** 冒犯、觸怒

The visitor's move offended the lion inside the fence.

遊客的舉動觸怒了柵欄裡面的獅子。

❸ emergency **n.** 緊急狀況、突發事件

Remember to call 119 when encountering an emergency situation.

遇到緊急狀況記得撥打 119。

❹ meantime **n.** 其間、同時

Substantial personnel changes of the management are ongoing at the company. In the meantime, the secret new product which takes three years of research and development is also about to launch.

公司的管理階層正在進行大幅度的人事調動，與此同時，秘密研發 3 年的新產品也即將上市。

❺ concentrate **v.** 集中、全神貫注

Last night, I stayed up late for studying today's exam, but I can't concentrate on answering the questions now.

我昨晚為了今天的考試熬夜讀書，結果反而無法集中精神作答。

❻ technology **n.** 工藝、技術
The government has decided to use this latest technology in our infrastructure.
政府決定將這項最新技術用在基礎建設上。

❼ depend **v.** 依賴
Pets must rely on the owners to survive, so please treat them well.
寵物必須依賴主人才能生存，所以請好好地對待牠們。

❽ smart **adj.** 使用電腦的、自動的
Today's smart phones have comparable functions of a computer.
現今智慧手機的功能已可媲美一台電腦。

❾ function **n.** 功能
The mother did not know what to do when the dehydration function of the washing machine failed.
洗衣機的脫水功能故障了，讓媽媽不知該如何是好。

❿ application **n.** 應用、運用
The electronic operating system has a wide range of applications that can replace a lot of manpower.
這個電子作業系統的應用範圍非常廣泛，可以取代不少人力。

30 秒會話教室

當對方提起某個話題，就可以用 Speaking of「說到、提及」來接續，如：Speaking of Mary, have you seen her recently?
說到瑪麗，你最近有見過她嗎？

情境 30 還留著前女友的物品

會話訓練班

新婚的 Marjorie 正在幫老公 Albert 整理要去巴黎度蜜月的行李，卻意外地在衣櫃角落發現了一疊明信片，從內容判斷應該是 Albert 的前女友寄給他的……

Marjorie, who is newly married, is helping her husband Albert packing his luggage for their **honeymoon** to Paris, but **accidentally** finds a stack of postcards in the closet's corner. Judging from the contents, they should be sent by Albert's ex-girlfriend...

Marjorie I've found the stack of **postcards** in the closet's corner...

我在衣櫃裡發現了這疊明信片……。

Albert Oh, I have no idea where they have been. I really miss them.

喔，我都不知道把它丟到哪裡去了，好懷念啊。

Marjorie Aren't you going to tell me something about the person who sent you the cards?

你不跟我說說寄這些明信片的人的事情嗎？

Albert Hmm, it was from my ex-girlfriend. She was a flight attendant. She sent me a postcard once she traveled to a city.

嗯，是我的前女友寄的，她是個空姐，每到一個城市就會寄一張明信片給我。

Marjorie What happened then? Why didn't you stay together?

後來呢？你們怎麼沒有繼續在一起？

Albert	She was a **sensitive** person, like she was born **melancholy**. She was always **pessimistic** to everything, so we ended up breaking up.	她是個多愁善感的人，骨子裡總有一股揮之不去的憂鬱，對任何事情都很悲觀，所以我們最後還是分手了。
Marjorie	Do you still have some feelings to her? If you don't, why didn't you just **throw** them away?	你對她還有感情嗎？不然怎麼不把這些東西丟了？
Albert	Actually I think there is no way to forget memories; it's just sometimes these memories have no emotional components. So I keep the postcards because they are simply something that have some meanings to me, but they do not represent the feelings still. You can assure that.	其實我覺得人的回憶是沒有辦法說忘記就忘記的，只是這些回憶已經沒有了感情的成分，所以我把明信片留著只是單純因為這是有意義的東西，並不代表感情還在，妳可以放心。
Marjorie	I can understand that, because I'm a **nostalgic** person, who likes to keep some **memorable** items.	我能理解，因為我也是個念舊的人，喜歡留一些值得懷念的物品。
Albert	Thank you for your **understanding**. Once we arrive in Paris, we'll also create a lot of our own memories.	謝謝妳的體諒，等我們到了巴黎，也會創造許多屬於我們的回憶的。

必會單字一手抓

❶ honeymoon n. 蜜月

The island countries have been the first choice of honeymoon location for newlyweds.

海島國家向來是新婚夫妻度蜜月的首選。

❷ accidentally adv. 意外地、偶然地

The sister unexpectedly found herself being the object of discussions among her male friends.

妹妹意外地發現自己成了男性友人間討論的對象。

❸ postcard n. 明信片

Grandpa's interest is to collect all kinds of beautiful postcards.

爺爺的興趣是收集各種漂亮的明信片。

❹ sensitive adj. 敏感的、易受傷害的

I have met a sensitive boy, who always needs to be carefully appeased his emotions.

我認識了一位敏感的男孩，總是要小心安撫他的情緒。

❺ pessimistic adj. 悲觀的

Pessimistic thoughts are easily transmitted to others, and let the people around become unhappy.

悲觀的想法容易傳染給別人，讓周圍的人都變得不快樂。

❻ melancholy n. 憂鬱

Cheerfulness is health; its opposite, melancholy is disease.

快樂就是健康；憂鬱即是疾病。

❼ throw v. 拋、扔

The mom shouted to the brother and asked him to throw way a frog holding in his hands.

媽媽對弟弟大喊，要他把手中抓著的青蛙丟掉。

❽ nostalgic **adj.** 懷舊的、鄉愁的
Recently, the nostalgic trends are getting popular even in the restaurants.
近來連餐廳都吹起一股懷舊風。

❾ memorable **adj.** 值得懷念的、難忘的
When I was at college, I participated in many memorable events.
我在大學時期參加過許多令人難忘的活動。

❿ understanding **n.** 理解、同情
The little boy's annoying actions, in fact, was simply trying to get everyone's understanding and concern.
那個小男孩無理取鬧的舉動，其實無非是想獲得大家的理解與關注。

Nostalgia for the good old days. 好懷念那些美好的時光。I really miss those good times. 我真的很想念那些好時光。

關鍵字搜尋

Romantic Movie Date

1.Think what movies both of you like. Romance is rooted in shared interests.
思考一下你和你約會的對象都喜歡的電影。浪漫是建立在共同的興趣上。

2.Bring your date a movie-related gift. For example, if the movie is "Notebook," bring your date a notebook.
給你的約會對象一個跟電影有關的小禮物。舉例，如果是看電影手札情緣，你可以給他一個筆記本。

3.Provide snacks for the movie date. Sharing a bag of popcorn can be romantic.
為你的約會對象準備零食，一起吃一袋爆米花也很浪漫。

情境 31 愛看辣妹

會話訓練班

Austine 跟曖昧對象 Jocelyn 一起去逛街，沿途 Jocelyn 卻注意到 Austine 的眼睛不時注意著身邊經過的辣妹，這讓她心裡很不是滋味……

When Austine goes out shopping together with Jocelyn, his potential date, on the way, Jocelyn has noticed that Austine can't take his eyes away from some **sexy** girls passing by. This has made her not too happy...

Jocelyn	You have been checking out some hotties and sexy girls. You are so **horny**!	你從剛才就一直在看辣妹，真是好色！
Austine	This is not being horny. This is male's **instinct**. It's the same with that girls like checking out handsome guys!	這才不叫好色，這是男性的本能，就跟女生也喜歡看帥哥一樣啊！
Jocelyn	That I can't **deny** for sure, but can you at least not check out so **brazenly**?	這我的確無法反駁，但是至少不要看得那麼明顯嘛！
Austine	I think that it's **human nature** to see beautiful things around. As for whether checking it out discreetly or not, that's just being a hypocrite on the surface, it seems to me that people like me are more **frankly**, right?	喜歡看美麗的事物是人類的天性，至於看得明不明顯，那只不過是表面上的偽裝而已，反而像我這樣的人比較老實不是嗎？

Jocelyn	I think you're right, but I still feel uncomfortable after your explanations. Can't a man at least show some respect and attention to the woman beside him?	你說的沒錯，但我聽了就是莫名地不高興，難道男人就不能至少對身旁的女性表現出專注和尊重嗎？
Austine	Hehe, you already start getting jealous before we're really together?	呵呵，我們還沒在一起妳就在吃醋了嗎？
Jocelyn	You love checking out hotties even before we're being together. What am I going to do if we're really a couple?	我們還沒在一起你就這麼愛看辣妹，真的在一起我怎麼受的了？
Austine	No worries, men are **visual animals**. Enjoying seeing and falling in love are two completely different things.	放心，男人是視覺上的動物，欣賞跟喜歡是兩碼子事。
Jocelyn	Sigh, aren't there any men in this world who don't like to check out hotties?	唉，難道世界上就沒有不愛看辣妹的男人了嗎？
Austine	No way, even **blind** people want to see them mentally; it's just that they can't see them for real.	不可能的，就連瞎子的心裡也是會想看的，只是他們看不到而已。

必會單字一手抓

❶ sexy adj. 性感的、迷人的

The male singer has a very sexy voice.

那位男歌手擁有非常迷人的嗓音。

❷ horny adj. 好色的

Adolescent boys inevitably have some horny thoughts.

正值青春期的男孩難免會有一些好色的思想。

❸ instinct n. 本能

Most wild animals have a hunting instinct. People must be careful even after they are tamed.

野生動物都具有狩獵的本能，即使經過馴服仍然要小心。

❹ deny v. 否認

Don't deny that the girl you like is Lynn, right?

不必否認了，你喜歡的女孩就是 Lynn 對嗎？

❺ brazenly adv. 厚臉皮地、無恥地

My loafing uncle always brazenly comes stay at our home for several days.

遊手好閒的叔叔總是厚臉皮地到我們家賴著不走好幾天。

❻ human n. 人的、凡人皆有的

We are just human; we inevitably make mistakes.

我們只是凡人，難免會犯錯。

❼ nature n. 天性、本質

All women are born to have motherhood in nature.

所有的女性都有與生俱來的母性。

❽ blind adj. 盲的

My sister went to a blind date and met several nice men.

妹妹去參加了一場盲目約會並且認識了好幾位不錯的對象。

❾ visual **adj.** 視覺的

The movies in recent years are advertised with 3D effects that are to enhance the visual enjoyment.

近幾年來的電影都標榜 3D，讓視覺上的享受更加提升。

❿ frankly **adv.** 率直地、坦白地

He told me frankly that he did not like my book.

他老實地告訴我其實他並不喜歡我的書。

30 秒會話教室

當要向人坦承心中的某些想法時，可以用以下說法起頭，如：Frankly speaking/ To speak frankly, I don't like this idea at all. 老實說，我一點都不喜歡這個主意。

情境 32 今天要看哪部電影？

會話訓練班

Miles 跟女友 Doris 約好下班後去看場電影，但是兩人對看電影的喜好不同，在電影院外面遲遲無法決定要看哪一部……

Miles and his girlfriend Doris have scheduled to see a movie after work, but the two have different preferences for movies so they cannot decide what movie to see outside the movie theater...

Doris Both of these two films are started in 10 minutes. We are not going to make it if we can't decide soon.

這兩部電影都是再過 10 分鐘就要開演了，再不趕快決定就來不及了。

Miles I know that, but I really don't want to see that **romantic comedy** movie. I will definitely **fall asleep**.

我知道，可是我真的不想看那部愛情喜劇電影，我一定會睡著。

Doris I've heard my friends say that film is extremely romantic and touching. They say you need to bring some extra packs of **tissues**.

聽朋友說那部電影很浪漫、很感人耶，她們說一定要多帶幾包面紙進去。

Miles **Give me a break**. Those are chick flicks for girls. The **trailer** of this **action movie** looks exciting with much tension and fast moving actions. Let's see this one.

饒了我吧，那是妳們女生在看的。這部動作電影的預告看起來緊張刺激，節奏又快，我們看這部好不好。

Doris But all action movies are all about killing and chasing, nothing like well-written plots. They are very **superficial**.

可是動作電影都在打打殺殺，沒甚麼劇情，內容很空洞耶。

Miles If you want some well-written plots, you shouldn't go see a romantic comedy at all. How about we see a **thriller**?

妳想看有劇情的電影，就更不該去看愛情喜劇才對啊。不如我們來看恐怖片吧？

Doris You mean the one starts in 20 minutes?

你說 20 分鐘後開演的那部電影嗎？

Miles Yes. It's the story about a group of youngsters encountering a horror killer while going on vacation. There are attractive men and women with **mystery** plots, also with many action scenes.

對啊，劇情標榜一群年輕人去度假時遇上恐怖殺人魔，有俊男美女又有懸疑劇情，還有不少動作場面。

Doris Okay, as long as it's not a **horror movie**. I can deal with a bloody movie like that.

好啊，只要不是鬼片，這種血腥的電影我還可以接受。

Miles Then let's go buy the tickets, and also get some popcorns and coke we can bring in the theater.

那我們趕快買票吧，順便買爆米花跟可樂進去吃。

必會單字一手抓

❶ comedy n. 喜劇

That comedy hits a box office record worldwide in a decade.

那部喜劇創下了十年來的全球電影票房紀錄。

❷ asleep adj. 睡著的

That little baby fell asleep after drinking milk.

那個小嬰兒喝完牛奶後就睡著了。

❸ romantic adj. 羅曼蒂克的

Most girls find it's difficult to resist the romantic atmosphere.

女生最難以抵擋羅曼蒂克的氣氛了。

❹ tissues n. 紙巾、面紙、衛生紙

Could you pass a tissue to me, please? Thank you!

可以請你遞一張紙巾給我嗎？謝謝。

❺ trailer n. 電影預告

Many people say that the movie trailer alone is so scary that people can't fall asleep after watching it.

許多人說光看那部電影預告就嚇到睡不著。

❻ action n. 行動、行為

Our son was bullied by the classmates without having a reason at school, so we must take action.

我們的兒子在學校被同學無端欺負，我們必須採取行動。

❼ superficial adj. 膚淺的、淺薄的

It is a very superficial idea thinking that women who have a beautiful appearance don't have much capability at work.

覺得擁有漂亮外貌的女性沒有能力工作是一種很膚淺的想法。

❽ thriller **n.** 驚悚電影
The thriller we just watched wasn't very scary.
剛才看的驚悚電影不怎麼嚇人。

❾ mystery **n.** 神秘的事物
Any mystery things are very appealing to me.
任何神秘難解的事物都非常吸引我。

❿ horror **adj.** 令人恐懼的事物
That classic horror movie is replayed on TV every Halloween.
每到萬聖節，電視一定會重播那部經典的恐怖電影。

30 秒會話教室

Give me a break 有「放我一馬」的意思，如:：Oh, Come On .Give me a break. 噢，得了。饒了我吧。

情境 33 藍綠立場大不同

會話訓練班

Derek 下班後到醫院的病房來照顧因車禍住院的女友 Fiona，他拿出蘋果準備削給 Fiona 吃，一邊將電視轉到他想看的頻道……

After Derek finishes work, he goes to the hospital **ward** to take care of his hospitalized girlfriend Fiona due to a car accident. When he is ready to **peel** an apple to Fiona, he also changes the **channel** to something he wants to watch...

Fiona I'm watching a drama series, turn the channel back.

我正在看連續劇呢，把頻道轉回去啦。

Derek Come one. Please let me watch it for a while. This show has always **criticized** the wrong doing of the **government party**, really vented out much of the **civilians**' anger for us the ordinary people.

讓我看一下嘛，拜託，這個節目總是在批評執政黨的不當作為，為我們這些小老百姓出了一口氣。

Fiona What venting out? I think the **opposition party** has also objected for making objections.

甚麼出一口氣？我看那些在野黨是專門為了反對而反對的。

Derek There must be an opposition party to **oversee** so the government party can seek the improvement.

本來就是要有在野黨的監督，執政黨才能有所改進啊。

Fiona	But there are some good policies also need the support of opposition parties, so the government party can execute them.	可是有些良好的施政，也需要在野黨的支持，執政黨才能執行呀。
Derek	It is supposed to be this way, but now the government officials only know about **taking bribes**, corruption, and never take the people into consideration, not to mention to promote a good **policy**.	本來應該是這樣沒錯，不過現在的政府官員都只知道收賄、貪汙，根本無心為人民著想，更遑論推動甚麼良好的政策了。
Fiona	Perhaps there are government officials they are still seriously make efforts, but we just did not see them. One swallow does not make a summer. In fact, if we can put aside our political prejudices and only consider the interests of the entire country, this country will be a better place.	或許也有認真努力的官員，只是我們沒看到，所以你不能以偏概全。其實如果大家能拋開固有的政黨成見，以整個國家的利益來著想，這個國家才會更好。
Derek	Didn't you get hospitalized by having your head hit, I did not expect for a quite clear thinking.	妳不是撞到頭住院嗎，沒想到思路還挺清晰的嘛！
Fiona	By telling you all this, my wounds have begun aching!	跟你講這些，我的傷口又開始隱隱作痛了啦！
Derek	OK, OK, the apple is peeled. Why don't you eat first, and let me watch for another 10 minutes.	好好好，蘋果削好了，妳先吃，再讓我看個 10 分鐘。

必會單字一手抓

❶ ward n. 病房、病室

A person was admitted to the emergency ward because he was hit by a drunk driver.

一位民眾因為被酒駕肇事者撞上而被送進急診病房。

❷ peel v. 削去…的皮

The master can finish peeling an apple within 30 seconds.

那位達人可以在 30 秒內削好一顆蘋果。

❸ channel n. 頻道

The movie channels on TV are the favorite of our whole family.

我們全家人最喜歡看的就是電視上的電影頻道。

❹ criticize v. 批評

Do not easily criticize others' appearance.

切勿輕易批評他人的外表。

❺ party n. 政黨、黨派

No matter which political party is in power, they should always hold the responsibility to be their own duties as of being the rise and fall of the nation.

不管哪一個政黨執政，都應該要以國家興亡為己任。

❻ civilians n. 平民、百姓（與軍警相對）

The protesting civilians had clashed with the police in the streets.

上街頭抗議的平民與警方發生武力衝突。

❼ opposition n. 反對黨、反對、對立
The main opposition comes from the students with much love and compassion after the school bans the feeding of stray animals.
學校明令禁止餵食流浪動物後，主要的反對聲浪來自於充滿愛心的學生。

❽ oversee v. 監督、監視
The financial department at the company is overseen by him.
公司裡的財政部門由他來負責監督。

❾ bribe n. 賄賂、行賄物
The police have found a large amount of bribe the candidate has received in his house.
警方在那位競選人的家中查出大批他所收下的行賄物。

❿ policy n. 政策
Honesty is the best policy.
誠實是最好的政策。

30 秒會話教室

One swallow does not make a summer. One grain does not fill a sack. One actor cannot make a play.
以上三個俚語皆有「以偏概全」的意思。

情境 34 愛車才是大老婆？

會話訓練班

Kenneth 只要有假期，就會開車到住在另一個城市的女友 Irene 家共度兩人時光。但他每到達目的地的第一件事情都不是向 Irene 噓寒問暖，而是先照顧他的愛車……

Whenever Kenneth is on holidays, he will drive to another city to live spend some time in the home of his girlfriend Irene. But each time when he arrives, he doesn't talk and check on Irene. Instead, he first takes care of his car...

Irene	Kenneth, how come you don't get tired after 5 more hours driving? Why don't you come inside and take a rest?	Kenneth，你開了 5 個小時的車不會累嗎？怎麼不先進來休息呢？
Kenneth	Let me check the **radiator** and **engine** first, and then wash the car. I'll go inside once I finish.	我先檢查一下散熱器跟引擎，然後把車子洗乾淨再進去。
Irene	Didn't you come **all this way** to have a date with me? Why now all you care about is your car then?	你大老遠開車過來不是為了跟我約會的嗎？怎麼只顧著你的車子呢？
Kenneth	Haven't you heard that a car is a man's first wife?	妳沒聽說車子是男人的大老婆嗎？

Irene	Huh, then fine, you go sleep with your first wife tonight!	哼，那你今晚就跟你的大老婆睡吧！
Kenneth	Alright, alright, I didn't really mean that. Seriously though, I need to drive back and forth between your and my places very often, what should I do when my car **breaks down** or **has a flat tire** if I don't well maintain the car?	好啦好啦！我不是那個意思，不過說真的，我要經常像這樣開車往返兩地，車子不好好保養，要是半路拋錨、或是輪胎爆胎怎麼辦？
Irene	You've got some points there too.	也是沒錯啦！
Kenneth	Besides, you would feel embarrassed if you sit in a filthy car. I don't think you would like to go out with me by sitting in a car looking like from a **junk yard**.	而且車子要是髒兮兮的，開在路上也很丟臉啊！妳應該也不會想坐在像從垃圾場開出來的車子裡跟我出門吧？
Irene	I don't want that **indeed**.	的確不想。
Kenneth	So please stop **striving for favor** with my first wife. Why don't you go get ready, and I'll be finished washing the car **by then**, so we can get rolling and have dinner.	所以妳就別跟我的大老婆爭寵了，妳先去準備一下，到時候我的車也洗好了，就可以開車上街吃晚餐囉。

必會單字一手抓

❶ radiator **n.** 散熱器

This car's radiator breaks down, so it is not temporarily drivable on the road.

這部汽車的散熱器故障了，暫時無法開車上路。

❷ engine **n.** 引擎

The engine actually looks like this originally.

原來引擎實際上看起來是長這個樣子。

❸ break down 故障

The van suddenly broke down on the way, and now it is currently waiting for towing on the side of the road.

那輛貨車在運送途中突然故障，目前拋錨在公路旁等待拖吊。

❹ tire **n.** 輪胎

Dad helped me make a swing with some old tires in the backyard.

爸爸用舊輪胎幫我在後院做了一個盪鞦韆。

❺ flat **adj.** 平的、洩了氣的

The little boy loves the bike he receives on Christmas so much that he continues riding it even the tires are flat.

小男孩非常喜愛那輛在聖誕節收到的腳踏車，騎到輪胎都扁掉了還是照騎不誤。

❻ junk **n.** 廢棄的舊物

Mom thinks that the bunch of rock magazines and CDs in my brother's room is simply junk.

媽媽覺得弟弟房間那一堆搖滾雜誌和 CD 簡直是廢物。

❼ yard **n.** 工場、堆場、庭院
Every month my family will hold a barbecue party in the backyard.
每個月我們全家人都會在後院舉辦一次烤肉派對。

❽ indeed **adv.** 確實、實在（加強語氣）
You're right, we do need to speed up our serving indeed.
您說得沒錯，我們確實需要加強上菜的速度。

❾ by then 到時候
I will try to study hard and get on the top three of the class. By then, you will agree to go out with me on a date.
我會努力用功讀書考進班上前 3 名的，到時候妳就要答應跟我出去約會。

❿ strive **v.** 努力、奮鬥
The little boy is striving to help the old lady go across the street by pushing her wheelchair.
小男孩努力地幫老奶奶推著輪椅過馬路。

30 秒會話教室

You came all this way just to buy a cup of coffee? 你大老遠跑來就只是為了買一杯咖啡？

情境 35 你一聲不吭跑去哪？

會話訓練班

Miles 經常不跟女友 Doris 報備一聲就出門或不回家，打手機也聯絡不到人，讓 Doris 非常擔心男友是不是瞞著她在外面亂來……

Miles often does not report his **whereabouts** to his girlfriend Doris before he goes out, or tell her he is not going to go home soon. He cannot be reached very often on his cell phone. It lets Doris feel very worried about whether her boyfriend is fooling around behind her back...

Doris	Miles, I finally get you here. I have been standing and waiting downstairs your place for four hours.	Miles，我終於等到你了，我在你家樓下站了4個小時！
Miles	What are you doing for waiting me here? Why didn't you give me a call first?	妳在這裡等我做甚麼啊？怎麼不先打個電話給我呢？
Doris	I've made hundreds of phone calls and they all went to your **voicemail**. The phone in your room has already awakened your **neighbors**.	我打了接近上百通電話，手機通通轉接到語音信箱。你房裡的電話也打到已經吵醒鄰居了。
Miles	Really? Let me see...Ah, my **battery** is **dead**, that's why you couldn't reach me.	真的嗎？我看看……啊，我的手機沒電了，難怪妳打不進來。

Doris	Miles, we don't live together. If you don't tell me where you are, I won't have a clue of your whereabouts. It sometimes worries me a lot, especially in a situation like this; your battery is dead and I can't reach you at all.	Miles，我們沒有住在一起，所以你不告訴我的話，我是不會知道你去了那裡的，這讓我很擔心。尤其又是遇上這種手機沒電、聯絡不到人的情形。
Miles	Are you worried about me **cheating** on you?	妳是擔心我在外面亂來嗎？
Doris	To be honest with you, it does come across my mind, but there's more than that. What if you got caught in an accident outsides and you had a desperate cry for help?	說真的，我的確是這麼想的，不過不單純是因為這樣，說不定你在外面發生了意外、急需幫助也有可能。
Miles	I just like to go out having fun and some food with my friends. Do I have to wait at home for your phone calls every day?	我不過是喜歡跟朋友去外面吃飯、玩樂，難道非得每天待在家裡等妳的電話不可嗎？
Doris	That won't be necessary. You just need to tell me **roughly** about why you're not home tonight and where you are, so I don't need to feel worried for not knowing your **whereabouts**. That's it.	不用這樣，只要你大略跟我說一下，今晚會因為去哪裡而不在家，讓我不會因為沒有掌握你的行蹤而為你擔心，這樣就可以了。
Miles	Well, perhaps it's because we have separated for a long time after we **re-encounter**, so I am so used to having a life going anywhere I want without much **solicitude**. I will slowly get used to having someone worrying my whereabouts in my life.	好啦，或許是因為我們分隔兩地很久之後才重逢，讓我習慣了一個人沒有牽掛、愛去哪裡就去哪裡的日子，以後我會慢慢去適應有人在為我的行蹤擔心的生活。

必會單字一手抓

❶ voicemail **n.** 語音信箱

The calls are transferred to his voicemail no matter how many times we call.

不管打他的電話幾次，都是轉入語音信箱。

❷ neighbor **n.** 鄰居

It drives me crazy that our next door neighbor likes to sing karaoke till early in the morning.

我們隔壁的鄰居總喜歡唱卡拉 OK 到清晨，快把我逼瘋了。

❸ battery **n.** 電池

The battery of the alarm clock is dead, which makes me oversleep and miss the school bus today.

鬧鐘的電池沒電了，害我今天睡過頭趕不上校車。

❹ dead **adj.** 無效的、不發揮作用的

This phone in the house is dead for the telephone line has long been cut off.

這台室內電話根本沒辦法發揮作用，原來電話線早就被剪斷了。

❺ desperate **adj.** 極度渴望的

The explorers caught in the desert are desperate to be rescued.

在沙漠中遇難的探險家極度渴望獲救。

❻ roughly **adv.** 粗略地、大約

The teacher just roughly called the roll and began the class without noticing some students were absent.

老師粗略地點了一下人數就開始上課，完全沒發現有同學沒到。

❼ whereabouts n. 行蹤、下落

The police did not know the whereabouts of that abducted child at all, which made the parents so anxious that they could not sleep at nights.

警察完全不知道那位被綁架兒童的下落，兒童的父母著急到夜不成眠。

❽ solicitude n. 焦慮、掛念、擔心的事情

My sister has much solicitude for her boyfriend who just leaves for his military service.

姊姊對剛出發去當兵的男友滿心牽掛。

❾ re-encounter v. 重逢

When can the separated lovers on the battlefield re-encounter again?

在戰場上分離的戀人不知何時才能重逢？

❿ cheat v. （夫妻等）表現不忠

The spouses who suspect if their husbands or wives are cheating hire a detective agency to investigate.

懷疑另一半不忠的人都會委託徵信社進行調查。

30 秒會話教室

To be honest, I don't like him very much. 說真的，我不太喜歡他。

To be honest with you, I'm still a student. 跟你說實話，我還是個學生。

名人怎麼說？

The first duty of love is to listen. —Paul Tillich

愛情的首要責任是傾聽。—保羅・田立克

情境 36 不懂撒嬌的女強人

會話訓練班

Victoria 獨立經營一家服飾店，生意做得有聲有色，儼然已經是一位事業成功的女強人。而男友 Harvey 只是個普通的上班族，這常讓 Harvey 在家中也像個員工一樣受到女友的指使……

Victoria independently operates a clothing store and runs the business very well. She has seemed to be a **successful businesswoman**. On the other hand, her boyfriend Harvey is just an **ordinary** office worker, which often makes him feel like an **employee** instructed by his girlfriend at home...

Victoria	Harvey, have you forgotten dumping garbage today again? How many times do I have to remind you until you remember it?	Harvey，你今天是不是又忘了倒垃圾？要我講幾次你才會記得啊？
Harvey	I'm sorry. I got off work a bit late today...	對不起，今天下班的有點晚……。
Victoria	And you also forgot buying some of the groceries I asked you to help out. You miss lots of them. There is no toothpaste to use in the house.	我叫你幫忙買的日用品你也忘東忘西的，根本就沒有買齊嘛！家裡已經沒有牙膏可以用了。
Harvey	Let me ask you one thing, are you forgetting that you are at home now? This is not your store, and I am not your employee.	我說妳呀，是不是忘了自己現在已經回到家了？這裡不是妳的店面耶，而我也不是妳雇用的員工。

Victoria I...

我……。

Harvey Sometimes I really hope that I can have a **sweet** girlfriend who waits me at home and cooks for me after I finish work. I know you're not the type of girl who behaves in a sweet and **helpless** way. I feel truly proud of you for running a business so well, but I hope you not to bring your work style home, okay?

有時候我真的很希望下班回到家能夠有個溫柔的女朋友做好飯菜等著我，我知道妳不是這種小鳥依人的類型，妳把事業做的很好，我也覺得與有榮焉，但我只希望妳不要把工作時的那一套作風帶回家裡來，好嗎？

Victoria Sigh, I'm sorry, my dear. I think I am so used to instructing the staff in the store, so when I see a bunch of house chores not taken care of, I become very **impatient**.

唉，對不起，親愛的，我想我是在店裡指揮員工習慣了，回到家看到一堆家事沒做，就顯得更不耐煩。

Harvey I am the same like you, so we must learn to understand and **cooperate**, rather than **blame** each other; otherwise our relationship would be no way to continue.

我也是一樣啊，所以我們都要學著體諒以及互相配合，而不是互相指責，不然我們的感情應該沒辦法繼續下去了。

Victoria I know you've also put some hard work on us for the past period of time. How can I improve it?

過去這一段日子，辛苦你了。我該怎麼改進呢？

Harvey Though you act tough at work, but at home, you can just relax and rely on me and be my Miss sweet.

妳在工作上盡管強勢，不過在家裡，妳就放心當個依賴我的小女人吧。

必會單字一手抓

❶ successful adj. 成功的、有成就的

Bill Gates is a successful businessman.

比爾蓋茲是一位成功的生意人。

❷ businesswoman n. 女實業家

That businesswoman who relies on her own strength to quickly climb the corporate ladder now has become the richest person in Taiwan.

那位女實業家靠著自己的實力一步步往上升遷，如今已成為全台首富。

❸ ordinary adj. 平凡的

This is not an ordinary dog; it has saved his master and his whole family in a fire incident.

這不是一隻平凡的小狗，牠可是從火場拯救過主人一家人呢。

❹ employees n. 受雇者

Many employees are protesting in the streets for that their wages haven't been raised for nearly a decade.

許多受雇者上街頭抗議薪資已經將近十年沒有調高了。

❺ sweet **adj.** 溫柔的
The mother is singing a lullaby with a sweet gentle tone to a newborn baby.
那位母親用溫柔的語調唱搖籃曲給剛出生的小嬰兒聽。

❻ helpless **adj.** 無助的
Dolly's wallet was stolen, and she felt helpless.
Dolly 的錢包被偷了，她覺得很無助。

❼ impatient **adj.** 不耐煩的
The front desk lady looks very impatient when she helps me deal with the application form.
櫃台小姐在幫我處理表格申請時看起來非常地不耐煩。

❽ blame **v.** 指責、歸咎於
You cannot blame the guests not to return the extra change. After all, it is your fault not to count it right and check first.
不能怪客人多收了找零不歸還，畢竟是你自己算錯在先又沒有檢查。

❾ rely on 依靠、信任
The old nanny relies on the nursing lady a lot who takes care of her living.
老奶奶非常依靠照顧她生活起居的看護阿姨。

❿ cooperate **v.** 合作、配合
Let's all cooperate to get the work done!
我們大家一起合力把工作做完吧！

30 秒會話教室

當對方對某些事情有疑慮的時候，可以很 man 地對他說：You can rely on me. 你可以依賴我。You can trust me. 你可以相信我。

情境 37 迷戀偶像

會話訓練班

Jocelyn 喜愛的韓國偶像即將來台舉辦演唱會，Jocelyn 為偶像瘋狂的模樣讓剛開始交往的男友 Austine 很難以想像……

Jocelyn's favorite Korean **idol** group is coming to Taiwan to perform in a **concert**. Her newly dated boyfriend Austine finds it very **unbelievable** seeing that Jocelyn is so **crazy about** her idols...

Jocelyn I am going out with friends tonight to get in the line for buying the concert tickets of a Korean idol group.

我今天晚上要跟朋友去排隊買韓國男子團體的演唱會門票。

Austine Tonight? How come someone begins to **sell** tickets at night?

今晚？怎麼有人是晚上才開始賣票的？

Jocelyn Nah, It starts **selling** the tickets from noon tomorrow. We **line up** during the night to have better seats.

不是啦，是明天中午才開賣，我們是利用晚上的時間先去排隊搶位置。

Austine So that means you girls are going to spend the night in the street? Would that be very dangerous?

也就是說妳們要在街頭度過一夜囉？那豈不是很危險嗎？

Jocelyn You don't have to worry. There are many **fans** they do just the same like us there.

不會啦，因為還有很多粉絲也是這樣啊！

Austine Are you girls all lost your mind? You don't sleep at home, but you are rather **willing to** stay on the roadside with chilly wind blowing just for some singing and dancing men.

妳們這些女生都瘋了嗎？有家不睡，為了幾個又唱又跳的男人甘願在路邊吹冷風！

Jocelyn You guys don't understand! Idols only come perform at a concert once in a while. I will regret it for the rest of my life if I don't get the tickets.

你們這些男生不懂的啦！偶像多久才來開一次演唱會，不買到票一定會抱憾終生的！

Austine I think the tickets must be very cheap, right? That's why there are so many fools rushing to line up.

我想一定是票很便宜吧？才會有那麼多笨蛋搶著排隊。

Jocelyn Just the opposite! A ticket in the front rock area costs NT$7300! And that does not include the **budget** for buying the merchandise.

才不呢！最前面的搖滾區，一張門票就要台幣7300元呢！而且還不包含到時候買周邊商品的預算喔。

Austine What! No wonder you said could understand before you found me like to check out hotties. You are much worse that I am, for being willing to spend so much money on seeing some handsome guys.

甚麼！難怪我之前愛看辣妹，妳說妳能理解，原來是因為妳比我還要嚴重啊！願意花那麼多錢去看帥哥！？

必會單字一手抓

❶ idol n. 偶像

That beautiful female teacher is the idol of the faculty and the students at school.

那位漂亮的女老師是全校師生的校園偶像。

❷ concert n. 演唱會

As long as my favorite band has a concert, I would certainly go against all odds.

只要我喜愛的樂團舉辦演唱會，我一定會排除萬難前往。

❸ crazy adj. 著迷的、狂熱的

Jimmy is very crazy about American football.

Jimmy 對美式足球非常狂熱。

❹ unbelievable adj. 難以想像的 字彙連結站 unthinkable

It's really hard to imagine that the elephants can use the trunk holding a brush and painting.

大象會用象鼻拿著畫筆畫畫？真是難以想像。

❺ sell v. 銷售

In addition to selling flowers at that flower shop, it also provides a service to write a love letter.

那間花店除了販售鮮花，還提供代寫情書的服務。

❻ fan n. 狂熱仰慕者、粉絲

I am a big fan of Angelina Jolie.

我是安潔莉娜・裘莉的大粉絲。

❼ willing adj. 心甘情願的
A father is always willing to do anything for his own daughter.
父親總是心甘情願為自己的女兒做任何事情。

❽ budget n. 預算
We must purchase the necessary office supplies for the department on the budget.
我們必須在預算內採購部門所必需的事務用品。

❾ line up 排隊
The teacher asked the class to line up, and got ready for the routine health checks.
老師要全班同學排成一隊，準備進行例行的健康檢查。

❿ mind n. 頭腦、理智
Lucy's mind is very clear, and her reaction is surprisingly fast.
Lucy 的頭腦非常清晰，反應出奇地快。

30 秒會話教室

看到別人難以理解的舉動時，可以用下列句型表達自己的質疑：Are you lost your mind? 你腦袋壞掉了嗎？Are you crazy? 你瘋了嗎？

情境 38 不擅甜言蜜語

會話訓練班

經歷過車禍意外的 Fiona 康復出院後，跟男友 Derek 恢復了平常的生活模式，但這也讓習慣了男友照料的 Fiona 無法適應，覺得 Derek 不像以前這麼溫柔了……

After Fiona **recovered** from a car accident and discharged from the hospital, she has resumed the normal life style with her boyfriend Derek. However, Fiona can't **adapt** to the new conditions since she is so accustomed to the **considerate** care of her boyfriend, but Derek is not as **gentle as** before...

Derek	I've cut some fruit and put it on the table. Have some now?	我把水果削好了放在桌上，快吃吧。
Fiona	You used to **feed** bite by bite and ask me whether it was sweet or not, or whether I still wanted to eat. Now you're just being cold.	你以前都會一口一口餵我，還會問我甜不甜？還要不要再吃？現在好冷淡喔。
Derek	That's how we always get along with each other. You feel differently because you were a **patient** before.	我們之間的相處本來就是這樣的啊，那是因為妳之前是病人。
Fiona	Do you mean you will only **treat** me gently when I am ill or hospitalized again?	你的意思是，要等我再次生病或住院，你才會用溫柔的一面對待我囉？

Derek It is not how it is. I was worried about your injury when you were in hospital so I was cautiously taking care of you. Are you **addicted** to be served so much you start to have some Princess **Syndrome**?

不是那樣子的，住院的時候是因為我擔心妳的傷勢，才會小心翼翼地伺候妳。難不成妳被服侍到上了癮、有公主病了嗎？

Fiona I am not. I just hope you can **sweet talk** to me more like you used to be, so I know how important I am to you.

才不是，我只是希望你能多像那時候一樣對我甜言蜜語、讓我知道自己對你有多重要。

Derek I just put some feeling in my heart without saying it, but that does not mean that my heart does not care. You should know how much I care about you.

有些感情只是放在心裡沒說出口而已，不代表心裡不關心。妳應該知道我有多在乎妳才對啊。

Fiona How should I know when you don't say it?

你不說我怎麼知道呢？

Derek You fool. When I thought you lost memory, didn't I say a lot of to you even I felt embarrassed myself? That is my feeling for you. You just need to remember those instant moments of feeling.

笨蛋，當我以為妳失去記憶的時候，我不是說出了許多連自己都感到難為情的話嗎？那就是我對妳的感情，妳只要記得那瞬間的感覺就夠了。

Fiona Well, those words have indeed touched me, but I still hope that you can occasionally sweet talk to me, okay?

好吧，那段話的確讓我很感動，不過我還是希望平常也能偶爾聽到一些情話，好嗎？

必會單字一手抓

❶ adapt v. 適應

The newly kept canary seems to be unable to adapt to the home, and it looks listless.

剛養的金絲雀似乎還無法適應新家的生活，看起來很沒有精神。

❷ recover v. 恢復健康

After the doctors' superb medical skills, the patient who had been pronounced incurable has gradually recovered.

經過醫生精湛的醫術，那位原本被宣告不治的病患已經逐漸恢復健康。

❸ gentle adj. 溫和的

That tiger's trait is very gentle, and it never shouts to people.

那隻老虎的個性非常溫和，從來不曾對人發威。

❹ considerate adj. 體貼的

Nora always has praised her son for being very considerate.

Nora 總是稱讚她的兒子非常體貼。

❺ feed v. 餵食

A story on the news says that, there was a forgetful pet owner who left home and his 14 cats without being fed, causing the cats starved to death.

新聞上說，有一位糊塗的飼主外出後一直沒有返家餵食家中的 14 隻貓咪，導致貓咪活活餓死。

❻ patient n. 病人

That doctor treats each patient like his own family.

那位醫生對每位病人都像對待自己的家人一樣親切。

❼ addicted **adj.** 入了迷的

She was addicted to smoking.

她對抽菸上了癮。

❽ syndrome **n.** 併發症

The patient has the postoperative complication syndrome after the surgery, and needs some immediate treatment.

那位病人出現了手術後的併發症，需要馬上治療。

❾ sweet talk **v.** 講甜言蜜語

Women do not mind to often hear some sweet talk.

女人並不介意經常聽到一些甜言蜜語。

❿ treat **v.** 對待

Nobody should treat an old gentleman like that.

任何人都不該像那樣對待一位老先生。

30 秒會話教室

糟糕啦！突然對某某東西上癮時你可以說這一句：I'm addicted to________.

I'm addicted to the Internet. 我對網路上癮。I'm addicted to this kind of food. 我對這種食物上了癮。

情境 39 運動寡婦

會話訓練班

Brian 非常喜愛籃球運動，只要電視上有比賽，他一定拋下所有事情守在電視機前為他喜歡的球隊加油，這讓女友 Phoebe 感到很無奈……

Brian is very fond of watching basketball games. Whenever there are **sport** games playing on TV, he must put aside everything and **root for** his favorite **team** in front of television, which makes his girlfriend Phoebe feel helpless sometimes...

Phoebe	Brian, I'm hungry. Didn't we talk about going out for dinner tonight?	Brian，我肚子餓了，我們不是說好今晚要出去吃飯嗎？
Brian	Wait a moment. It's the last 3 minutes **countdown**. I'll take you out after the **result** comes out.	等一下，比賽正進入倒數 3 分鐘，等分出勝負之後我就帶妳出門。
Phoebe	What's the excitement about watching the game anyway? If you want to know which team wins, why don't you just check the final result of the game **announced** on TV at the end?	球賽到底有甚麼好看的？想知道哪一隊贏球，直接等電視公布比賽結果不就得了？
Brian	You don't understand it. The **process** is more important than results! Gosh, the two teams **drew**...The game goes into **overtime**.	妳不懂的啦，過程比結果重要啊！天啊！兩隊竟然打成平手……要進入延長賽了

Phoebe	What?? I'm starving. How long is the overtime?	甚麼？？我肚子已經很餓了耶，延長賽還要比多久啊？
Brian	Each playoff game lasts five minutes. If there's no winning and losing, there will be one more. Can you go look for something to eat in the fridge, please?	延長賽一場 5 分鐘，如果還是分不出勝負的話就再次延長，妳先去冰箱找找有沒有東西吃啦，拜託。
Phoebe	There's nothing left to eat in the house. That's why I keep rushing you.	就是家裡都沒東西吃了，我才會一直催你啊！
Brian	This game is too important to miss. I've got to finish it.	這場比賽對我很重要，我一定要看完才行。
Phoebe	Never mind, give me the car key. I'll drive to the town and get something to eat. I'm nothing but a sports **widow**.	算了啦，車鑰匙給我，我自己開車去鎮上買東西吃。我簡直像個運動寡婦一樣。
Brian	You want to go by yourself? That's great! Can you also buy me some dinner and beer?	妳要自己去啊？那太好了！可以順便幫我買晚餐跟啤酒回來嗎？

必會單字一手抓

❶ sport n. 運動

Badminton is one of the sports that are more suitable for the elderly.

羽毛球是較為適合老年人的運動之一。

❷ root for 為…加油

Last night all the people of Taiwan had rooted for Jeremy Lin in the front of the TVs.

昨晚全台灣的民眾都守在電視機前面為林書豪加油。

❸ team n. 隊伍

There are 25 teams participating the national basketball game this time.

這次的全國籃球大賽共有 25 支隊伍參加。

❹ countdown n. 倒數計秒

When the game entered the final countdown, the boxers were still fighting till the last minutes on the stage.

當比賽進入倒數計秒時，台上的拳擊選手仍舊咬牙苦撐。

❺ announce v. 宣布、發布

The referee announced the victory of the red team that was suspected of cheating causing extreme dissatisfaction with the white team.

裁判宣布有作弊嫌疑的紅隊勝利，引發白隊極度不滿。

❻ result n. 比賽結果

Judging by the result of the competition, although the team did not win, but the sportsmanship they were showing is worth learning.

由比賽結果來看，那一隊雖然沒有贏，但是他們所展現的運動家精神值得學習。

❼ process n. 過程

This process will affect the degree of fermentation of the dough.

這個過程會影響麵團的發酵程度。

❽ draw v. 打成平手

All the audience felt extremely surprised that the two teams actually drew.

那兩隊竟然打成平手，令所有觀眾大吃一驚。

❾ overtime n. 延長時間、超過時間、加班時間

In order to complete the work, I have worked overtime for two days.

為了完成工作，我這兩天都在加班。

❿ widow n. 寡婦

It is extremely rude to call a person a widow in someone's face.

當面稱呼人家是寡婦，是一件非常無禮的行為。

30 秒會話教室

「某某寡婦」是指另一半熱衷於某事而忽略了自己，如：Are you a sports widow? 妳是個運動寡婦嗎？

名人怎麼說？

If you wished to be loved, love.—Lucius Annaeus Seneca

你果你想被愛，去愛吧。—古希臘哲學家

情境 40 男友被電玩搶走了？

會話訓練班

Austine 跟剛交往的女友 Jocelyn 度過熱戀期，他開始恢復每天打電動的宅男本性，讓 Jocelyn 覺得受到了冷落……

After Austine and his newly dated girlfriend Jocelyn have just passed the honeymoon period of their relationship, he starts to resume the **character** of an **indoorsman** playing video games every day. That has made Jocelyn feel out in the cold...

Jocelyn	Austine, what are you doing right now? I'm downstairs your dorm, do you want to go out for dinner?	Austine，你現在在做甚麼呢？我就在你的宿舍樓下，要不要一起去吃個晚餐？
Austine	I'm busy now, can't talk to you on the phone. You can go eat by yourself if you're hungry. I gotta hang up the phone.	我現在正在忙，不方便講電話，妳餓了的話就自己先去吃吧，我要掛電話了。
Jocelyn	What are you busy with? You don't even have time talking on the phone? Are you taking a girl to you room and fooling around with her?	你在忙甚麼啊？連講通電話都沒時間？該不會帶女生回房間亂來吧？
Austine	Nah! I'm playing an online game now. If I don't concentrate on the game, I will be a **burden** to my **teammates**.	才不是呢！我正在玩線上遊戲啦。我不趕快專心玩的話，會拖累我的隊友的。

Jocelyn	An online game? Are your teammates in the **virtual** world are more important than your girlfriend?	線上遊戲？在虛擬世界的隊友有比我這個女朋友重要嗎？
Austine	It's totally different. I can't **quit midway**, my teammates need my help to accomplish a mission now. You can eat by yourself anyway.	這不一樣，我的隊友現在需要我幫忙解任務，我不能中途退出，而妳可以自己去吃東西啊。
Jocelyn	Austine Newman, you're a jerk! You become **quite** a different person before and after we start dating. You would never leave me alone and be always my company before.	Austine Newman 你這個混蛋，跟交往之前簡直判若兩人！你以前絕不會丟下我一個，不管到哪裡都會陪我的。
Austine	Didn't you leave me alone to see your idol's concert before? Alright, alright, can you wait till I finish this game?	妳還不是一樣丟下我一個人去看偶像演唱會？好啦，先等我把這場玩完再說。
Jocelyn	I would never expect that I need to **compete** with online games. I'm an **unperson**.	沒想到我竟然要跟電玩爭男朋友，我真是個不受重視的人。
Austine	I'll call you after I finish, bye!	玩完我再打給妳喔，再見。

必會單字一手抓

❶ indoorsman n. 宅男

Is "indoorsman" regarded as a curse word?

宅男算是一種罵人的詞彙嗎？

❷ character n. 品質、性格

A person's character determines the fate of his/her life.

一個人的品格決定了他一生的命運。

❸ unperson n. 不受重視之人

That unappreciated politician is an unperson who has been deployed the powers and the duties, and assigned to an unimportant position.

那個不受重視的政治家被調配到權力的邊緣擔任無關緊要的職務。

❹ burden v. 重擔、加負擔於……

On the battlefield, once a person is injured, it becomes the brothers' burden.

在戰場上，只要一受傷就會成為兄弟們的重擔。

❺ teammate n. 隊友

I have developed a close friendship with my teammates.

我與我的隊友之間發展出緊密的情誼。

❻ virtual adj. 虛擬的

There is a virtual fish tank on the teacher's computer screen.

老師的電腦螢幕上有著一個虛擬的魚缸。

❼ quit v. 退出

You cannot quit halfway the race, which is to raise a white flag to the opponents.

妳不能中途退出比賽，這樣等於是向對手認輸了。

❽ midway **adj.** 中途的

That leading sailing ship capsized on the midway in the game.

領先的那艘風帆在比賽中途翻覆了。

❾ quite **adv.** 完全、相當、很

Julia is quite a cautious person.

Julia 是個非常謹慎的人。

❿ compete **v.** 競爭、對抗

We also need to do a lot of work to be eligible to compete with that team.

我們還要做許多努力才有資格與那隊強隊競爭。

30 秒會話教室

「冷落」用英文要怎麼說呢？看看下面的句型就知道囉：You can't leave a guest out in the cold. 你不能冷落客人。

名人怎麼說？

So it's not gonna be easy. It's going to be really hard; we're gonna have to work at this everyday, but I want to do that because I want you. I want all of you, forever, everyday. You and me... everyday. —Nicholas Sparks

這一點都不簡單。這會很難，我們必須每天經營，但是我想要去做因為我想要你。我想要全部的你，永遠，每天。你跟我……每天在一起。—小說家

情境 41 老公是媽寶

會話訓練班

Marjorie 與 Albert 兩人結婚後，Albert 的母親便經常來看他們，經由觀察 Albert 母子之間的相處模式，Marjorie 發現丈夫對母親所說的話異常地順從……

After Marjorie and Albert get married, Albert's mother often calls on them. By **observing** the **model** for **interaction** between Albert and his, Marjorie has found that he is unusually **obedient** to what his mother says...

Marjorie	Honey, how come the cookies I put in the fridge has gone? Did you eat them?	親愛的，我擺在冰箱裡的餅乾怎麼不見了，你吃掉了嗎？
Albert	My mom stopped by this afternoon. She said the cookies had too much starch and sugar, and they were bad for health, so she threw them away.	今天下午我媽來家裡，她說那種餅乾都是澱粉跟糖分，吃多了對身體不好，所以把它丟了。
Marjorie	What! But I only have a box once in a while when I have cravings for cookies. How could she go through our fridge without our permission?	甚麼！可是我偶爾嘴饞才吃一盒啊，她怎麼可以亂動我們家的冰箱。
Albert	This is not just "our" home. She's my mom, and my stuff also **belongs** to her.	這不只是「我們」家，她是我媽媽，我的東西當然也是屬於她的。

Marjorie	But I'm your wife. Shouldn't she also respect the **daughter-in-law**?	但我是你老婆啊，她是否也該尊重一下我這個媳婦？
Albert	My mom has endured a lot of hardship **raising** us three brothers alone. Her words are everything. Since she thinks eating that kind of stuff is bad for health, you should listen to her.	我媽一個人含辛茹苦地把我們三兄弟養大，她說的話就是一切，既然她說那種東西吃了不好，妳應該聽她的。
Marjorie	What if she had told you not to marry me, would you have also been willing to give up our relationship?	那如果她當初叫你不要跟我結婚，你也願意放棄我們的感情囉。
Albert	If that had been the case, I would have respected my mother's decision, but the good thing is she pretty much likes you.	如果真的是那樣，我會尊重我媽的決定，但好險她還挺喜歡妳的。
Marjorie	Should I feel **honored** with it? You're nothing but a mama's boy.	我該為此感到光榮嗎？你這樣根本就是媽寶。
Albert	I personally think it's **filial piety**.	我比較認為這是孝順。

必會單字一手抓

❶ observe v. 觀察

The homework of the physics/chemistry class is to observe ants' way of marching.

理化課的回家功課是要觀察螞蟻的行進方式。

❷ interaction n. 互動

The interaction between the teachers and children can be seen through the class cameras at this tutorial school.

這間補習班可以透過攝影機看到老師與孩子們上課時的互動方式。

❸ model n. 雛形、原形

This is a model of an apartment building.

這是一棟公寓的建築模型。

❹ obedient adj. 順從的

We are obedient to that spoiled kid and sit down to play with her playing house.

我們順從那位被寵壞的小孩，坐下陪她玩扮家家酒。

❺ belong v. 屬於

The land piece of the school's backyard belongs to the county government.

學校後院那塊地是屬於縣政府的。

❻ daughter-in-law n. 媳婦

The daughter-in-law is also someone else's daughter, so please treat her with the same love and care.

媳婦也是別人家的女兒，要將心比心好好對待。

❼ raise v. 養育

That single mother has raised three kids alone.

那位單親媽媽一個人養育三個小孩。

❽ honor n. 榮耀

I want to dedicate this honor to my parents and teachers, as well as all the people who have supported me.

我要將此榮耀獻給我的父母以及師長，還有所有曾經支持過我的人。

❾ filial adj. 子女的、孝順的

It is chilling to see that children nowadays have less and less filial piety to their parents.

現代的孩子對父母越來越不孝順，看了就令人心寒。

❿ piety n. 虔誠的行為或言語

The behavior of filial piety needs to be shaped up in childhood so the child can have much gratitude.

孝順父母的行為需要從小教育，讓孩子充滿感恩的心。

30 秒會話教室

mama's boy 指被家裡呵護的太好、沒有擔當、不夠成熟的男子。這個說法有輕視的意味，所以除非是很熟的對象，否則千萬不要亂用喔。如：Why Women Don't Like Mama's Boys? 為什麼女生都不喜歡媽寶？

情境 42 岳父看未來女婿

會話訓練班

Heather 介紹剛交往的男友 Patrick 給父母認識，但 Heather 的爸爸似乎對女兒的男友充滿敵意，不停地查問 Patrick 的私事……

Heather is introducing her boyfriend Patrick to her parents, but Heather's father seems to have much **animosity** to his daughter's boyfriend, and constantly question Patrick about his privacy...

Heather's father	I've heard that you met my youngest daughter Celia first?	聽我大女兒說，你是先認識我的小女兒 Celia？
Patrick	Yes, sir.	是啊，伯父。
Heather's father	What are you up to? I'm warning you, don't you dare to fool with both of my daughters!	你在打甚麼主意啊？我警告你，你可別想同時玩弄我的兩個女兒！
Heather	Dad, you've got the wrong idea. Celia and he met at the airport for mistakenly taking each other's luggage. Then, Celia, introduced him to me.	爸爸你誤會了啦，他跟 Celia 是因為在機場拿錯行李認識的，後來 Celia 才把他介紹給我。

Patrick	Yes, sir. I'm dating Heather. I only see Celia as a baby sister.	對啊，伯父，我是跟 Heather 交往，然後把 Celia 當成妹妹一樣看待。
Heather's father	Fine, then. Did you say you work in a law firm? Can you assure that you can **support** my daughter's living?	那就好。你說你是在律師事務所上班？你保證以後能養活我女兒嗎？
Heather	Dad, we just start dating each other. You're embarrassing me by asking so many questions.	爸爸，我們才剛開始交往而已，你問那麼多，多不好意思啊？
Heather's father	Of course I need to ask all these questions. I don't want you to **devote** all your **sentiment** into him and then break up. That will be totally **wasting** your **youth**.	這些當然要問啊，不然等到投入感情了才來分手嗎？多浪費妳的青春啊！
Patrick	Heather, I agree. A man should take the responsibilities even they are dating. I am looking **forward** to having a **serious** relationship with you, with possibility of marriage.	Heather，伯父說的對，即使還是交往，男人也該負起責任。我是認真地看待我們兩人的關係，並以結婚為前提在交往。

Heather's father That's more like it. Come and **keep** telling me about your **job**.

這還像樣一點，來，你繼續跟我說你的工作狀況吧。

必會單字一手抓

❶ animosity n. 敵意

The neighbor's dog in the front always has animosity to me.

鄰居家門前的狗總是對我充滿敵意。

❷ support v. 扶養

That old granny has no family or relatives to support so she is entirely dependent on the government.

那位老奶奶沒有任何親人扶養，完全依賴政府。

❸ waste v. 浪費

Don't waste your time on the unreliable man.

不要浪費你的時間在這不可靠的男人上。

❹ youth n. 青春時代

Mom always refreshes memories of her youth while singing songs back then.

媽媽總是一邊回憶著青春時代一邊哼唱當時的流行歌曲。

❺ devote v. 將…奉獻給

The Veterans have devoted the lifetime to the country, but do not get any care and respect.

老兵將一生都奉獻給國家，卻沒有得到任何照顧與尊重。

❻ sentiment **n.** 感情

When the students at the school sing the national anthem, everyone is full of patriotic sentiment.

全校齊唱國歌的時候，讓大家充滿了愛國的情感。

❼ forward **adv.** 向前

The customs officers ordered us to move forward.

海關人員示意我們向前移動。

❽ serious **adj.** 認真的

James is very serious when he describes his strange dream last night.

James 非常認真地敘述他昨晚夢到的怪夢。

❾ keep **v.** 繼續不斷

A person should keep surpassing himself/herself in life in order to move towards a better future.

人生就是要持續不斷地超越自己，才能邁向更好的未來。

❿ job **n.** 工作

The employment agencies not only help the unemployed people find jobs, but also offer many courses.

職業介紹所除了幫失業者介紹工作，還提供許多進修課程。

30 秒會話教室

對於巴不得快點發生的事情，可以用以下的片語：I'm looking forward to seeing you again. 我很期待再次見到你。

to 後面的動詞為 V-ing 喔。

兩人世界 ByeBye

情境 43 幫女友向老師請假

會話訓練班

Austine 的女友 Jocelyn 一夜之間突然得了重感冒，同時上吐下瀉，根本無法到校上課。因此 Austine 先將女友暫時安頓好，親自前往 Jocelyn 教授的辦公室幫她請假……

Austine's girlfriend Jocelyn catches a **severe** cold overnight, with **vomiting** and **diarrhea**, which makes her unable to attend her class. For that reason, Austine first takes care of his girlfriend for the time being, then goes to of Jocelyn's professor's office to ask for a sick leave for her in person.

Austin	Excuse me, Professor Green. I am Austine Newman, a senior student in history department. I'm here for requesting a sick leave for a student of yours, Jocelyn Wagner.	Professor Green，抱歉打擾了，我是歷史系四年級的 Austine Newman，我來幫您的一位學生，Jocelyn Wagner 請假。
Professor Green	Oh, is that the hard studying girl with a **ponytail**, who always carries a dictionary to class? You must be her boyfriend, right?	喔，是那位綁著馬尾，總是會抱著字典來上課的認真女孩。你應該是她的男朋友吧？

Austine	Yes, I am. She still insists on looking up words in a dictionary even now with an easy access to an **electronic** dictionary. She thinks she can get more detailed **explanations** from a dictionary.	是的，明明現在早就有電子字典了，她還是堅持用字典查，說是字典上的解釋比較仔細。
Professor Green	It is this kind of **spirit** for learning a **language** well. I have a high expectation for her. What's wrong with her?	學語言本來就是要有這樣的精神，我非常看好她。她怎麼了嗎？
Autine	Oh, she has started vomiting and having diarrhea this morning when she got up. She has been so **faint** and weak that she can't even stand up straight. I think she has a cold.	喔，她一早起來就上吐下瀉，有氣無力地，根本無法站穩，應該是感冒了。
Professor Green	That doesn't sound just like having a cold according to your description. Do you have class later? You'd better take her to see a doctor. This could be stomach flu caused by viruses.	聽你這麼說起來不像是單純的感冒，你等一下有課嗎？最好趕快帶她去看醫生，可能是腸胃型的感冒病毒。
Austine	I don't have class this morning. I come here for requesting a sick leave for her only.	我這個上午沒課，我是專程過來幫她請假的。

Professor Green Why didn't you just call the office of the department?

你怎麼不打個電話到系上辦公室說一聲就好了呢？

Austine Jocelyn told me she was supposed to give a report to the class in her German class today. She was thinking of hanging on to get up firmly. I told her to take a good rest.

因為 Jocelyn 說今天的德文課輪到她上台做報告，她本來還想硬撐著起來，是我要她好好休息的。

Professor Green Ah, Jocelyn is such a diligent student. Don't worry, tell her to rest and get well soon. It won't be too late for her to give the report after she gets better. And you, you are also a very **reliable** young man.

唉， Jocelyn 真是個認真的好學生，你放心，叫她好好休息，等她病好了再報告也不遲。而你，也真是個有肩膀的好孩子。

必會單字一手抓

❶ severe **adj.** 嚴重的、劇烈的
The child has severe ADHD (Attention Deficit/Hyperactivity Disorder).
那個孩子患有嚴重的過動症。

❷ vomiting **n.** 嘔吐
I start vomiting every time I eat the fat in meat.
我只要吃到肥肉就會嘔吐。

❸ diarrhea n. 腹瀉
One should go see a doctor when having severe constant diarrhea.
只要有嚴重不止的腹瀉症狀就應該馬上去看醫生。

❹ ponytail n. 馬尾（髮型）
Some girls look good with ponytails, but some don't.
有的女孩綁馬尾非常好看，有的則不是那麼適合。

❺ explanation n. 解釋
The suspect couldn't explain why he happened to be around the corpse at the time of the crime.
嫌犯無法解釋在案發當時為什麼剛好會在屍體附近。

❻ language n. 語言
Keeping a language alive is the best way to pass down the culture.
語言是將一種文化傳承下去的最重要方法。

❼ spirit n. 精神
When the flesh dies eventually, the spirit will remain.
人的肉體終究會消滅，但精神會長存。

❽ electronic adj. 電子的
Using electronic devices is prohibited during take-off.
飛機起飛時嚴禁使用電子設備。

❾ faint adj. 虛弱的、昏倒
The female student suddenly felt weak and faint at the knees for her not having breakfast this morning.
女同學突然感到虛弱站不穩，原來是因為她今早沒吃早餐。

❿ reliable adj. 可靠的
Cars made in Germany are very reliable in quality.
德國出產的汽車品質非常可靠。

30 秒會話教室

I'd like to take a day off. 我想要請一天的假。I will take a half -day off this Friday afternoon. 我這個周五下午會請半天的假。

情境 44 與女友及室友相處

會話訓練班

Miles 在約好的時間到女友 Doris 的租屋處準備載她出門約會，不過此時 Doris 才正要去洗澡，於是請 Miles 先進屋等待，不過較為尷尬的是，Doris 還有一位女室友——Chloe……

Miles is picking up his girlfriend Doris for a date at her place at the time they are supposed to meet. Doris is just about to take a shower, so she sends Miles to the house waiting. Awkwardly Miles finds out Doris has a female **roommate**—Chloe...

Chloe	Hi, you must be Doris' boyfriend, Miles. **I have heard a lot about you.** I'm Chloe.	嗨，你就是 Doris 的男朋友 Miles 吧。久仰大名，我是 Chloe。
Miles	Hi, nice to meet you. Are you going to **attend** the National Judicial Examination, aren't you? I've heard a lot about you too from Doris.	妳好，妳正準備參加司法考試對吧，我也常聽 Doris 提起妳。
Chloe	That's right! Let me get this **straight** with you. Last time you let Doris wait for you for hours downstairs your place in the chill wind. Do you know my heart **bled** for her when she called me and told me about this?	沒錯，因此廢話不多說，上次你讓 Doris 在你家樓下冒著寒風等了好幾個小時，你知道當她打電話跟我說這件事時，我有多心疼嗎？

Miles	I...I know. I'm sorry. It's my fault. I also explained that to Doris. I won't do it again.	我……我知道，對不起，是我的錯，我也跟 Doris 解釋過了，以後不會再犯了。
Chloe	I asked her to come back immediately but she was so worried about your safety and insisted on waiting for you to come home. You should really treasure her for having a girlfriend who loves you so dearly, **or** I won't **forgive** you!	我要她趕緊回來，她卻不放心你的安危，堅持要等到你回家，你有一個這麼愛你的女朋友，真的應該好好珍惜。否則我第一個不饒你！
Miles	I will for sure. In this regard, I feel much **relieved** knowing Doris have a roommate who **defends** her and stands by her. Please keep looking out for her if needed.	我會的。話說回來，Doris 有這麼為她打抱不平的室友，我也就放心了。以後也還請妳多多照顧她。
Doris	Sorry for keeping you waiting. I'm ready to go. What were you two chatting about?	Miles 對不起，讓你久等了，我已經準備好可以出門了。你們剛剛在聊甚麼啊？
Chloe	Oh, ya, we were talking about "treasure".	對啊，我在跟 Miles 聊「珍惜」這件事。
Doris	You two get so **congenial** first time you meet? Chloe, come join us to the dinner. Miles, don't you think it's a good idea?	你們第一次見面就這麼投機？Chloe 妳也跟我們一起去吃飯吧，Miles 你說好不好？
Chloe	No, thanks. I hate being the third **wheel**. Miles, I'll talk to you later. I'm going back to my room for the test.	不了，我不想當你們倆的電燈泡，Miles，有機會再聊吧。我先進房準備考試了。

必會單字一手抓

❶ roommate n. 室友

I have three roommates after I move in the college dormitory.

搬進大學宿舍之後，我就多了三位室友。

❷ attend v. 出席、參加

My mom was too busy to attend the PTA meeting at our school yesterday.

媽媽因為太忙，所以沒有出席昨天我們學校的家長會。

❸ straight adj. 坦率的

I prefer the straight answers even though that would be not pleasant.

我寧願得到坦率的答案即使不會令人很愉快。

❹ bleed v. 流血、心疼

My heart bleeds for the old man who is abandoned by his children.

我很同情那位被子女拋棄的老先生。

❺ forgive v. 原諒

The elderly woman forgives the young man who robbed her purse.

老太太原諒了那個搶她錢包的年輕人。

❻ defend v. 防衛、保護、為…辯護

The students are gathering to protest to the media and to defend their freedom of speech.

學生們群起對抗媒體，誓言捍衛自己的言論自由。

❼ relieve **v.** 緩和、使寬慰
The elderly people feel very relieved seeing the children show much filial piety after growing up.
看到孩子們長大後都如此孝順，老人家感到非常欣慰。

❽ congenial **adj.** 意氣相投的、協調的
I've met many congenial friends with common interests on the Internet.
我在網路上遇到了不少意氣相投的同好。

❾ wheel **n.** 輪子、方向盤
He lets his girlfriend who just got her driver's license take the wheel.
他讓剛考到駕照的女友開車。

❿ or **conj.** 否則、要不然 字彙連結站 otherwise
Get up soon or you'll be late for work.
快點起床，不然你上班要遲到了。

30 秒會話教室

I have heard a lot about you. Your reputation precedes you. 以上這兩句都是「久仰大名」的意思喔。

關鍵字搜尋

《宅男行不行》（英語：The Big Bang Theory）自2007年開播以來擁有世界各地的眾多粉絲。住在一起的兩個天才宅男與他們生活周遭所發生爆笑故事。他們書呆子式的人際相處模式是本劇的笑點。

情境 45 靈感來了！別打擾我！

會話訓練班

Albert 是一位作家，專門寫一些散文及小說，他生性浪漫，讓妻子 Marjorie 的生活充滿驚喜，但是等他腦中出現靈感時，就像變了個人似的……

Albert is a writer who writes **prose** and **novels**. Romance is in his nature that brings his wife, Marjorie, surprises in life. However, he turns into a different man, when he has **inspiration** in his mind.

Marjorie	…Honey, are you **nodding**? You kept silent when I knocked on the door of the study.	……親愛的，你在打瞌睡嗎？我一直敲書房的門你都不出聲。
Albert	What...? Oh, I'm sorry. I've been pondering over the materials for the **column**.	甚麼……？喔，不好意思，我在想這次的專欄要寫些甚麼？
Marjorie	Do you mean the weekly column, which the newspaper came invite you? Isn't there a regular **deadline**?	你說那個報社找你合作，每周一次的專欄啊，那不是有固定的截稿日嗎？
Albert	That's right. The deadline is tomorrow morning. That's why I'm trying to rack my brains and get some inspiration. I have no idea where to start.	對呀，明天一早就要交了，所以我現在正在苦思靈感呢！完全不知道該由哪個方向下筆。

Marjorie	I'm going out to get something for making the dinner. I was wondering what would you have in mind for dinner?	我正準備要出門買晚餐的材料，是想問你有沒有想吃甚麼？
Albert	Ah, I'll leave that to you. My brain is in a mess.	哎呀，那個交給妳決定就好，我現在腦子裡一團亂。
Marjorie	It's not helping if you just dig yourself in. Try to relax a bit. How about going shopping with me?	光這樣埋頭苦思也沒有用啊，稍微放鬆一下吧，要不要陪我一起去買？
Albert	Could you please leave me alone? How can I finish it in the **timely** fashion if you don't let me think?	可以請妳離開書房讓我一個人靜一靜嗎！？妳不讓我思考，我要怎麼及時交差？
Marjorie	But I seemed to have something I wanted to tell you about...Oh, right, I had a very interesting dream last night. I dreamed about falling in love with an **alien**. He brought me back to their **planet**. Surprisingly, the **civilization** in that planet was almost identical to the earth...	可是我記得有甚麼事想跟你說……對了，我昨晚做的夢真是有趣，我夢見我和外星人談戀愛，他把我帶回外星人的星球，沒想到那個星球的文明跟地球幾乎一模一樣……
Albert	Ah! I got it! My dear, thank you so much! That's what I'm going to write about!	啊！我想到了！親愛的真是謝謝妳！就決定這麼寫了！

必會單字一手抓

❶ prose n. 散文

He writes down the journey of his study in prose.

他以散文寫下自己的求學歷程。

❷ novel n. 小說

The classmates love to bring some romantic novels for distributing them in class at school.

班上同學最愛帶言情小說到學校傳閱。

❸ inspiration n. 靈感

The most desperate part for a person who makes a living by writing is to run out of inspiration.

對一個靠寫作維生的人來說，沒有靈感是最痛苦的一件事。

❹ nod v. 打瞌睡 字彙連結站 doze off

He stayed up too late last night so he keeps nodding in class today.

他昨晚太晚睡了，今天上課一直打瞌睡。

❺ column n. 專欄

The relationship column in this paper offers some interesting perspectives.

這份報紙上的兩性專欄有很多有趣的觀點。

❻ deadline n. 截止時間

Following the deadlines of the publisher is a very important thing for the writers.

遵守出版社的截止時間對文字工作者來說是一件非常重要的事情。

❼ timely **adv.** 及時地

The appearance of the police officers saved them from the punks in the timely fashion.

警察的出現及時地從小混混手中解救了他們。

❽ alien **n.** 外星人

Do you believe in the existence of the aliens in the universe?

你相信宇宙中有外星人嗎？

❾ planet **n.** 行星

All the planets orbit the sun.

所有的行星都繞著太陽轉動。

❿ civilization **n.** 文明

The ancient Maya civilization predicted the end of the world in the year of 2012.

馬雅文明預言了 2012 年的世界末日。

30 秒會話教室

leave me alone 有「留我一個人」以及「讓我獨處」的意思，因此可以用在請求方面，如：Could you please leave me alone? 可以讓我一個人靜一靜嗎？

情境 46 男友是工作狂

會話訓練班

Fiona 的副導男友 Derek 總是忙於電影拍攝的工作，就算人回到家中，還是電話接個不停，或是埋首思考工作內容，讓本來就覺得男友不夠熱情的 Fiona 更是感到受冷落⋯⋯

Fiona's boyfriend, who is an **assistant director**, is always busy with filming work. Even though he's at home, he never stops answering phone calls, or buries himself in work thinking about the work. It makes Fiona, who thinks her boyfriend is not passionate enough, even feels more left out...

Fiona My dear, didn't you say that you wanted to come back early today to watch a movie's premiere in the movie channel with me?

親愛的，你不是說好今天要早點回來陪我看電影頻道首播的電影嗎？

Derek I'm so sorry. The director wanted to **shoot** a **scene** in a rush **unexpectedly**, so all the **staff** had no choice but to continue working overtime. Even those big shot **actors** did not say a word. What else could I do?

對不起，導演臨時說要趕拍一場戲，所有的工作人員也只能留下來繼續加班，連那些大牌演員都沒吭聲了，我能怎麼辦呢？

Fiona Then I guess there's nothing else you could do. By the way, can we go to the country side and take a nice walk since it's a holiday tomorrow? The weather has finally gotten sunnier and warmer lately.

那也沒辦法，對了，明天放假，我們一起到郊外走走好不好，難得最近天氣放晴了。

Derek I'm so tired now. I don't think I can do it if I have to get up early tomorrow, drive and walk all day.

我現在好累，如果明天還要我早起開車、走路，可能沒辦法耶。

Fiona It's a wonderful holiday with a great weather. Do I have to stay home with you until you wake up when you want to?

難道一個難得好天氣的假日，我就非得在家裡陪你睡到自然醒嗎？

Derek If you really want to go out to relax, you can find other friends of yours! After I get enough sleep tomorrow, I also need to run some errands for our director.

如果妳真的很想出門散心，可以找其他朋友啊！我明天睡飽以後還要幫導演做一些庶務的工作。

Fiona Besides those money which is **barely** enough to live on, what else do you get from working days and nights? I'm worried that you'll lose your health and leisure life for that.

你這樣沒日沒夜的工作，除了勉強可以餬口的薪水以外，還能得到甚麼？我怕你會因此賠上了你的健康跟休閒生活。

Derek I think you already know I have always wanted to be a director on my own! I can learn so much by working for this director, which is more **priceless** than my weekly **wage**.

妳也不是不知道，我一直很想自己出來當導演啊！現在跟在這位導演身邊可以學到很多東西，這是比薪水還要無價的資產。

Fiona Then what about our relationship? Am I not important to you?

那我們的感情呢？難道我就不重要嗎？

Derek (Sigh) Haven't we had this talk before? I really love you, but I hope you can support my work and decisions.

唉，我們之前不是談過了嗎？我真的很愛妳，但是也希望妳能支持我的工作和決定。

必會單字一手抓

❶ assistant n. 助理
All the legislators have assistants with them.
立法委員的身邊都有助理。

❷ director n. 導演
Director Ang Lee is the pride and glory of Taiwan in our people's minds.
李安導演是國人心目中的台灣之光。

❸ shoot v. 拍攝
He likes shooting the funny pictures of the pets at home.
他很喜歡拍攝家中寵物逗趣的畫面。

❹ scene n. 一場（戲）、一個鏡頭
My favorite scene is in Titanic when the leading actor and actress are holding each other at the front of the ship.
男女主角在船頭相擁是電影「鐵達尼號」當中我最喜歡的一個鏡頭。

❺ staff n. 工作人員
The staff behind the curtain are all nameless heroes.
一場表演幕後的工作人員都是無名的功臣。

❻ priceless adj. 無價的
I think a person's sincerity is priceless.
我覺得一個人的真心是無價的。

❼ barely adv. 勉強、幾乎沒有
That elderly lady has barely nothing in the house, not even a decent piece of furniture.
那位老奶奶的家中家徒四壁，幾乎沒有像樣的家具。

❽ wage **n.** 薪水、報酬
Her weekly wage is NT$5,000 dollars.
她的週薪為五千元新台幣。

❾ actor **n.** 男演員、演員
I have seen every movie that actor plays. He is my idol.
那位男演員演的每一部電影我都看過，他是我的偶像。

❿ unexpectedly **adv.** 意外地
The news is unexpectedly surprising that the entrepreneur passed away in his prime
那位壯年實業家的過世消息令人意外。

30 秒會話教室

We had a deal before. 我們之前說好的。這句話可以用來提醒對方履行之前答應過的承諾。

名人怎麼說？

If you love life, don't waste time, for time is what life is made up of. —Bruce Lee
如果你熱愛生命，別浪費時間，因為生命是由時間組成的。—李小龍

情境 47 探視當兵男友

會話訓練班

Austine 大學一畢業就接到了兵單，今天正是他入伍後的第一次懇親會，女友 Jocelyn 迫不及待地前往軍中探視他……

After Austine graduated from college, he received the **military** service notification right away. Today it's the first family reunion **visit** for him after he **enrolls** for military service. His girlfriend Jocelyn cannot wait to go visit him in the army...

Jocelyn	Hello, do you know how to get to the fifth meeting room according to this?	你好，請問這上面寫的第五會客室該怎麼走呢？
Larry	Are you the family member of the new **recruit**? Have you registered yet at the reception outside?	妳是要來探望新兵的家屬嗎？有先到外面的報到處報到了嗎？
Jocelyn	Not yet...This is the first time I visit here. I don't know the **procedures** here.	還沒有耶……我是第一次來探視，不太清楚流程。
Larry	It's okay. Please come this way. Let me take you there.	沒關係，來，請往這邊走，我帶妳去。
Austine	Jocelyn, finally I get to see you here! Sorry I made you come here alone! Was it easy to find your way here?	Jocelyn，我終於等到妳了！讓妳一個人來真是辛苦了！這邊好找嗎？

Jocelyn	Good thing I had this soldier took me here, otherwise I would get lost in the army camp.	是這位士兵帶我過來的，要不然我應該還在軍營裏面迷路呢！
Austine	This is not a soldier! You must have to entertain an angel unawares! This is our **platoon** leader. I'm so sorry about that, Sir!	甚麼士兵，妳真是有眼不識泰山，這位是我們的排長啦，排長真是失敬失敬！
Larry	Oh, that's okay! Although Austine Newman is just a new recruit, his **energetic** attitude has left a great impression. Keep up the good work! Spend some quality time with your girlfriend! Excuse me for leaving you two here.	呵呵，沒關係的！Austine Newman 雖然是剛入伍的新兵，但是精神抖擻的態度已經讓人留下了深刻的印象，以後也要好好努力喔！今天的懇親會以及接下來的懇親假就好好陪陪女朋友吧！我先失陪了。
Austine	Yes, sir!	是的，長官！
Jocelyn	I've never seen you wearing a military **uniform**, so **heroic bearing** and disciplined. Boys really have to go through the military training to become a real man!	我從沒看過你身穿軍服又如此英姿煥發又有紀律的模樣耶，男生果然要經過當兵才會蛻變成一個真正的男人！

必會單字一手抓

❶ enroll v. 入伍

Her boyfriend was enrolled for military service two months ago.

她的男朋友於兩個月前入伍。

❷ military n. 軍隊、軍方

The military has received commands from the top government officials asking to practice some military exercises on that deserted island.

軍方收到政府高層的命令，在那座無人小島上進行軍事演習。

❸ visit v. 拜訪、探望

Since that elderly man was admitted to hospital, there hasn't been any of his family coming to visit him.

自從那位老爺爺住院後，就沒有任何親人來探望他。

❹ platoon v. 排（軍隊）

That humorous and funny platoon leader has been favored by the soldiers.

那位幽默風趣的排長非常受到士兵們的喜愛。

❺ recruit n. 新兵

New recruits are all trained at the boot camp.

新兵都要在新兵訓練營接受訓練。

❻ procedures n. 手續、步驟、程序

The new coming secretary has familiarized with the procedures of the meetings.

新來的秘書已經熟悉了開會的程序。

❼ uniform n. 制服、軍服

Once men put on uniforms they look handsome and masculine.

男人穿上軍服就會顯得帥氣又有男人味。

❽ heroic **adj.** 英勇的

There are many heroic figures in Greek mythology that are still praised by people.

希臘神話中有許多英勇的人物仍被後人所歌頌。

❾ bearing **n.** 舉止、風度

She has been educated to be a girl of noble bearing

她從小就被教育成一位舉止端莊的女孩。

❿ energetic **adj.** 精神飽滿的

She is an energetic gymnast.

她是一位精神飽滿的體操選手。

30 秒會話教室

Entertain an angel unawares. 在無意中招待了一位天使，也就是中文「有眼不識泰山」的意思。

情境 48 秘書女友與老闆

會話訓練班

Patrick 剛接女友 Heather 下班準備散步去吃晚餐，Heather 馬上就又接到老闆的來電，等 Heather 掛完電話後 Patrick 不悅地問……

Patrick just picked up his girlfriend Heather after work to take a walk to have dinner. Heather gets a phone call from her boss right after that. After she finishes talking, Patrick is being upset and asking her something...

Patrick	It's time after work. Why did your boss have to call you?	都已經下班了，妳的老闆還打電話給妳做甚麼？
Heather	(Sigh) He said he is going to have a social **engagement** with the clients. There is an important **contract** I need to bring him there.	唉，他說他現在要去跟客戶應酬，有一份重要的合約要順便帶過去。
Patrick	What? So now he wants you to go back to work overtime so you can help him type the contract?	甚麼？所以他要妳現在回去加班幫他打合約嗎？
Heather	No, you got it wrong. I have finished the contract. It's just I **locked** the contract in my file **cabinet** and I've got the key...	不是啦，那份合約我已經完成了，只是我臨走前鎖在我的檔案櫃裡了，而鑰匙在我這邊……。

Patrick	So now you need to send the key back? It's like 15-minute away from where we're now to your company! Being a **secretary** is just like being a **slave**!	所以妳現在要把鑰匙送回去？我們都已經距離妳的公司有 15 分鐘的路程了耶！當老闆的秘書簡直就像奴隸一樣！
Heather	In fact, he is not like having no **humanity** or something. He said he would drive over to get the key from me. Let's first find a **conspicuous** place and wait, and he should be coming soon... Look! Speak of the **devil**... Hey, Tim, I'm here.	其實他沒那麼沒人性啦！他說要開車過來找我拿，我們先在路邊找個顯眼的地方等一下，他應該快到了…你看！說人人到……Hey, Tim，我在這裡。
Tim	Heather, I'm sorry to **disturb** your off work time. Is this your boyfriend? I am Heather's boss, Tim Morgan.	Heather，不好意思，耽誤妳的下班時間。這是妳男朋友吧？我是 Heather 的老闆 Tim Morgan。
Patrick	Hello, I'm Patrick Larsson.	你好，我是 Patrick Larsson。
Tim	I'm sorry I have a social engagement with the clients, can't talk to you long. Next time let me buy you two a dinner. Heather, I will take that key with me then. Have a wonderful evening, good night.	很抱歉我還有應酬，無法跟你多聊聊，下次有機會我再請你們吃頓飯。Heather，那鑰匙我先拿走囉，祝兩位有美好的一夜，晚安。
Heather	See, I told you his is pretty nice.	你看，我就說他人不錯吧。

必會單字一手抓

❶ engagement n. 約會

He has an important engagement with a client this afternoon.

他今天下午和客戶有個重要的約會。

❷ contract n. 合約

According to the contract, you have to keep your lips sealed for the company's business.

依照合約，妳必須為妳的公司保守業務方面的秘密。

❸ secretary n. 秘書

Being a secretary is not as easy as most people think it is. It is much more than just answering phone calls.

當秘書並非如同一般人所想的，只要接接電話那麼輕鬆。

❹ slave n. 奴隸

Legend has it that it was many slaves that made it possible to complete the ancient Egyptian pyramids.

據說古代埃及的金字塔是動用了許多奴隸才得以完工的。

❺ humanity n. 人性、人道

That country gives humanity treatments to the refugees.

那個國家非常人道地對待偷渡者。

❻ conspicuous adj. 顯眼的、易看見的

Only conspicuous road signs can serve the purpose of warning pedestrians.

顯眼的交通號誌才能達到警示用路人的作用。

❼ devil **n.** 魔鬼、惡魔

Any women with slight intelligence would be considered witches who believed in devils during the medieval times.

中世紀稍微有智慧的女性都會被認為是信奉惡魔的女巫。

❽ disturb **v.** 妨礙、打擾

Sorry to disturb you, but I really need your help.

很抱歉因為自己的私事而打擾你，但我真的需要你的協助。

❾ cabinet **n.** 櫥、櫃

The teacher's office is occupied by file cabinets one after another.

老師辦公室裡的空間全被一個個的檔案櫃給佔據了。

❿ lock **v.** 鎖、鎖上

The elderly lady locked herself up on the balcony.

那位老奶奶把自己反鎖在陽台上了。

30 秒會話教室

Speak of the devil and he does appear.——說到惡魔、惡魔就出現了。
也就是中文的「說曹操，曹操到」。

情境 49 家庭醫生前來看診

會話訓練班

從 Marjorie 小時候，家裡就有請家庭醫師看診的習慣，長大後個性較為內向的 Marjorie 更是不習慣讓其他的醫生看診，甚至連結婚後也是如此……

Since Marjorie was a child, the family has been used to seeing a family doctor. Marjorie, who is shy and introverted, can't get used to seeing other doctors after growing up, even after getting married.

Albert	Honey, I'm home. What's for dinner tonight?....Wait, Who is this man! ? Why is he in our house? You get the heck out of here!	老婆，我回來囉！今天晚餐要吃甚麼？等等……，這個男人是誰啊！？怎麼會在我們家裡？快給我滾出去！
Marjorie	Albert, **calm down**! This is my family doctor, Dr.Chastain.	Albert，你先別激動！這位是我的家庭醫生，Dr.Chastain。
Dr.Chastain	Hello, you must be Marjorie's husband. We were just talking about how you proposed to her.	你好，你是 Marjorie 的先生吧。我們剛才才在聊你是怎麼跟她求婚的呢。
Albert	Family doctor...? Oh... Now I do remember you have mentioned that you have seen a family doctor since you were little...but I didn't put that in my mind.	家庭醫生……？喔……我現在才想起來妳好像有提過從小都找家庭醫師看診這件事……但我當時沒放在心上。

Marjorie Look at you being all surprised and shocked. I thought you were coming to **punch** Dr.Chastain.

看你剛才那副又驚訝又激動的模樣，我還以為你要衝過來揍 Dr.Chastain 一拳呢！

Albert Hmm... because I saw your clothes were open on your chest, and there was a man getting so closed to you. I thought you two were doing something **shady**.

嗯……因為看妳胸前的衣服是敞開的，又有一個男人靠妳那麼近，我還以為你們倆個在做甚麼見不得人的事情呢？

Dr.Chastain I was an old doctor. Marjorie's family has been seeing me since her mother's **generation**. Marjorie is like my daughter, you can be assured that. I just was using a stethoscope to listen to her heart sounds.

我已經是個老醫生了，從 Marjorie 的媽媽那一代開始就是找我看診的，Marjorie 就像是我的女兒一樣，你大可放心，我剛才是在用聽診器聽她的心音！

Albert I'm so sorry and please accept my apology! To tell you the truth, judging by the **sight** of your back, It's really hard to tell you're an old doctor. Presumably you must take a very good care of and maintain your physical health. By the way, honey, is there something wrong with you?

真是失敬了！說實話，從醫生您的背影真的看不出來有年紀了，想必非常注重身體的健康與保養。對了，老婆妳的身體怎麼了嗎？

Dr.Chastain	Marjorie said she recently easily feels **dizzy**, and often has **nausea** and vomiting. After I **diagnose**, I think she might be **pregnant**, but still she needs to go to a large hospital for a prenatal visit. Congratulations!	Marjorie 說最近容易感到頭暈目眩，又經常覺得噁心想吐，經過我的診斷，應該是有喜了，之後還是要到大醫院進行產前檢查，恭喜你們。
Marjorie	Oh, my! Honey, isn't this a nice surprise?	喔，我的天啊！老公，這是個很棒的驚喜吧？

必會單字一手抓

❶ calm **v.** 鎮定下來

Please calm down, and tell me what happened slowly, so I know how to help you.

請妳冷靜一點，慢慢告訴我發生甚麼事了？我才知道該如何幫妳。

❷ punch **v.** 用拳猛擊

That boxer mercilessly hit the opponent's chin.

那位拳擊手狠狠地猛擊對手的下巴。

❸ shady **adj.** 見不得人的、可疑的

She was entangled with a shady character.

她跟一個可疑人物有所牽連。

❹ generation n. 世代、一代
People who were born in the 90s are called "The Millennial Generation."
1990 年以後出生的孩子被稱為「富裕的一代」。

❺ sight n. 景象
He saw a familiar figure; not until he ran up to that person did he realize it was the wrong person.
他看到一個熟悉的背影，直到追了上去才發現自己認錯人了。

❻ dizzy adj. 頭暈目眩的
She didn't eat breakfast; no wonder she felt dizzy only ten minutes after listening to the lecture.
她沒吃早餐，難怪才聽十分鐘的演講就感到頭暈目眩。

❼ nausea n. 噁心、作嘔
My sister has nausea and vomiting every time she rides through some winding mountain roads.
妹妹只要搭車經過蜿蜒的山路就會感到噁心想吐。

❽ diagnose v. 診斷
The doctors diagnosed that my uncle's tumor is benign with no immediate threats.
醫生診斷出舅舅罹患的腫瘤是良性的，暫時沒有大礙。

❾ prenatal adj. 產前的、出生以前的
Every time his wife goes to the hospital to have a prenatal visit, he will take a leave and go with her. He's such a considerate husband.
每次太太要到醫院去做產檢，他都會請假陪同，真是一位體貼的好先生。

30 秒會話教室

當你身體不舒服，卻又說不出確切的症狀時，可以直接說：I feel under the weather.
我覺得身體不舒服。或是 I feel sick.

情境 50 男友的錄取通知

會話訓練班

和經營服飾店的女友 Victoria 不同，Harvey 只是個普通的白領階級，在大環境不景氣之下還被公司裁員，他只好努力地投履歷找工作……

Being different clothing from his girlfriend Victoria who runs a clothing store, Harvey is just an ordinary **white-collar** worker. He lost his job during the **depression**, so he has to **summit resumes** to look for a job...

Hal Hello, may I speak to Harvey Ross?

喂，請問是 Harvey Ross 的家嗎？

Victoria Hello, who's calling, please?

是的，你好，請問哪裡找？

Hal I am the human **resource** manager of XX Technology, Hal Garcia. We have received Mr. Ross the resume that he **applied** for the job. We think he is very suitable for this opening position so we would like to **notify** him to attend the **final stage** of the interview.

我是 XX 科技公司的人力資源經理，Hal Garcia，我們收到了 Mr. Ross 的應徵履歷，覺得他非常適合我們正在徵才的這份職務，因此想通知他前來進行最後一個階段的面試。

Victoria Oh, that's really great! He's not home now, could you please tell me the place and time for the interview, also anything regarding this matter? I'll let him know when he comes back.

喔，那真是太好了！不過他現在剛好不在家，能麻煩您將面試的時間與相關須知告訴我嗎？等他回來我馬上轉告他。

Hal	Yes, please. Please tell Mr. Ross come find me at the Human Resources Office on the 8th floor at 10:00 am the day after tomorrow. He only needs to show up in person.	好的，那就麻煩妳了，請 Mr. Ross 於後天上午 10:00 至敝公司 8 樓的人力資源辦公室找我，只要人來就可以了。
Victoria	I've really appreciated that your company offers this great opportunity. Harvey will surely strive to do the best. He will not let you down.	真的非常感謝貴公司給予的寶貴機會，Harvey 一定會好好努力表現、不會讓您失望的。
Hal	I'm really looking forward to his contribution to our company. That would be all. I wish you have a good day, ma'am.	我也非常期待他的發展，那就先這樣了，祝妳日安，女士。
Harvey	I'm back. Who were you just talking on the phone? Why are you looking all excited?	我回來了。妳剛剛在跟誰講電話啊？怎麼一副歡天喜地的樣子？
Victoria	It was a phone call from XX technology to notify to attend the final stage of the interview. They seem to much value your abilities. That's really great!	剛剛有一間 XX 科技公司打來通知你去進行最後階段的面試，他們好像很看重你的能力，真是太好了！
Harvey	Really? I would have thought a big company like that would never accept me. I did not think I still have some value in this job market! I've started to have more **confidence** in my own future.	真的嗎？我本來以為那麼大間的企業應該不會錄取我，沒想到我還是有些價值的！我開始對自己的將來有信心了！

必會單字一手抓

❶ white-collar adj. 勞動的

His parents are white-collar workers.

他的父母親都是白領階級的勞工。

❷ depression n. 景氣、蕭條

Many workers still work hard and strive for good performance during the time facing the economic depression.

有很多勞工在面對不景氣的時期仍舊努力地工作力求表現。

❸ resume n. 履歷

There are many freshmen newly graduated from colleges do not know how to write their resumes.

有很多剛從大學畢業的新鮮人不知道該如何寫好自己的履歷。

❹ submit v. 提交、呈遞

That teacher who physically punished the children couldn't handle the pressure from the public, and finally submitted his resignation to the school.

那位體罰學童的老師受不了輿論壓力，終於向校方遞交了辭呈。

❺ resource n. 資源、物力

If people still do not limit the exploitation of natural resources, they will lead the earth to destruction.

倘若人們仍舊對自然資源的開發不知節制，將會導致地球走向滅亡。

❻ confidence n. 自信、信賴

That model feels very confident to her appearance.

那位模特兒對自己的外貌非常有自信。

❼ apply n. 申請、請求
She applies for transferring to a smaller clinic only a month after starting working in this hospital.
她才到這間醫院報到一個月，就申請調職到較小的診所去了。

❽ notify n. 通知、告知
Please notify me when you will arrive in Taiwan, so I know when to pick you up.
請通知我您何時會抵達台灣，好讓我前往接機。

❾ final adj. 最後的、最終的
This is your last chance. If you don't go talk to her, she will leave soon.
這是最後一次的機會，你再不去跟她搭訕，她就要離開了。

❿ stage n. 階段、時期
A caterpillar must go through the cocooning stage to become a butterfly.
毛毛蟲必須經過蛹的階段才能變成蝴蝶。

30 秒會話教室

You should have confidence in yourself. 你應該對自己有信心。I have confidence in you. 我對你有信心。

情境 51 第一次見女方父母

會話訓練班

今天 Louis 是第一次和女友 Eliza 的父母見面，他提早到達了約定的餐廳想給對方一個好印象。等 Eliza 與父母在約好的時間進入餐廳就坐，他馬上有禮貌地主動打招呼……

Today it's the first time Louis meets the parents of his girlfriend, Eliza. He has arrived earlier at the restaurant than the meeting time hoping to leave a good impression on the parents. He **greets** them **politely** soon after Eliza and her parents arrive and get seated at the restaurant at the scheduled time…

Louis	Hello, uncles and auntie, I'm Louis Thompson. I am recently graduated from department of **programming** at XX university.	伯父、伯母，你們好，我是 Louis Thompson，今年剛從 XX 大學的程式設計系畢業。
Eliza' father	You are such a lively, energetic young man, but look at you being all nervous and **shivering**. Come sit down first.	真是有朝氣的男生，不過看你緊張的直發抖，先坐下吧。
Eliza' mother	Yah, don't stand on **ceremony**. Let's go have a seat first.	是啊，不用這麼拘束，我們坐下再說。
Eliza	Dad, mom, there's a company finds Louis to design the websites before Louis gets graduated.	爸、媽，Louis 還沒畢業，就已經有企業找他幫忙設計網站了喔。

Eliza' mother	That's very impressive, so you sort of already found a job, right? What is your monthly **salary** now?	這麼厲害呀，那麼你已經算是找到工作囉？你現在的月薪是多少？
Eliza' father	Eliza's mom, how come you started the conversation by asking such a personal question. No matter how much salary he makes every month, that's the money he earns by working hard. Eliza, you should go find a job soon, don't just **spend** the hard earned money Louis has got.	孩子的媽，妳怎麼劈頭就問這麼私人的問題，不管薪水高不高，那都是他自己的錢，Eliza 妳也要趕緊找工作，可別都花 Louis 辛苦賺的錢啊。
Eliza	Yes, I'm working on that. Hey, didn't I tell you my father is a very open-minded person?	是的，我正在努力了。呵，我就跟你說過我爸爸很開明吧？
Louis	I was very nervous at the beginning, but after I meet your parents, I feel they are just like my family...Am I being too **self-righteous** by saying that?	本來一開始非常緊張，等真的看到伯父伯母之後，就覺得像自己的家人一樣親切……咦？我突然這樣說會不會太自以為是了？
Eliza' mother	Why so? We only have daughters in our family. To be honest with you, we really hope to see you and Eliza get married so we can have a **son-in-law**.	怎麼會呢？我們家都生女兒，其實我們很希望你能跟 Eliza 修成正果，讓我們多一個半子呢。

必會單字一手抓

❶ greet v. 問候、招呼、迎接
The hostess is standing at the door greeting the guests to the dinner party tonight.
女主人站在大門外迎接今晚晚宴的客人。

❷ politely adv. 有禮貌地
My niece is politely saying Hello to all the elderly relatives.
姪女很有禮貌地向所有的長輩打招呼。

❸ salary n. 薪資、薪水
She has earned the salary people are envy of based on her own effort since she first started working.
她剛出社會就憑著自己的努力領到人人稱羨的薪水。

❹ spend v. 花費（時間、金錢）
I've spent 6 hours on making that stuffed bear doll.
那隻布製小熊花了我六個小時才縫好。

❺ self-righteous adj. 自以為是的
John is a self-righteous man thinking all the girls like him.
John 是一個自己為是的人，總以為所有女生都喜歡他。

❻ programming n. （電腦）編制程序
I only know that he's the new professor in the department of computer programming. I don't know his name yet.
我只知道他是程式設計系的新任教授，還不知道他的名字。

❼ shiver v. 發抖、打顫
Models always shiver in the cold weather because they usually

need to wear less clothes.
模特兒經常要穿著清涼，在寒冷的天氣裡總是冷的直發抖。

❽ ceremony **n.** 儀式、典禮
She will the MC (Master of Ceremonies) in that grand ceremony.
她將在那場盛大的典禮當中擔任司儀。

❾ son-in-law **n.** 女婿
Many mothers all wish the future sons-in-law has a job with steady income.
許多作母親的都希望未來的女婿擁有一份穩定的職業。

30 秒會話教室

Q：What's your expected salary? 你期望的薪水是多少？A：I'm hoping a monthly salary of 20,000 dollars. 我希望的待遇是月薪兩萬元。

關鍵字搜尋

First Impression
Dress sharp: Make yourself look presentable. Don't wear anything too weird. If your clothes need ironing, iron them.
衣著俐落：讓自己衣著得體，不要穿太古怪的衣服，如果衣服該燙就燙。
Give a friendly greeting. When you meet her parents, look them in the eye, smile and offer a handshake to both parents.
友善的打招呼：當你見到她的父母，眼神要對到，保持微笑並與兩位家長握手。
Don't act nervous. Much of us judge a man relate to his confidence and bearing.
不要表現出緊張：通常大部分的人會以自信神色與行為舉止來判斷一個男人。

情境 52 鄰居的閒言閒語

會話訓練班

Miles 和女友 Doris 各自在外租屋，因為 Doris 還另有室友較不方便，因此只有 Doris 偶爾會到 Miles 的租屋處小住幾天，但這卻讓 Miles 的鄰居開始有些閒言閒語……

Miles and his girlfriend both have their own rental places. Doris occasionally goes to Miles' place to stay for a few days since she has a roommate, but this has made the neighbor start **gossiping** behind their backs...

Doris	Excuse me, could you help me press the floor button for me? I'm going to the 11th **floor**, thank you.	不好意思，可以幫我按一下電梯嗎？我要到 11 樓，謝謝。
Neighbor A	Is she the girl you saw last time with Mrs. Wong, who always come stay with a man?	她就是妳上次跟王太太看到的，老是跑來男生家住的女人嗎？
Neighbor B	That's right. She always stays for two or three days. It's so **shameless** on her staying with a man she doesn't marry to, maybe she threw herself at him.	對呀，而且一住就是兩三天，明明兩個人就還沒結婚，真是不要臉，說不定是她倒貼人家的。
Doris	Excuse me, this is my floor. Excuse me.	對不起，我的樓層到了，請借過。

Miles Doris, you come back! Why the long face? Is the stuff you're carrying too heavy? Please, let me help you to put them away.

Doris，妳來啦！咦？怎麼一臉不高興的樣子，東西太重了嗎？來，我幫妳拿去放好。

Doris There were two ladies from the neighborhood in the elevator while I was carrying all bags of the groceries. I asked them to press the floor button for me, but they just totally **ignored** me. The **worse** thing was they started badmouthing about me in the **narrow** space of the elevator, like they didn't care at all if I could hear them. I was so furious that I would almost say a few words in **retort**.

我剛剛雙手拿著大包小包的東西搭電梯，電梯裡面剛好有兩位太太，我請她們幫我按一下電梯，結果她們竟然完全不理我。更可惡的是，她們竟然就在電梯那麼狹小的空間裡講起我的壞話，絲毫不怕我聽到的樣子，害我一度氣到想回嗆她們？

Miles How could that happen? The neighbors I've met at all time are pretty **decent**. What did they say about you?

這麼會這樣？我平常遇到的鄰居對我都還挺親切的。她們說了甚麼？

Doris A woman with **curly** hair said that she and Mrs. Wong saw me always come stay with a man, and something about me being shameless and throwing myself at you.

有一個捲頭髮的太太說甚麼她跟一位王太太看到我老是跑來男人家住，還說我不要臉、倒貼你。

Miles I think you met Mrs. Lee and Mrs. Chen who are good friends with Mrs. Wong. They are very friendly to me all the time and often ask me if I need anything.

那妳遇到的應該是跟王太太很好的李太太和陳太太，她們平常對我很熱情，常常問我有沒有缺甚麼東西耶！

Doris Great! Then they must have **hostility** to me because they like you. It's such a bummer for me.

那她們應該是因為喜歡你，所以才對我懷有敵意，我真是倒楣！

必會單字一手抓

❶ gossip **v.** 閒話、聊天

The whole community was gossiping about the couple.

整個社區都在說這對夫妻的閒話。

❷ shameless **adj.** 無恥的、不要臉的

That shameless politician keeps denying all the mistakes he has made even in the presence of the evidence of his embezzlement.

那個無恥的政客，貪汙的罪證確鑿卻仍舊矢口否認自己的錯誤。

❸ floor **n.** 樓層

I've been to her place on the 11th floor in that building.

她住在那棟大樓的 11 樓，我曾經去過一次。

❹ ignore **v.** 忽視、不理會

There's no passer-by responding to that old woman's shouting and letting the burglar rob her purse.

沒有任何路人理會那位老婦人的呼喊，任憑小偷搶走她的錢包。

❺ narrow **adj.** 狹窄的

That narrow alley would be in serious danger if there was a fire breaking out.

那條巷弄非常狹窄，萬一發生火警可就糟糕了。

❻ decent **adj.** 親切的、樂於助人的

The new security guard of the building is very decent.

大樓的新警衛非常親切。

❼ hostility **n.** 敵意、敵視

That problem kid has always had hostility to everyone.

那個問題兒童總是對所有人充滿敵意。

❽ retort **v.** 回嘴、反駁

My sister retorted that she only fought back when the little boy started hitting her.

妹妹反駁說是鄰居小男孩先動手打人，她才還手的。

❾ worse **adj.** 更糟的

The flood caused by the typhoon are not ebbing yet in the disaster area; the worse thing is, there's another flood tide coming alongside the coastal area.

颱風造成的災區淹水還沒退，更糟的是，沿海地區又要漲潮了。

❿ curly **adj.** 捲曲的、有捲髮的

That woman with curly hair bargains with one vender after another every time she comes to the market.

那位捲髮的婦人每次來到市場都會一攤一攤地殺價。

30 秒會話教室

The worse thing is / To make matters worse, I locked myself out of my house. 更糟糕的是，我把自己反鎖在門外了。

情境 53 年節親戚逼婚

會話訓練班

Derek 是第二次於農曆新年期間陪女友 Fiona 回家探望家人，席間親戚眾多，難免會被問到令人尷尬的問題例如婚事……

This is the second time Derek goes visit the family of his girlfriend, Fiona on Chinese New Year. It's very hard for them to avoid the **awkward** questions about "when are you getting married" when there are many **relatives** around.

Fiona's aunt	Dear, are you turning 30 soon after a few years, right?	親愛的，妳再幾年就 30 歲了吧？
Fiona	Yes, I'm 28 this year.	對啊，今年滿 28 歲了。
Fiona's aunt	Then why don't you get married soon? Don't you know you will be an **elderly primigravida**?	那妳還不趕快結婚嗎？你知道這樣可是會變成高齡產婦的喔？
Fiona's uncle	It's not like you are not in a relationship with someone. Ask your boyfriend to marry you soon. Derek, come over here, Let me ask you something. How come you haven't given Fiona a **promise** yet?	妳又不是沒有交往的對象，叫男朋友趕快娶妳啊！ Derek，你過來，舅舅問你，你怎麼還不趕快給我們家 Fiona 一個承諾呢？

Derek We've talked about this, but we think it's better for us to work on our careers for another few years before we tight the knot.

我們有談過這件事，我們想說再拚個幾年事業再結婚比較好。

Fiona's aunt Career? You can still build up your career after getting married! There's a Chinese **proverb** saying that a man has his best luck before having a wife and after having a baby. Men should always get married first and then start a career!

事業？結了婚一樣可以繼續拚事業啊！中國有句俗諺叫做：『娶某前，生子後』，男人就是要先成家才會立業嘛！

Fiona Auntie, he's been really busy at work lately. Besides, we've already moved in together, what really makes the difference is just a marriage **certificate**. There's really no rush for us to get married.

阿姨，他現在的工作真的很忙，而且我們住在一起，實際上只差一張結婚證書而已，結不結婚真的不急啦！

Fiona's uncle There's really no guarantee for girls in this case. What if you two break up later? Her youth and time will all go down the drain!

可是這樣對女孩子很沒有保障啊！萬一你們最後還是分手，妳的青春就全白費了！

Derek	Uncle, auntie, I promise, I won't let that happen. I will provide Fiona a brighter future. After I **improve** my **circumstances** of my work and finance, Fiona and I will start **undertaking** the wedding plans.	舅舅、阿姨，不會的。我一定會給 Fiona 一個未來，等我的工作更加穩定、經濟狀況有了改善，就會開始著手計畫婚事了。
Fiona's mother	You two old folks stop **interrogating** the couple. It's time for dinner.	你們兩位長輩不要再逼問小倆口了啦，可以過來吃飯了。

必會單字一手抓

❶ relative **n.** 親戚
The only relative that poor little boy who lost his parents has is his old grandmother.
那位失去父母的可憐小男孩唯一的親人就剩下年邁的奶奶了。

❷ awkward **adj.** 難對付的、棘手的
That government official has been asked several awkward question in the press conference.
那位政府官員在記者會上被問到了幾個棘手的問題。

❸ primigravida **n.** 初產孕婦
Women tend to get married at earlier ages than men do mostly because they want to avoid being an elderly primigravida.
女性會比男性更急於走入婚姻，多半是為了避免成為高齡產婦的關係。

❹ promise **v.** 承諾
I promise you I'll never abuse any small animals.
答應我你絕對不會再傷害小動物了。

❺ proverb **n.** 諺語、常言

Lydia, who studies in the language department of Chinese, buys a book introducing Chinese proverbs.
就讀中文系的 Lydia 特地買了一本介紹中國諺語的書。

❻ certificate n. 證明書、執照
The detailed birth time is certainly recorded on one's birth certificate.
一個人的出生證明上一定會記載著詳細的出生時間。

❼ improve v. 增進、改善
A person who never makes good use of time to better himself ends up accomplishing nothing.
從不利用時間改善自己各方面能力的人，最終會一事無成。

❽ circumstances n. 經濟狀況
The financial circumstances have been going downhill since that family lost the father.
自從那家人失去父親之後，經濟狀況就陷入了困境。

❾ undertake v. 試圖、著手做
The government sends out a team to undertake some research on the study of the recently discovered historic relics.
政府派出了一支隊伍對那項剛出土的文物著手進行研究。

❿ interrogate v. 審問、質問
The detective keeps interrogating him about his whereabouts on the spot.
偵探不停質問他事發當時人在哪裡？

30 秒會話教室

I will get married. 我將來會結婚。I'm getting married. 我要結婚了。
I will marry her. 我要娶她。

關鍵字搜尋

Only do what your heart tells you.—Princess Diana
只做你的心所跟你說的事。—黛安娜王妃

情境 54 上門提親

會話訓練班

Brian 和 Phoebe 已經私下許諾互訂終生，Phoecy 也已經見過 Brian 的家人，接下來就等 Brian 到 Phoebe 家提親……

Brian and Phoebe already get engaged in privacy. Phoebe has already met Brian's family. Now they are going to **propose** marriage to Phoebe's family.

Brian	Uncle and auntie, I'm here today for an important matter that I'd like to ask your **permission**.	伯父、伯母，我今天來是有重要的事情想徵求兩位的同意。
Phoebe' father	I think we've already heard something about it. Please tell us your request.	我們已經有所耳聞了，請說。
Brian	Will you let your daughter marry me, uncle and auntie?	伯父、伯母，請問你們願意把女兒嫁給我嗎？
Phoebe' father	(Sigh) You two have been dating for quite a while. Despite how much I don't want her to leave us, **sooner or later** she has to make her own family.	唉，你們也交往很久了，雖然捨不得我的寶貝女兒，但她遲早還是得嫁人的。

Phoebe' mother	You have been **pampered** and **spoiled** since **childhood**, please change some of your old habits once you stay with another family. Remember to do the housework **industriously**, and don't **pull** a long face anytime you feel upset, okay?	妳從小嬌生慣養，嫁到人家家去可不能偷懶啊，家事要勤勞地做，也不可以隨便板著一張臉，知道嗎？
Phoebe	Mom, I know.	媽，我知道。
Phoebe' father	Brian, please take a good care of my daughter.	Brian，我的女兒就交給你了。
Brain	Thank you, Sir. I'll love her dearly for the rest of my life. Auntie, don't you worry, you can be **assured** that my family all like Phoebe very much.	謝謝伯父，我一定會好好愛她一輩子！也請伯母放心，我的家人也都很喜歡 Phoebe。
Phoebe' father	Don't treat me as an **outsider**. Just call me dad. When are you going to have the wedding? What kind of wedding do you want to have? Do you **plan** out everything?	以後就不用這麼生疏了，叫我爸爸就好。那婚期預計在甚麼時候呢？要辦怎麼樣的婚禮？你們都計劃好了嗎？
Brian	Yes, pretty much. Let me have some more discussion with Mom and Dad about the wedding.	是的，我這就跟爸、媽討論一下婚禮的方式。

必會單字一手抓

❶ propose v. 提議、求婚

Someone proposes that we should give our flyers at the door for attracting more customers.

有人建議我們在門口發放傳單吸引更多客人。

❷ permission n. 允許、同意

No entry without permission and no trespassing.

未經許可不得入內參觀，不得擅自闖入。

❸ pamper v. 縱容、嬌養

It's not love if the parents only pamper them; it's in fact to sabotage their lives.

縱容孩子不是在疼他，而是在害他。

❹ spoiled adj. 被寵壞的

Every spoiled child has something in common, which is the lack of consideration for others.

被寵壞的孩子都有一個特徵，就是不懂得為別人著想。

❺ childhood n. 童年時期

He spent most of his childhood with his fisherman father on the fishing boat.

他的童年時期幾乎是和漁夫父親在漁船上度過的。

❻ industriously adv. 勤奮地

That cleaning lady industriously cleans up the toilets in the whole building every day.

那位打掃阿姨每天都勤奮地清掃整棟大樓的廁所。

❼ assured **adj.** 確定的、得到保證的

You can be assured that your resume will be greatly accepted by the boss of the company.

請你放心，你的履歷一定會順利得到公司老闆的青睞的。

❽ outsider **n.** 局外人

I'm an outsider, even though I have lived in Japan for five years.

我是一個局外人，就算我已在日本住了 5 年。

❾ pull **v.** 拉

Those students all pull long faces because the teacher announced the makeup test after school.

那群學生因為老師說放學後要補考，個個愁眉苦臉的。

❿ plan **v.** 計劃、打算

The management plans to fully delegate this project to us. What are you going to do with that?

上頭把這件企劃案全權交給我們負責，你打算怎麼做？

30 秒會話教室

Sooner or later you will thank me. 你遲早會感謝我的。You will leave your parents sooner or later. 你遲早會離開父母的。

Part 5

讓夢想的種子萌芽

情境 55 熱血棒球夢

會話訓練班

仍在就讀大學的 Celia 是棒球社的經理，她喜歡上棒球隊的主將 Joshua，而 Joshua 也常在練習之餘跟她吐露自己對棒球這項運動的熱愛……

Celia, who is still at college, is the manager of the baseball club. She falls in love with the **chief commander** of the baseball team, Joshua. In the meantime, Joshua often shows his **passion** for baseball to Celia after the practice...

Celia	What a hard day of practice! You hit some perfect **swings** with great poses today at the practice. Come have some **mineral** water and towels.	辛苦了！今天的揮棒練習姿勢很標準喔！來，礦泉水和毛巾。
Joshua	Thank you. It might have something to do with the **scout** coming. That made me practice even harder.	謝謝妳。可能是聽說球探要來的關係，所以練習得特別起勁。
Celia	I think it's more than that. I can tell you have extreme passion on baseball than most people do. Other players don't seem to care even when they know about the scout is coming.	我覺得不光只是這個原因，我看得出你對棒球有異於常人的熱情，其他球員即使知道球探要來，好像也不特別放在心上。
Joshua	Really? I didn't **notice** of other people's reactions? Perhaps I've just **focused on** practicing. Playing baseball has been like my dream since I was little.	是嗎？我沒有注意到其他人的反應耶，或許是我太專注於練習了吧。因為棒球真的是我從小的夢想。

Celia	I think you have a pretty good chance of being selected by the scout. I believe you can make your dream come true by playing in MLB(Major **League** Baseball).	我覺得你很有機會被球探選上，你一定可以如願到大聯盟打球的。
Joshua	Really? How come? I still think I need to improve a lot.	真的嗎？怎麼說？我覺得自己還有很多不足的地方。
Celia	That's because...because you always come for the practice earlier than anyone else, make sure you make every pose right, and put on a smile facing all of this. I can feel your genuine love and passion for baseball.	因為……因為你總是比其他人早到開始練習，動作也做得比別人確實，而且永遠都是面帶微笑地面對這一切，我可以感覺到你是真心喜愛著棒球。
Joshua	So you have been observing me **silently**. It would be great if there was a cute manager like you in MLB.	原來妳一直在默默觀察我呀。如果大聯盟也有像妳這麼可愛的球隊經理就好了呢。
Celia	You…Don't make fun of me! I'm off to pick up the bats and balls scattering all around.	你……你別取笑我了啦！我要去整理球場上散落一地的球棒和球了。
Joshua	Let me help you with that. Let's have some coffee after we put everything in the equipment room.	我來幫妳吧。等東西都收進器材室之後，我們去喝杯咖啡吧。

必會單字一手抓

❶ chief adj. 為首的、主要的

He has devoted himself to this company for 8 years. Finally now he's assigned as the chief engineer supervising this construction project.

他在公司熬了八年，終於被委任為監督這項工程的總工程師。

❷ commander n. 指揮官、領導人

One must follow the orders of the commander in the military.

在軍隊裡一定要服從指揮官的命令。

❸ swing v. 揮舞、使擺動

That player hit a upright swing and sent the ball to the left field.

那位選手一記高揮棒把球打到了左外野。

❹ mineral adj. 礦物的

The United States possess rich mineral resources in its vast land.

美國國土廣大，擁有非常豐富的礦物資源。

❺ scout n. 球探、星探等發掘新人者

Young women have to be careful with people who disguise themselves into a star scout and allure them to fall for their schemes.

有些壞人會偽裝成星探誘騙年輕女性上當，不得不防。

❻ league n. 同盟、聯盟

The countries located in the coastal area form a defense league.

位於沿海的幾個國家組成了防禦聯盟。

❼ silently adv. 寂靜地、沉默地

The brothers are silently eating dinner after being lectured by their mother.

那對剛被媽媽罵完的兄弟沉默地吃著晚餐。

❽ passion n. 熱情、酷愛

My brother has so much passion for playing the guitar.

哥哥對彈吉他充滿熱愛。

❾ notice v. 注意、注意到

The noisy students didn't notice that the teacher had walked into the classroom with anger.

吵鬧的學生們沒注意到老師已經生氣地走進教室。

❿ focus v. 使集中

Those children are now focusing on the butterflies that fly in the classroom.

那些小孩的注意力全部集中在飛進教室的蝴蝶身上。

30 秒會話教室

Don't make fun of me. 取笑我。這句話也有「別拿我開玩笑啦、別逗我了」的意思。

情境 56 渾身戲胞無處發揮？去當演員吧！

會話訓練班

Fiona 一直覺得自己有很強烈的表演慾望並渴望被人注意，但她不知道該如何踏進相關的行業，因此她向男友 Derek 提起了這個想法……

Fiona has always had an **overwhelming** desire to be noticed, but she doesn't know how to get into the **acting industry**, so she mentions this idea to her boyfriend, Derek...

Fiona Honey, do you know any movies or TV shows are looking for some ordinary actors or actresses?

親愛的，你知道最近有甚麼電影或節目在徵求素人演員嗎？

Derek I do know about some, but why are you asking me this?

有是有，不過妳問這個做甚麼？

Fiona I want to sign up for that! Will I get selected more easily if I use your **connections**?

我想去報名啊！如果透過你這層關係，會不會比較容易入選呢？

Derek Although the assistant director can **participate in** the process of **selecting** the actors, you still need to have what it takes you to be casted! Why are you all being interested in acting without a **cause**?

雖然助理導演可以參與遴選員的過程，但是妳也要真的有實力才能讓妳入選啊！妳怎麼無緣無故突然開始對演戲有興趣呢？

Fiona	Don't you think I've got some talent in acting?	你不覺得我很有演戲的天分嗎？
Derek	Why makes you think so?	何以見得？
Fiona	Huh, didn't you remember the time I was in the hospital, I acted like I lost all my memories, and I got you really **believe** that. Did you forget?	唉唷，就是我之前住院的時候，不是演了一齣喪失記憶的戲，你還真的相信了，你忘了嗎？
Derek	You called that acting? Do you really think those actors win their Oscar **Awards** by having some **flat** acting skills? I think you just use this as an excuse so you can spend time with me days and nights, right?	這哪叫演戲的天分？妳以為那些演員都是用像妳一樣的蹩腳演技得到奧斯卡獎的嗎？我認為妳只是想進入電影圈，好跟我朝夕相處吧？
Fiona	Hmm, busted! You got me!	唔，被你發現了！
Derek	Alright, alright. I know you feel lonely. I will try get off work early so we can spend more time together. As for being an actress, let's wait and see if you really have some interest in it.	好啦，我知道妳感到寂寞。我會盡量早點下班回家陪妳的，倒是演戲一事，等妳真的有興趣再說吧。

必會單字一手抓

❶ overwhelming adj. 勢不可擋的、壓倒性的
That senator won the election for his second term in the House with overwhelming votes.
那位議員以壓倒性的高票數當選連任。

❷ industry n. 工業、行業
The car industry in Germany is not compatible in the world.
德國的汽車工業是放眼世界無人能敵的。

❸ acting n. 演戲、演技
That experienced actress has received life achievement award based on her acting techniques.
那位老牌女演員憑著她的演技得到了終身成就獎。

❹ select v. 挑選、選拔
That diligent and responsible girl was selected to the class leader by the whole class.
那個認真負責的小女孩被全班同學選為班長。

❺ award n. 獎、獎項
The short stories earned her a literary award.

❻ connection n. 關係、往來
He's just a business connection.
他跟我只有生意上的關係。

❼ participate v. 參與
Everybody can participate in this charity bazaar.
每個人都可以參加這次的義賣活動。

❽ believe **v.** 相信、信任

She never believes whatever men tells her since her ex-boyfriend lied to her and took away all her savings.

自從她被前男友騙走積蓄以後，她就再也不相信男人說的話了。

❾ flat **adj.** 單調的、無聊的

He feels everything in his life flat and monotonous since he lost his wife.

失去心愛的妻子之後，他覺得生活中的一切都是單調乏味的。

❿ cause **n.** 原因、根據

The investigation team can't still find the real cause to the plane crash.

調查小組還是無法找出造成飛機失事的原因。

30 秒會話教室

由日文演變而來的「素人」也就是指一般人的意思，例：The Internet have brought fame to a lot of ordinary but talented people. 網際網路使很多有才華的素人成名。

情境 57 天生歌喉「讚」

會話訓練班

Olivia 平時很喜歡哼哼唱唱，有時唱到高興的時候還會忘情高歌，讓老公 Wesley 驚訝於她的好歌喉，常常勸她去參加歌唱比賽……

Olivia usually likes to hum and sing, and sometimes she sings so happily, she just sings like there's no one around. Her husband Wesley is so surprised with her good singing **voice**, and often encourages her to go to the singing contest...

Wesley	Dear, your singing voice just came out of the **bathroom** that was really good. It sounds like **heaven**.	老婆，妳剛剛在浴室唱歌傳了出來，真的好好聽喔，讓我彷佛置身天堂。
Olivia	Oh, did I sing that **loudly**? I'm really sorry for waking you up.	呵，我唱得有那麼大聲啊？真是不好意思，吵醒你了。
Wesley	Not at all. I think it's a pity if I'm the only person who gets to enjoy your **angelic** voice. Do you want to enroll in a singing competition?	不會啊，我都覺得妳的天籟美聲只讓我一個人欣賞太可惜了，妳要不要報名參加歌唱比賽呀？
Olivia	A singing competition? That does come across my mind, but I don't know by what means that I can participate in. I always think it something **unattainable** for me.	歌唱比賽？我是有想過啦。但是不知道要藉由甚麼管道才能參加？總覺得是一件遙不可及的事情。

Wesley	Aren't there many singing talent shows on TV? Everyone can sign up for it. Let me go online to take a look.	現在電視上不是有許多歌唱選秀節目嗎？大家都可以報名的。我上網查查看。
Olivia	Your great **efficiency** actually makes me nervous. I'm afraid I might have stage **fright** in front of so many people if I really join the competition.	你說做就做的效率，反倒讓我緊張了起來，我怕真的去參加比賽，在那麼多人面前會怯場耶。
Wesley	Found it! There is an "Asia's new talent singing contest" All you have to do is to fill out the **form** and attach a clear video clip about 3-5 minutes in length. You don't have to sing in front of everyone. I think it will help you build some confidence first.	找到了，有個「亞洲新人歌唱大賽」，只要下載報名表填寫，並附上清楚的視訊片段，約 3 到 5 分鐘就可以了。這就不用在大家面前演唱了，很適合幫妳先建立信心。
Olivia	Can I...can I really make it? Do you really have that much confidence in my singing?	我……我真的可以嗎？你對我的歌喉真的這麼有信心？
Wesley	We should have the courage to pursue our dreams. I think you really have the strength. I am not joking. Let me tell you what, let's sign up first. If you get selected, you'll have confidence in yourself and to be bold in the competition. If not selected, there's nothing for you to lose.	有夢想就要勇於追尋，妳是真的有這個實力的，我不會騙妳。不然這樣吧，我們先報名看看，如果成功入選，妳就對自己有信心，放膽去參加比賽。如果沒入選，也沒什麼損失啊。

Olivia	Okay, I am willing to give it a try. Let's make the video when I'm ready.	好，我願意試試看。等我準備好就來錄製影像吧。

必會單字一手抓

❶ voice **n.** 聲音、嗓子

I know she is in a bad mood now only by listening to her voice.

我光聽她的聲音就知道她現在心情不好。

❷ bathroom **n.** 浴室

She puts some pots of plants in the bathroom, which looks green and lush.

她在浴室擺放了幾盆植栽，看起來綠意盎然。

❸ angelic **adj.** 天使的、似天使的

The baby in the photograph has an angelic smile.

照片中的小嬰兒帶著天使般的笑容。

❹ heaven **n.** 天堂（常大寫）、天空

When I was little, my parents always said my grandmother went to the Heaven. I didn't understand what this meant until I grew up.

小時候父母都說奶奶到天堂去了，等我長大後才明白這是甚麼意思。

❺ unattainable **adj.** 達不到的、做不到的

Having a room of my own was an unattainable dream in my mind.

擁有一間屬於自己的房間，在我心中曾是遙不可及的夢想。

❻ efficiency **n.** 效率、功效

The harvesters have increased farmers' work efficiency.

收割機的問世使農夫們的工作更有效率。

❼ fright **n.** 驚嚇、恐怖、令人吃驚的人事物

That caterpillar almost made the girls in fright in the class.

那隻毛毛蟲差點讓班上的女生嚇得半死。

❽ loudly **adv.** 高聲地、吵鬧地

The next-door neighbor's new born baby has been crying loudly.

隔壁鄰居剛誕生的小嬰兒高聲地哭鬧。

❾ form **n.** 表格

Please fill your basic information in the blank space of this form, thank you.

請在這張表格的空白處填上你的基本資料，謝謝。

30 秒會話教室

daring to dream、go for it 都是勸人勇於追夢的片語，還有 Don't be afraid to dream a little bigger. 別害怕作大一點的夢想。

名人怎麼說？

At the touch of love everyone becomes a poet. —Plato

一旦碰到愛情，每個人都成為了詩人。—柏拉圖

情境 58 幫助非洲難民

會話訓練班

天生悲天憫人的 Eliza，對弱勢族群，如老人、小孩、肢障者總是展現出無比的同情心，並會盡一己之力幫助他們……

Eliza always expresses her **humanitarianism** and great **compassion** to **disadvantaged** people, like elderly people, children, disabilities, and does her best to help them...

Eliza	Every time I see the news about **famine** in Africa on television, my heart goes broken.	每次看到電視上播出非洲飢荒的新聞，心裡就好難過喔。
Louis	Yeah, it's really tragic looking at those hungry and **bony refugees** who can only drink dirty water like water in ditches.	對呀，看那些難民們一個個餓的骨瘦如柴，只能喝像水溝水一樣的髒水，真的很悲慘。
Eliza	Don't you want to help them after you see that?	你看了都不會想幫助他們嗎？
Louis	Of course I do, but the land of Africa is not suitable for planting crops and being self sufficient. That's something we can't help.	會呀，可是那是非洲整個國土不適合栽種作物、自給自足的緣故，這我們也幫不上忙。
Eliza	Anyway, I'm just waiting for graduation. I think I should go to Africa to participate in the Red Cross as a **volunteer** after graduation.	反正我現在只是在等畢業而已，乾脆畢業後就參加紅十字會，到非洲當義工好了！

Louis　You...Are you serious? But we just meet your parents and expressed the willingness to be in a long-term relationship. If you really want to go to Africa, what about me? I can't just leave my job that I just found!

妳……妳是認真的嗎？可是我們才剛見過妳父母，表達要長久交往的意願，妳要是真的跑到非洲去，那我怎麼辦？我可不能放著已經找到的工作不管呀！

Eliza　But I really can't just sit and watch it happen without doing anything. My conscience will be so sorry for that.

可是我真的無法坐視不管，這樣我的良心會過意不去的。

Louis　You are such a **tender-hearted** person. I really don't recommend you to go to Africa as a volunteer. How about we **donate** to the Red Cross if we can't be there as a volunteer?

妳這個人就是心軟。我真的不建議妳貿然跑去非洲當義工，不然這樣吧，不能出力，我們就出錢，捐款到紅十字會怎麼樣？

Eliza　That sounds nice, but...I am not making any money yet. It won't help if I only donate some pocket money...

好是好，可是……我還沒開始上班賺錢。只捐一些零錢也無濟於事……。

Louis　No wonder you want to go there as a volunteer. You think you don't have enough money to donate? Well, judging by your great **sentiment**, let me help you by donating my first month's salary. As for the rest, let's wait till you start making money, okay?

難怪妳想用出力的方式，原來是沒有錢可以捐啊？好吧，看在妳偉大情操的份上，我先幫妳捐出我第一個月的薪水，其他的等妳開始賺錢了再捐，好嗎？

必會單字一手抓

❶ sentiment n. 情操、感情

That piece of news provoked the patriotic sentiment of the people.

那則新聞激起了人民的愛國情操。

❷ humanitarianism n. 人道主義、博愛

The Red Cross has helped many refugees in different countries based on the spirit of humanitarianism.

紅十字會組織本著人道主義的精神幫助了許多國家的難民。

❸ disadvantaged adj. 弱勢的、下層社會的

The distribution of the public welfare lottery has helped many disadvantaged people in the society.

公益彩券的發行幫助了不少社會中的弱勢族群。

❹ compassion n. 同情心

That police officer feels much compassion for the poor man who couldn't help but steal some bread owing to suffering from hunger and cold.

那位警察十分同情因飢寒交迫而忍不住偷麵包的窮人。

❺ famine n. 饑荒

The weather and geographic conditions cause the long-term famine in many African countries.

氣候和地理條件造成非洲國家長年的饑荒。

❻ bony adj. 骨瘦如柴的、骨的

There are many bony stray dogs wondering on the street.

有許多骨瘦如柴的野狗在街頭流浪。

❼ refugee n. 難民、流亡者

The World War II made a lot of people in many countries become refugees losing their homes.

二次世界大戰讓許多國家的人民成了難民，流離失所。

❽ volunteer n. 義工、自願者

There are many volunteers coming to the beach for cleaning every weekend.

每到周末假日，海邊就會有許多自願者前來淨灘。

❾ donate v. 捐贈、捐獻

People in my country have donated money and expressed compassion during the Japan 311 earthquake incident.

日本發生 311 地震時，國人紛紛捐錢表達慰問。

❿ tender-hearted adj. 慈悲的、有同情心的

She is such a tender-hearted girl who donates her pocket money to the charity.

她是一位有同情心的善良女孩，懂得把零用錢捐出來。

30 秒會話教室

Are you serious? Do you mean it? 這兩句都有「你是認真的嗎？你說的是真的嗎？」之意。回答可用：I am in earnest. 我是認真的。

情境 59 重返校園

會話訓練班

Jocelyn 從德文系畢業之後，如願當上了德文口譯的工作，開始有機會跟著公司到德國出差，這也讓她對德國的人文歷史更加有興趣，終於動了想重回學校學習的念頭……

After Jocelyn's graduation from school, she becomes an **interpreter** as she has always wanted and starts having the chance to take business trips to Germany with the company. It makes her more interested in German culture and history, and also starts the idea of going back to school...

Jocelyn	Here you are. This is the **souvenir** I buy for you from Germany.	這個送你，是我從德國買回來的紀念品喔！
Austine	Wow, you are so sweet! Let me see...it's a Swiss army knife! How come you didn't get the Berlin **mascot** bear, United Buddy Bears?	喔，這麼好！我看看……是一把瑞士刀！妳怎麼不買一隻德國的吉祥物、柏林熊公仔啊？
Jocelyn	The Swiss army knives made in Germany are the best of qualities. You should bring one with you in case you need it, and you will thank me one day. I buy one for myself too. As for the Berlin mascot bear, you can see painted United Buddy Bears in different colors everywhere. They are so cute!	德國製的瑞士刀品質最好了，可以隨身帶著以防不時之需，說不定你哪天會感謝我的！我自己也買了一把。至於你說的柏林熊，我這次去德國，大街小巷都可以看到彩繪柏林熊耶，好可愛！

Austine	Look at you being all excited. I guess you really find the right job as a German interpreter.	看妳說的興高采烈的，看來妳做德文口譯的工作真的是選對了！
Jocelyn	Of course! I have so much passion for what I do with the language of German. Speaking of that, I really want to go back to school and study German culture and history.	當然囉！我對德文可是有滿腔的熱忱呢！說到這裡，我真的好想重回學校學習德國的人文歷史。
Austine	Didn't you graduate from the department of German? You should have already gotten a lot of **knowledge** in this field.	妳不就是德文系畢業的嗎？當初應該學了不少相關知識才是啊？
Jocelyn	Our department only focuses on the study of the language. Although I've taken geography and history classes, you know there's only little you can know in one semester. I've only scratched the surface.	我們學校的德文系主要專注在學習德文上面，地理、歷史雖然有選修過，但你也知道，一學期的時間哪能學到多少？所以我只有學到一些皮毛。
Austine	Are you sure you want to give up the job you've always wanted and go back to school for another four years? I feel overwhelmed already by knowing the idea.	不過妳要放棄好不容易找到的好工作，重新當四年的學生嗎？光聽我就受不了了。

Jocelyn Of course not! I've already made the **inquiry**. I can attend class as an **auditor** during the time I don't have to do my **interpreting** work. I think I can get the permission from the manager if I tell them I'm going to take the **refresher course**.

當然不是囉！我已經打聽好了，有另一間大學可以旁聽，我只要每周利用不用口譯的時間去上課，跟經理說我是要去參加在職進修課程就好，應該可以得到同意的。

Austine That sounds acceptable to me too. It feels like being young again if I could go back to school though. I've really missed the **school days** living in a **trouble-free** life since I started working.

這樣聽起來我也可以接受。不過能重返校園當學生感覺真青春呢，自從開始工作以後就好懷念學生時代無憂無慮的生活喔。

必會單字一手抓

❶ interpret v. 口譯、翻譯

She is interpreting some concerns the boss has to the representatives overseas.

她將老闆的疑慮翻譯給國外的廠商代表聽。

❷ interpreter n. 口譯員、通譯員

Being a simultaneous interpreter is considered the most challenging on the top of the profession.

同步口譯員是口譯當中最難最厲害的一種。

❸ souvenir n. 紀念品

The tour guide is going to take us to buy some souvenirs at a shopping mall according to the schedule for this morning in London.

這個上午在倫敦的行程，導遊安排我們去暢貨中心買紀念品。

❹ mascot **n.** 吉祥物

The mascot of this baseball team is a platypus.

這支棒球隊的吉祥物是一隻鴨嘴獸。

❺ knowledge **n.** 知識、學問

It is the idea that her father has instilled in her: knowledge is power.

「知識就是力量」，這是她的父親不停灌輸給她的觀念。

❻ auditor **n.** 旁聽生，聽者

She took many courses of the department of Economics as an auditor.

她以旁聽生的身份上了很多經濟系的課。

❼ refresher courses **n.** 在職進修課程

His new company offers many refresher courses.

他的新公司提供了許多在職進修的課程。

❽ school days **n.** 學生時代（用複數）、學校上課日

That child who has been bullied feels very resistant to going to school whenever the school days are.

每到學校要上學的日子，那個曾被同學霸凌的小孩就會感到非常抗拒。

❾ trouble-free **adj.** 無憂無慮的、輕鬆自如的

Many people yearn for a trouble-free life just like a bird does.

很多人都嚮往像小鳥一樣過著無憂無慮的生活。

❿ inquiry **v.** 打聽、詢問

Please call the operator if there are any inquires.

如果有任何問題，請打電話向總機詢問。

30 秒會話教室

當你為某人做出了某項有遠見的付出，但當時卻不受到認同，就可以說：You will thank me one day. 有一天你會感謝我的。

情境 60 時裝設計師

會話訓練班

經營服飾店起家的 Victoria 已經拓展了兩家分店，除了原有的成衣，她也開始嘗試自己繪製草圖，再請工廠完成成品在自家店內販賣，頗受顧客歡迎……

Victoria who started her business by running a clothing store has already opened two **branch** stores. In addition to selling the **ready-made** clothes, she also starts trying to draw her own sketches. Then produce by OEM factory (Original Equipment Manufacturer) and sell them in her store. The clothes are quite popular with the customers...

Harvey Honey, why aren't you sleeping at this late hour? Are you drawing sketches again?

親愛的，這麼晚了妳還不睡嗎？妳又在畫圖了呀？

Victoria This is the **garment sketch**. I need to finish it so I can let the patternmaker make the pattern a few days later. I have to get it done ASAP(as soon as possible).

這是服裝草圖啦，過幾天就要交給打版師打版了，我得趕快完成才行。

Harvey I felt that the business was doing better than usual the other day I passed your store. Is it because these new clothes you design?

我那天經過妳店裡，總覺得比平時看到的生意還要好，是因為妳設計的這些新衣服的緣故嗎？

Victoria Perhaps I think. There have been more customers come ask the clothes since I started designing my own clothes and displayed them in the display windows.

或許是吧，自從我自己設計的衣服放進櫥窗展示之後，多了好多客人進來詢問喔。

Harvey	There are so many women's clothing brands in the market, what features do you think your clothes attract the customers?	市面上的女裝這麼多，妳覺得妳設計的衣服是甚麼地方吸引了顧客呢？
Victoria	According to the **feedback** received from customers so far, they think the soft-tone colors I **design** draw their attention at first they see them. Next it's the **elegant** design that is suitable for whether some formal occasions or casual wearing.	目前從客人口中收到的回饋都是，覺得我設計的衣服用色很柔和，讓人第一眼就會被吸引，再來就是典雅大方的款式，不論正式場合或是平常上街穿都很適合。
Harvey	Hmm, some famous designer brand clothes are innovative and bold, but they are not suitable for ordinary people to wear when going out.	嗯，有些名牌服飾的設計雖然新穎又大膽，但真的不太適合普通人出門的時候穿。
Victoria	Yeah, so at first I thought maybe I could design some **wearable** but **classic** styles. I didn't expect the reactions were surprisingly good. It seems that I really can continue to work in the field of fashion design.	是呀，所以我當初才想自己設計一些實穿又不退流行的經典款式，沒想到反應出奇地好。看來我真的可以繼續走服裝設計的這條路。
Harvey	Yes, and that is a designer who never goes to the school of fashion design.	對呀，而且是個完全沒讀過設計學院的服裝設計師。
Victoria	Stop embarrassing me! I will keep up learning in this regard. Although I don't expect to be able to enter the Fashion Week in Paris, I should have no problem with launching my own **brand**.	你別糗我了啦！這方面我會好好學習的，雖然不奢望未來能進軍巴黎時裝周闖出名號，但推出自有品牌還是可行的。

必會單字一手抓

❶ branch n. 分店

That sushi house has braches all over Taiwan.

那家壽司店在全台灣都有分店。

❷ ready-made adj. 預先製成的、現成的

He bought a ready-made suit for the interview.

他買了一套現成的西裝準備穿去面試。

❸ garment n. 服裝、衣著

You can buy all kinds of garments at the department store.

到百貨公司裡可以買到各式各樣的服裝。

❹ sketch n. 草圖、素描

He secretly drew a sketch of that affectionate old couple in the park.

他為公園裡那對鶼鰈情深的老夫妻偷偷畫了一張素描。

❺ design n. 設計、構思

The design of that clothing has won the designer all positive comments from the media.

那件服裝的設計為設計師贏得了媒體的一致好評。

❻ feedback n. 反饋的信息

Have you received any positive feedback for your proposes in the meeting?

你在會議上的提議有得到好的反饋嗎？

❼ elegant adj. 優美的、雅致的
That beautiful woman with elegant gestures makes all the men helplessly adore her.
那位美女的舉手投足非常優美，讓所有男性都傾倒在她的石榴裙下。

❽ classic adj. 經典的
That old classic car attracts all the attention of the car lovers.
那款經典的老爺車吸引了愛車族的目光。

❾ brand n. 品牌、商標
My grandfather likes to smoke this tobacco brand the most.
我爺爺最喜歡抽這個品牌的煙草。

❿ wearable adj. 耐穿的、可以穿戴的
Jeans are the clothing pieces that are very wearable and easy to match.
牛仔褲是非常耐穿又好搭配的單品。

30 秒會話教室

When he saw the car, he fell in love with it at first sight. 當他看到那輛車子，便一見鍾情。

名人怎麼說？

Love is like war: easy to begin but very hard to stop. —H. L. Mencken
愛情就像戰爭：開始很容易但結束很難。—評論家

情境 61 徜徉花海的蝴蝶小姐

會話訓練班

花店店員對從小就喜歡蒔花惹草的 Phoebe 來說是個不可多得的好工作，最近花店老闆娘因長年身體不適，只能提早退休並將店面頂讓，Phoebe 便有意接手經營……

Being a clerk in a flower shop is a dream job for Phoebe who has green fingers since she was little. Because the owner of the flower shop has been ill for many years, she has to **retire** early and make a **disposal** of the store. Phoebe has intended to take over the business...

Phoebe	Honey, Have I told you my boss recently often goes to see a doctor in the middle of the work and let me take care of the store?	親愛的，我不是跟你說過最近老闆娘時常工作到一半跑去看醫生，讓我一個人顧店嗎？
Brian	Yeah, is your boss okay? What did the doctor say?	對呀，老闆娘沒事吧？醫生怎麼說？
Phoebe	According to the doctor's initial diagnosis, it's the unbalanced diet that causes some cardiovascular diseases. Then he has to continuously keep track of it and give further treatment. Plus my boss also wants to retire so she can take some good rest and recuperation as she feels getting older and more tired.	醫生初步診斷是因飲食不均衡而引起的一些心血管方面的疾病，接下來還要持續追蹤、治療，而老闆娘也覺得年紀大、累了，想要退休好好養病。

Brian	Retired!? Doesn't that also mean you will become **unemployed**?	退休！？那妳不就要失業了嗎？
Phoebe	There is a way to avoid unemployment , even to make it better than ever--that is to take over the boss' store!	有一個方法可以避免失業，甚至比目前過的還要好，就是把老闆娘的店面頂下來！
Brian	You want to be a **florist** in your own! I know you always like pruning flowers and putting flowers into a beautiful **bouquet**, but running a shop is different from taking care of flowers!	妳要自己當花商啊！我知道妳一直都很喜歡修剪花草、把一朵朵鮮花包裝成漂亮的花束，但經營一家店跟照顧花草可是兩回事呀！
Phoebe	Don't you worry about that. My boss usually assigns me to place orders from the **wholesalers**, sometimes to make delivery. I can even do accounting. As long as I take over the shop, I'll be able to get started right away.	這你別擔心，平常老闆娘就會交代我一些跟批發商訂購的工作，有時還要兼出外送貨，連記帳這些我也會，只要把店頂下來我馬上就能上手。
Brian	Hmm, so it sounds pretty feasible. However, where do you expect to get the money for taking over the business?	嗯，這樣聽起來可行性不小。不過頂下店面的錢，妳預計從哪裡來呢？
Phoebe	My boss says that if it's me, she is willing to give me a **discount**. I still need some extra even with all my **personal savings**, so I'd like to **borrow** some from you.	老闆娘說如果是我的話，願意給我打折，用我平常存下來的私房錢，還差一點，我想先跟你借。
Brian	Well, I think I'll help my little butterfly fulfill her dream of wandering in the flowers.	好吧，我就幫我的小蝴蝶，完成徜徉在花海中的夢想！

必會單字一手抓

❶ florist **n.** 花商、種花者

My mother orders several different types of flowers from the florist for decorating the living room as Chinese New Year is coming.

過年快到了，媽媽向花商訂購了幾種不同的花來布置客廳。

❷ retire **v.** 退休

My high school teacher retires at the age of 65 to enjoy the rest of his life.

我的高中老師一到 65 歲就退休，去享受人生了。

❸ unemployed **adj.** 失業的、無工作的

The government arranges some refresher courses for those unemployed workers so they can successfully find a new job.

政府為那些失業的勞工安排了進修課程，以便他們順利找到新的工作。

❹ bouquet **n.** 花束、一束花

The valedictorian takes the bouquet from the principal to formally finish their four years of college life.

畢業生代表從校長手上接過花束，正式結束他們四年來的大學生活。

❺ wholesaler **n.** 批發商

The shop owner decides to order potatoes from the places of the production instead of through the wholesalers.

那位店主決定不透過批發商，自己向產地訂購馬鈴薯。

❻ personal **adj.** 個人的、私人的

It's a matter of personal choice to like what kind of person as a partner.

喜歡甚麼樣的對象純粹是個人的選擇問題。

❼ savings **n.** 儲蓄、存款

She never has unnecessary spending so she has accumulated a lot of savings

她從來不做多餘的消費所以她有不少存款。

❽ borrow **v.** 借入

The lady next door often comes borrow sugar or some ingredients, but we all know there is no way she will return these things.

隔壁的太太經常跟我借糖或是一些食材，但我們都知道這些東西根本沒辦法還。

❾ discount **n.** 打折扣

Except the items on sales, everything in the store has a discount of 20% off.

除了特價商品外，本店全面打八折。

❿ disposal **n.** 出售、轉讓

That tycoon states the disposals of his assets in his will.

那位大富豪在遺囑中註明了財產的轉讓去向。

30 秒會話教室

「green fingers」（綠手指）指的是從事園藝的才能，例：My father has green fingers. 我的父親極有園藝天賦。

情境 62 暢銷作家

會話訓練班

原本的 Albert 是個尚未成名的普通作家，上次偶然從妻子 Marjorie 脫口而出的夢境得到創作靈感，所寫出的文章竟讓他大獲好評……

Albert has been an ordinary writer who isn't famous yet. Last time he accidentally got the inspiration from a dream of his wife, Marjorie. Unexpectedly, the article gets overwhelming positive feedback...

Albert	Honey, do you remember last time the column I wrote based on the inspiration I got from your dream?	親愛的，妳還記得我上次以妳的夢境為靈感所寫的那篇專欄嗎？
Marjorie	You mean the one about me falling in love with an alien? Of course I remember that. It gets a lot of responses after being **published** in the newspapers.	你是說跟外星人談戀愛那一篇嗎？我記得呀，報紙刊出後還得到不少迴響呢！
Albert	Yes, that's right. You know what? Today there is a publisher asking me if I could make the article into a **full-length** novel.	對，就是那次，結果妳知道嗎？今天竟然有出版社問我能不能將那篇文章寫成長篇的小說耶！
Marjorie	Oh, isn't that great? Did you say yes to them? Did you ask questions about the **copyright** and **commission**?	喔，那不是很棒嗎？你答應他們了嗎？有沒有問清楚版權和抽成的問題？

Albert	I first expressed a great **intention**, but also asked them to give me a few days to think about it.	我先表達的強烈的意願，但要他們給我幾天考慮看看。
Marjorie	Why do you still need to consider it? This is a golden opportunity you have wished for! Aren't you afraid the opportunity might just **sneak away**?	為什麼還要考慮呢？這可是求之不得的好機會耶！你不怕機會就這樣溜走嗎？
Albert	It's because...it is derived from your dream. I'm not sure if I could use this as a **skeleton**, and come up with a more **absorbing** story...	其實是因為……那是由妳的夢境所衍生出來的，我沒有把握能以這個為概略，想出更引人入勝的故事……。
Marjorie	How could you **deserve** being a writer with so little **imagination**?	你這樣也配稱為作家嗎？竟然這麼沒有想像力！
Albert	My...my specialty is literature, not having creativity! What do you think I should do?	我……我的專長是文學，不是搞創意嘛！妳說我該怎麼辦？
Marjorie	(Sigh) Let me describe the dream I still remember in detail to you. It should be helpful.	唉，我把那個夢境我還記得的部分鉅細靡遺地描述給你聽好了，應該會有幫助。

必會單字一手抓

❶ publish **v.** 出版、發行、刊登

It has created worldwide sensation after Harry Potter being published, which even made into a series of films.

《哈利波特》出版之後在全球造成轟動，甚至拍成系列電影。

❷ full-length **adj.** 未刪節的

I feel sleepy instantly as long as I read that full-length novel before going to bed.

我只要在睡前閱讀那本長篇小說，馬上就會產生睡意。

❸ copyright **n.** 版權、著作權

The author sold the copyright of the novel to the publisher.

作者將這本小說的版權賣給了出版社。

❹ commission **n.** 佣金

He can get a 10% commission whenever he sells a set of encyclopedias.

他只要推銷出一套百科全書就可以抽到 10%的佣金。

❺ sneak **v.** 溜、偷偷地走

Tom secretly sneaked out and played with friends while his mom didn't pay attention.

Tom 趁媽媽不注意，偷偷溜出去找朋友玩。

❻ skeleton **n.** 概略、大綱

I heard that the skeleton of this best-selling book came out while the author was in the toilet.

聽說那本暢銷小書的大綱是作者在上廁所時無意中想到的。

❼ absorbing adj. 引人入勝的

The captain with 20 years of fishing experience has many absorbing and fascinating adventure stories in the sea.

出海捕魚 20 年的船長有許多引人入勝的海上驚險故事。

❽ deserve v. 應受、該得

I'm sorry for that woman. She deserves a better life.

我為那女人感到遺憾。她應得更好的生活的。

❾ intention n. 意圖、目的

I had no intention to harm innocent children when set this trap.

我設這個陷阱並不是意圖要傷害不知情的孩童。

❿ imagination n. 想像力

Spoon-feeding education will stifle the child's imagination.

填鴨式的教育會扼殺孩子的想像力。

30 秒會話教室

要向人介紹自己的專長可以用以下的句型：My specialty is English. 我的專長是英文。或 I'm good at English. 我很擅長英文。

情境 63 正義的代言人

會話訓練班

Patrick 一邊準備律師資格考試一邊在律師事務所工作，如今考取的他也直接在原事務所擔任律師，準備在法庭中大展長才……

Before Patrick was preparing for the bar exam while working in the **law firm**. Now he is an **attorney** working in the original law firm as he's qualified. He's going to show what he's got in **court**...

Heather	Today it is your first time you defense a client in the courtroom after you become a **defense** lawyer. How did it go?	今天是你當上律師後第一次進法庭擔任客戶的辯護律師，一切還順利嗎？
Patrick	It's really an intensive and interesting day. I used to think it was easy when I saw lawyers have some heated debates in the courtroom before. In fact, I just totally went blank when I interrogated the **witness**, or stammered the law statues.	真是緊張又有趣的一天，以前看律師在法庭上激辯如流，總覺得很簡單，沒想到實際上輪到我詰問證人，反而腦袋一片空白，不然就結結巴巴地背不清楚法條。
Heather	What did you do? Didn't you feel so embarrassed?	那怎麼辦？豈不是很糗？
Patrick	I did at first. Fortunately I reorganized my thoughts. Also, it was more favorable for us with all the **evidence**, so I was more confident during the process.	那是剛開始的時候，還好後來我重整情緒，又加上種種證據對我方比較有利，所以對答起來也就更有信心了。

Heather	So your first defense should be considered successful?	所以你的第一次辯護應該算是成功囉？
Patrick	Yes, my client got an **acquittal** in court. In fact, he is indeed an innocent good man.	沒錯，我的客戶當庭無罪開釋了。而事實上，他也的確是無辜的好人。
Heather	I am not going to ask too much of the case, but what I want to know more is that will you ignore your conscience and defend for a client who has committed a crime, and asked you to be his attorney?	案件的內容我就不多問了，不過我比較想要知道的是，如果以後有真的犯了罪卻想委託你辯護的客戶，你也會昧著良心幫他開罪嗎？
Patrick	Even if the existing court system has many loopholes, and sometimes good people lose their confidence, but do not think one can be fine once out of the courtroom. The bad guys will still get punishment.	即使現存的法庭制度還有很多漏洞，甚至有時會叫善良的人失去信心，不過不要以為出了法庭就沒事，壞人還是會有報應的。
Heather	You said punishment, is the same as lynching law on one's own?	你說的報應，是指像動私刑一樣的私法制裁嗎？
Patrick	I'm talking about **conscience**'s condemnation. No one can escape that, which is what I believe in **justice**.	我說的是良心的譴責。沒有人能夠逃過這一關，這就是我所相信的正義。

必會單字一手抓

❶ law n. 法律

Drink-driving is a violation of law.

酒後開車是違反法律的行為。

❷ firm n. 商號、公司

Ten years ago my father left his former company and opened a new firm.

爸爸十年前離開前東家自己開了一間公司。

❸ attorney n. 律師

That mob boss hired a famous attorney to defend him.

那個黑幫老大請了知名的律師幫他辯護。

❹ court n. 法庭、法院

The court sentenced the murderer to life sentence.

法院判那個殺人犯無期徒刑。

❺ defense n. 被告及其辯護律師、辯護

The defense lawyer has strong and powerful argument which makes the jury unanimously agree.

那位律師的辯護強而有力，讓陪審團一致認同。

❻ witness n. 證人、目擊者

The witnesses testified that he did see the suspect flee the murder scene.

目擊者作證說他確實看到嫌犯逃出命案現場。

❼ evidence n. 證據、證人、證詞

The prosecutor presents some evidence which is strongly against the defendant.

檢察官舉出的證據對被告相當不利。

❽ acquittal n. 宣告無罪
The jury brought in an acquittal, so the family was so relieved and pleased in tears.
陪審團宣告無罪，所以家屬高興地落下淚來。

❾ conscience n. 良心、善惡觀念
Let conscience be your guide.
讓良心指引你吧。

❿ justice n. 正義、公平
In order to let the justice be done, he goes on the street to protest at all costs.
他為了伸張正義，不惜走上街頭抗議。

30 秒會話教室

I got nothing to hide. My conscience is clear. 我沒有甚麼好隱瞞的，我問心無愧。

名人怎麼說？

Come live in my heart, and pay no rent. —Samuel Lover
進來我的心房吧，不用付房租的。—作家

情境 64 踏出人類的一大步

會話訓練班

畢業於航空工程系的 Miles 如願進入美國太空總署進行太空船維修的工作，不過他的夢想更為遠大，他希望能成為一位登上太空的太空人……

Graduated from the Department of Aerospace Engineering, Miles get into NASA (National Aeronautics and Space Administration) for a **spaceship** maintenance job as he has always wanted, but his dream is more ambitious, and he hopes to become an **astronaut** who can travels to spaces...

Miles	Doris, you'd never know how excited I am after I started to work in NASA these days.	Doris，妳絕對猜不到這幾天我開始到 NASA 工作之後有多興奮！
Doris	Oh, do you get to wear the spacesuit yet? Like in the movie "Apollo 13".	喔，你有穿上那些太空衣了嗎？就像電影「阿波羅 13」裡的那樣。
Miles	I'm just a maintenance **mechanic**, not a **regular** astronaut. What makes me really excited about is to go inside the cabin and check up everything. I get nervous and start to **sweat** every time I think of a possible malfunction the space shuttle could have, even of a tiny **screw**. However, I realize that what I'm in **charge** of is a very crucial link.	我又不是正規的太空人，只是個維修技師而已，讓我興奮的是進入太空艙裡面檢查的時候，一想到每一顆小螺絲的鬆緊度都關係著太空梭上太空以後能否正常運作，就讓我緊張地全身冒汗，但也更覺得自己負責的是很重要的環節。

Doris Huh, I don't understand what fun it is of locking screws, but when it comes to space travel, everyone should have thought about it but cannot achieve the dream.

呵呵，我是不懂鎖螺絲有什麼好玩的，不過說到上太空，應該是所有人都曾經想過卻無法實現的夢想吧。

Miles Yeah, so now I have been so close to that dream. I have to work harder on that!

是呀，所以我現在已經離那個夢想這麼近了，我可更要加油才行！

Doris I'm not surprised you want to be an astronaut, but only the best of the best can really be selected as the astronauts.

你想當太空人我一點都不意外，但是真正能獲選為太空人的可都是少數菁英中的菁英耶！

Miles I know that, since I get to work as the entry-level in NASA, I can come into more contact with the actual **operation**. As for the professional knowledge, I will use my spare time to pursue further studies, and I will do additional physical training at regular hours.

這我知道，既然我現在已經進入 NASA 的基層工作，就可以接觸到實際的操作面，至於各種專業知識我會利用工作之餘繼續進修，平常也會再增加體能的訓練。

Doris It sounds like a long way to go. Although I don't want you to spend years floating in **zero-gravity** space instead being with me, let's wait for you to successfully become the candidate! The standard is extremely high for becoming an astronaut.

聽起來就是一條辛苦的路，雖然我不希望你真的長年在無重力的太空裡漂浮而不在我身邊，但還是等你成功獲選再說吧！要成為太空人，門檻可是很高的。

Miles	Why do you keep putting a damper on my enthusiasm and have such low expectation on me?	妳怎麼一直潑我冷水，完全不看好我嘛！
Doris	It's not the case! One hand I hope that your dreams can be realized; on the other hand I don't want you to leave me. I feel very ambivalent.	才不是這樣，我一方面希望你的夢想能實現；一方面又不希望你離開我，心情很矛盾。

必會單字一手抓

❶ spaceship n. 太空船

The little boy's room is filled with spaceship models.

小男孩的房間裡堆滿了太空船模型。

❷ astronaut n. 太空人、宇航員

Do you know what's on an astronaut's training program?

你知道太空人的訓練有哪些項目嗎？

❸ regular adj. 正規的

In order to be the regular player in the team, he practices two hours more than others every day.

他為了爭取成為球隊中的正規出賽者，每天比別人多練習 2 小時。

❹ mechanic n. 維修工、技工

The mechanic gives a major maintenance to my scooter.

那位修車技工幫我的機車進行大保養。

❺ screw **n.** 螺絲釘、固定、擰緊

Daddy screwed the broken door again on the door frame.

爸爸用螺絲釘把壞掉的門重新固定在門框上。

❻ sweat **n.** 汗

Do you sweat when you're nervous?

當你緊張時會出汗嗎。

❼ charge **v.** 委以責任、負責

The teacher asks the class leader to be solely responsible for the weekly class meeting.

老師要班長全權負責召開每周一次的班會。

❽ operation **n.** 操作、運轉

Not everyone can operate this machine. One has to take at least 200 hours of training.

不是每個人都可以操作這台機器的，至少要先經過 200 小時的培訓。

❾ gravity **n.** 地心引力

Newton discovered gravity under the apple tree.

牛頓在蘋果樹下發現了地心引力。

30 秒會話教室

sweat 也有辛苦工作的意思，如：He was sweating over her English books all day. 他整天都埋首苦讀英文課本。

情境 65 不求回報的程式設計師

會話訓練班

在科技公司擔任程式設計師的 Louis 非常樂在自己的工作中，除了完成上司交代的任務之外，他也常利用空閒時間寫出令人意想不到的創意程式……

Working as a programming designer in a technology company, Louis enjoys his work very much. In addition to completing the tasks the supervisors assign, he often uses his free time to write unexpectedly creative **programs**...

Louis	Eliza, **input** the name of your favorite idol in this **blank**.	Eliza，妳在這個空白處輸入妳喜歡的偶像的名字。
Eliza	Did you write a fun program again? Done. What does this program do?	你又寫了好玩的程式啊？輸入好了，這是要做什麼的？
Louis	I write a program that can detect how far you are away from your idol. The result just came out. You see, you and your idol are 30 kilometers from each other, you can find him easily by driving for a short while.	我寫了一個可以測試妳和偶像現在距離多遠的程式，結果出來了，妳看，妳和妳的偶像距離 30 公里，只要開車一下子就可以找到他了耶！
Eliza	Let me see, how did you do that? This result isn't just **bluffing**, right?	我看看，你是怎麼辦到的呀？這結果該不會是隨便唬人的吧？

Louis	Let me explain it to you. Listen, this program uses the Internet to **search** for the idol's public **schedules**, such as attending an event, a **press conference**, a concert, etc. to locate the idol's current **location**. So your idol should have an activity 30 km away.	我解釋給妳聽，這個程式會利用網路搜尋該偶像的公開行程，比如出席活動、記者會、開演唱會等等公開訊息，來定位該偶像目前人在什麼地方。所以妳的偶像應該在 30 公里以外的地方有活動。
Eliza	Oh God, you're **incredible**! I'm going to my idol's concert tomorrow. Today, he is flying here from Japan. There are a lot of fans going to the airport to welcome him.	你真的好神喔！我明天就是要去參加偶像的演唱會，他今天會從日本搭機過來，有好多粉絲都去機場接機了。
Louis	Oh yes, so this program is considered a successful testing.	呵呵，所以這個程式就算是測試成功了。
Eliza	You write these programs that cannot make money, and put them on the Net so everyone can download for free. I really don't understand you.	你寫這些不能賺錢的程式，還放到網路上讓大家免費下載，真的是搞不懂你耶。
Louis	Like someone is trying to help the refugees in Africa, I am doing this for the benefit of people. By the way, how come you don't go welcome your idol?	就像有人想幫助非洲難民一樣，我這也算是在造福人群啊。對了，那妳怎麼不一起去接機呢？
Eliza	I'll be **satisfied** tomorrow I can see him on the stage. I'd rather spend time with my boyfriend for the rest of my time.	明天可以看到舞台上的他我就心滿意足了，其他時間還是陪我的男朋友比較實在。

必會單字一手抓

❶ program n. 程式、設計程式

Do you know how to put this program back to the original settings?

你知道該如何將這個程式恢復為初始設定嗎？

❷ blank n. 空白處

Please fill in the blanks with the job that you want to apply for, thank you.

請在空白處填上您要申請的職位，謝謝。

❸ input v. 輸入

The boss asked her to input the customer's information into the computer and archive it.

老闆要她將客戶的資料都輸入進電腦並歸檔。

❹ bluff v. 虛張聲勢嚇唬人、愚弄

We all know she's just bluffing; she has no support behind her like what she said.

大家都知道她只是在虛張聲勢，背後根本沒有她所說的靠山可以撐腰。

❺ search v. 搜尋

The town mobilized a large number of manpower in the forest to search for the missing boy.

鎮上動員大批人力在森林中搜索那個失蹤的小男孩。

❻ schedule n. 日程表

The coach arranged tight practicing schedule for the players before the competition. .

教練為選手們安排了一個緊湊的賽前練習行程。

❼ press **n.** 新聞界、記者們
Those press reporters were constantly chasing the star who kept having rumors coming out.
那些記者們不停追著傳出緋聞的明星跑。

❽ location **n.** 位置、所在地
They arrived in the riverbank where the fireworks set off half day early, and picked a good location with a good view.
他們提早半天到達施放煙火的河畔，選了個視野好的好位置。

❾ incredible **adj.** 難以置信的、驚人的
Those big appetite eaters on the program can eat incredible quantity of food.
節目上那些大胃王的食量大的驚人。

❿ satisfy **v.** 使滿意、使高興
Only to get an award has been unable to make him satisfied
只拿到一座獎項已經不能使他滿意了。

30 秒會話教室

I was only giving you a bluff. 我只是在嚇唬你而已。I think he is just bluffing. 我覺得他只是在唬人而已。

情境 66 守護交通的人民保母

會話訓練班

交通警察 Fred 平時主要的工作就是指揮交通或是取締違規，雖然這樣的工作也是在為民服務，但他仍希望能加入打擊犯罪的行列……

Working as a **traffic** policeman, Fred's regular work is to direct traffic or crack down on violations. Although he is providing public service by doing such work, he still hopes to join the frontline of fighting **crime**...

Fred Irene, It's me, Fred. Long time no see. I didn't expect to meet you again in the same street.

Irene，是我，Fred。好久不見了，沒想到又在同一條路上遇見你。

Irene I was shocked that the police waved to me in the middle of driving. I thought I was speeding again!

開車開到一半有警察跟我招手，我嚇了一大跳，以為自己又超速違規了呢！

Fred No, you didn't. I stopped you 'coz I saw your familiar license plate. It's quite a coincidence that this is my last day of duty on the road today! I didn't think that I could meet you.

沒有啦，我是看到妳熟悉的車牌才叫住妳的。說來也真巧，今天可是我在道路上執勤的最後一天喔！沒想到竟然能遇見妳。

Irene Oh, is it like you are getting **promoted**? Or you don't want to be a policeman?

喔，難不成你要升官了？還是你不想當警察了？

Fred	It's not really like promotion. I am finally transferred to be the **criminal** police.	說升官也不是，我終於被調職為刑警了。
Irene	Criminal police? Why? I thought being the traffic police is more at ease.	刑警？為什麼呢？當交通警察感覺上不是比較輕鬆嗎？
Fred	That's because I have been very keen to participate in the work of the investigation of criminal cases, to use the remaining **clues** and evidences of the crime scene to find out the real reason behind and the **motives**, and to catch the criminal and put him behind **bars** in person.	因為我一直很希望能參與偵查刑事案件的工作，利用犯罪現場遺留下來的線索和證據做推理，找出事件背後真正的原因和動機，並親手抓到犯人將他關進監獄。
Irene	Sounds like someone have watched too much CSI!	聽起來有人 CSI 看太多囉！
Fred	Perhaps! I know the criminal police in the real world don't look as glamorous as they are in the show, cases are not that complicated and **confusing**, but it's the same sense of mission I want to **arrest** criminals. I hope to **decrease** the numbers of the villains in the world.	或許是吧！我知道真實世界的刑事警察絕對不像影集裡面那樣光鮮亮麗，案件也不至於那麼撲朔迷離，但想逮捕犯人的使命感是一樣的，我希望能幫忙減少世界上的壞人。
Irene	Congratulations, really. Speaking of which, you am not probably going to give me a ticket again next time I meet you here, are you?	真是恭喜你，話說回來，以後開在這條路上就不會遇到你來開我罰單囉？

必會單字一手抓

❶ traffic n. 交通、交通量

Taipei has the highest traffic flow in Taiwan.
台北市的交通流量是全台之冠。

❷ crime n. 犯罪、罪行

To see someone in mortal danger without saving him is also considered crime.
見死不救的旁觀行為一樣屬於犯罪。

❸ promote v. 晉升

He has never been promoted during the time of working in that company for 15 years.
他在那間公司做了 15 年，卻從未受到晉升。

❹ criminal adj. 刑事上的、犯罪的

Singapore has its unique criminal law.
新加坡有他們獨特的刑法。

❺ clue n. 線索、跡象

For the case of the woman reporting a missing child, the police have no clues to solve the case.
對於婦人所舉報的兒童失蹤案件，警察沒有任何線索可以破案。

❻ motive n. 動機、目的

The sole motive for he to do this is to draw me to vote for him.
他做這件事的唯一目的就是想拉攏我投他一票。

❼ bar n. 條狀物

My sister ate a whole chocolate bar before dinner; no wonder she can't eat much of the dinner.

妹妹在飯前吃了一整條巧克力，難怪晚餐吃不下。

❽ confusing adj. 令人困惑的

I'm sorry my gestures were confusing you. Please forgive me for that.

很抱歉我的舉動讓你困惑了，請你別放在心上。

❾ arrest v. 逮捕、居留

The illegal immigrants were arrested and taken into custody by the Customs right on the spot.

那些非法移民遭到海關當場居留。

❿ decrease v. 減少

Doing regular recycling helps decrease the waste of resources.

勤做資源回收有助於減少資源的浪費。

30 秒會話教室

behind bars 在鐵條後面，也就是被關進牢裡的意思。例：He will put behind bars for seven years. 他會被關進牢裡 7 年。

名人怎麼說？

I can live without money, but I cannot live without love. fiJudy Garland

我可以沒有錢，但是我不可以沒有愛。—美國女演員

情境 67 鐵面無私的檢察官

會話訓練班

司法考試放榜當日，Chloe 發現自己的名字名列榜上，高興地立刻打電話向室友 Doris 報告這個好消息……

On the day the judicial examination's result releases, Chloe finds her name on the list. She is so pleased and immediately calls her roommate, Doris, to tell her the good news

Chloe	Doris, are you still taking a nap? I'm sorry to wake you up. Listen, I passed the judicial examination!	Doris，妳還在午睡呀？抱歉吵醒妳，是這樣的，我通過司法特考了！
Doris	What, really? That's wonderful! I see you **stay up late** every night, and work part time during the day. Your effort finally gets paid off!	甚麼，真的嗎？太好了，看妳每天熬夜到那麼晚，白天還要打工，妳的付出終於有回報了！
Chloe	Yes. I can prepare for reporting in the **Ministry** of Justice! Finally I no longer need to memorize those law statutes, and I can actually participate in the investigation processes.	是啊，我可以準備到法務部報到了！終於不用再背那些法條，可以實際參與偵查了。
Doris	I remember you told me about the work content of being a **prosecutor**, but at this moment, I can't recall any of it.	我記得妳好像跟我說過檢察官的工作內容，但我一時回想不起來。

Chloe	The work content of being a prosecutor is to **investigate**, to the **public prosecution**, to assist the **voluntary prosecution**, and to execute the criminal judgments. Sometimes I also need to work on duty, overtime or travel	檢察官的工作內容就是實施偵查、提起公訴、協助自訴及指揮刑事裁判之執行。有時還需要配合業務輪值、加班或出差。
Doris	That sounds pretty boring! No wonder I forgot right after I heard it. Why are you interested in this career?	聽起來很無聊耶！難怪我聽過就忘了。妳為什麼會對這個職業有興趣呀？
Chloe	In fact, my father was prosecuted for **negligently** causing serious injury when I was little. The prosecutor didn't want to adopt the evidence and insisted on that my father was not out of **self-defense**. Although the sentence was very short, that has **casted** a **shadow on** my family ever since.	其實我父親小時候曾因為過失傷人而被起訴，當時的檢察官不願採納證據，堅持我父親不是出於正當防衛。雖然事後的刑責很輕，但也讓我們家從此蒙上了一層陰影。
Doris	I didn't know about this part of your past.	原來妳還有這一段過去呀。
Chloe	So I've wanted to be a prosecutor for justice since I was little, not only for my father, and also for the **innocent** people who are wrongly accused.	所以小小年紀的我就立志要當一個維護正義的檢察官，不僅是為了我父親，也為了還許多被冤枉的被告一個清白。
Doris	This is a tough way to go; you have to insist on it!	這條路不好走，不過妳一定要堅持下去喔！

必會單字一手抓

❶ ministry **n.** 政府的部門（常大寫）

She works as the entry-level staff in the Ministry of Executive Yuan department.

她在行政院交通部擔任基層員工。

❷ prosecutor **n.** 檢察官、公訴人

There are many prosecutors start their own business as being a lawyer after the retirement.

有許多檢察官退休以後自己開業當律師。

❸ investigate **v.** 調查、研究

The firefighters are investigating the cause of the fire.

消防員正在調查造成那起大火的原因。

❹ prosecution **n.** 起訴、告發

The government called for the prosecution of those responsible for the deaths.

政府要求起訴那些該為死者負責的人

❺ voluntary **adj.** 自願的、自發的

The witness voluntarily provides the evidence to the prosecutor.

那位證人自發性地向檢調單位提供證據。

❸ negligently **adv.** 疏忽地、粗心大意地

She negligently locked the child in the car and went shopping that almost suffocated the child to death.

她粗心大意地把孩子反鎖在車內就下車購物，差點沒把孩子悶死。

❼ self-defense **n.** 正當防衛、自衛

The old man shot and wounded a robber who broke into with a knife out of self-defense.

老爺爺出於正當防衛，開槍打傷了那位持刀闖入的強盜。

❽ shadow **n.** 陰影

According to experts, there will be a layer of shadow marked in the hearts of the children whose parents get divorced.

據專家說，父母離異的孩子心中都會有一層陰影。

❾ cast **n.** 投射

It's so magnificent seeing the bright moonlight casting on the lake.

明亮的月光灑在湖面上，甚是好看。

❿ innocent **adj.** 無罪的、清白的

Being kept in prison for 20 years, that inmate who constantly appealed during his sentence was finally acquitted as being innocent.

被關了 20 年，期間不斷上訴的那位受刑人終於獲判無罪。

30 秒會話教室

stay up 指的是通宵、不睡，Don't stay up too late. 不要熬夜熬得太晚。I stay up late doing homework. 我熬夜寫作業。

情境 68 打電動也能出頭天？

會話訓練班

在旁人眼中，Austine 只是個喜歡坐在電腦前玩線上遊戲的宅男，他們都不知道，其實 Austine 在遊戲界裡是神一般等級的存在，甚至已經有遊戲業者想要培養他成為電競選手……

For most of the people around, Austine is just a computer **nerd** who like sitting in front of the computer playing online games. Little do they know, in fact, Austine has the existence of God's level in the online game world, and even some online game companies want to **train** him to become the contestant of the online game competition…

Jocelyn	Austine, are you going to nest in front of the computer playing games this weekend, right? Then I'll go out with my BFFs (best friends forever).	Austine，你這個周末又要窩在電腦前玩遊戲了對不對？那我跟姊妹淘出去玩囉？
Austine	How come you suddenly don't **threaten** me with **smashing** my computer? I'm not getting used to it.	妳怎麼突然不威脅要把我的電腦砸掉了？讓我好不習慣喔！
Jocelyn	Because it won't work no matter how much I threat and induce! You're an **unpromising** nerd anyway.	還不是因為你怎麼威脅利誘都沒有用！我已經看開了，反正你就是個沒出息的宅男。

Austine	Who says that playing online games is unpromising? Recently, there are online game companies want to find me to join their team to participate in the World **Cyber** Games competition!	誰說玩線上遊戲就沒出息了？最近可是有遊戲廠商想要找我加入他們的隊伍去參加世界電玩大賽喔！
Jocelyn	Their team? Playing the game can be considered a sports competition? Is it just about moving fingers and mouse?	隊伍？玩遊戲也算一種運動競賽嗎？還不就是動動手指和滑鼠？
Austine	This is something you don't understand. It takes **strategies** and teamwork besides reacting fast enough to play the game. There have been professional online game completions around.	這妳就不明白了，玩遊戲除了反應夠快，還要懂得戰略和團隊合作，早就已經有專業級的比賽項目了。
Jocelyn	Oh, that's something I've never heard. How does it work? With connections global wide?	喔，這我倒沒聽說過。那是要怎麼比賽呢？全球連線嗎？
Austine	There'll be a specific location for the competition. By then, the players from all over the country will get together and play the actual game in front of the audience. The winning **prize** is incredibly high, and the winners get the trophies too.	比賽會特別找地方舉行，到時候全國的遊戲玩家都會齊聚一堂，在現場的觀眾面前實際比賽。贏了的獎金可是高的嚇人喔，而且還有獎盃呢！

Jocelyn Really? I never expected that a person could win money and **glory** by playing online games. Then you really have to work hard on it. If you don't win some money back, I will never forgive you!

真的嗎？真沒想到玩遊戲也能玩到有錢拿又能贏得榮耀耶，那你真的要好好加油喔，要是沒抱著獎金回來，我絕對不饒你！

Austine I'm having a discussion with the company about the time of the training. As long as I have some intensive practice, I can **definitely** win the prize.

我正在跟遊戲廠商洽談培訓的時間，只要我密集練習一下，肯定會得第一名的！

必會單字一手抓

❶ nerd **n.** 討厭的人、笨蛋

That nerd who only knows to study doesn't have a clue how to interact with people.

那個只會讀書的書呆子完全不懂得和人交際。

❷ train **v.** 訓練、培養

His ballerina mother has trained him to become a male ballet dancer.

他的芭蕾舞者母親培養他成為男性芭蕾舞者。

❸ cyber **n.** 意指與電腦相關之任何事物

Many safety problems are hidden in cyber dating.

網路交友潛藏著許多安全上的問題。

❹ threaten **v.** 威脅、恐嚇

That big muscle guy threatened him to turn out his wallet,

otherwise he would kill him.
那位壯漢威脅他把錢包交出來，否則就要殺了他。

5 unpromising adj. 沒出息的、沒希望的
Her unpromising second son came back again asking her for money.
她那沒出息的次子又回來向她伸手要錢了。

6 strategy n. 戰略、謀略
There are people everywhere study Art of War for learning strategies.
國內外都有人研究孫子兵法來學習謀略。

7 prize n. 獎賞、獎金
She uses the money receiving from the prize of the essay contest to pay for the tuition in full.
她將作文比賽得到的獎金全數拿去繳交學費了。

8 glory n. 榮耀、光榮、榮譽
The other players feel angry that only the captain has won all honor and glory.
只有隊長贏得了所有的榮譽和掌聲，其他隊員都感到憤憤不平。

9 definitely adv. 肯定地、當然
We must have faith in believing the rescue will definitely come.
救援一定會來的，我們要有信心。

10 smash v. 打碎、打破
As a little child, I had seen my father drunk and begin to smash things to vent out his anger.
小時候曾看過父親喝醉酒開始砸東西出氣的畫面。

30 秒會話教室

要表達從未聽過某些資訊，可以說：I've never heard that song before. 我從沒聽過那首歌。That's new to me. 這對我來說是個新鮮事。

情境 69 跟著我玩就對了

會話訓練班

就讀觀光科系的 Celia 即將畢業，她也像許多同學一樣，目標是成為導遊。此時她正和已獲選為職業棒球隊一員的 Joshua 談論願景……

Celia who is studying in the tourism department is going to graduate. Like many of her classmates, Celia's goal is to become a **tour guide**. At this moment she is having a discussion about their **visions** with Joshua who has been selected as a team member by a professional baseball team...

Celia	Time has passed so fast, it's time to graduate. You have been selected to a professional sport team, but I just start preparing the travel guide license examination.	好快唷，就要畢業了，你已經被選入職業球隊，而我才剛要開始準備導遊執照的考試。
Joshua	You have studied in the tourism department for four years, you'll certainly have no problem! But I wonder how people can find you when you're their tour guide since you're so **tiny**.	妳都讀了四年的觀光科了，一定沒問題的！不過看妳這麼嬌小，當導遊大家找的到妳嗎？
Celia	You always like embarrassing me! Tour guides always hold a small flag, and my voice is so loud; thanks for the training I've got being the manager of the baseball club. People don't need to worry about not hearing me.	你最愛糗我了！導遊會拿著小旗子的啦，而且我嗓門這麼大，都是擔任棒球社經理鍛鍊出來的，不怕大家聽不見。

Joshua	I was just joking, but why do you want to be a tour guide? Why don't you go work in a travel agency having an easier job?	我只是開開玩笑，不過妳為什麼會想當導遊呢？怎麼不到旅行社工作就好，感覺比較輕鬆。
Celia	I always like to travel leisurely. When I was at high school, I even went **backpacking** in Japan. After I study at university, I realize the work of a tour guide is not just about going abroad and having fun. I even love this profession more after I get this straight.	我從小就很喜歡旅行的悠閒，高中時還一個人到日本自由行。讀大學才知道導遊的工作並不只是出國玩那麼輕鬆，但我明白之後反而更愛導遊這個職業了！
Joshua	What made you say that? Is it because you like to take care of people? I can see that from how you taking care of the baseball team members.	怎麼說呢？是因為妳很喜歡照顧人嗎？這點我從妳平時照顧棒球社員的行為看的出來。
Celia	Perhaps that's why! I think by taking a tour, I can meet people from many different places. Although it's only a few days **journey**, people can develop a relationship like family or friends. I think this **ascribes** to the sense of being open that people have on the trips.	或許是吧！我覺得藉由帶團可以認識許多來自不同地方的人們，雖然只有短短幾天的行程，彼此卻能夠發展出情同家人、朋友的感情。我想這都歸功於旅遊的開放感所賜。

Joshua **Indeed**! We are more or less **mutually interested** with the people we meet in everyday life, so we need to pay attention to many small details after developing a long-term relationship. It's actually the people we meet on traveling we can get along without pressure but with happiness and passion.

的確，平常生活中認識的人彼此之間都或多或少有些利害關係，長期相處下來更要注意許多小細節，反而是在旅行中認識的朋友最熱情，相處起來快樂又沒有壓力。

Celia And I won't be getting tired of seeing everyone's happy expression when I introduce the delicious food, the fun places, and the must-buy things to people.

而且把國外好吃、好玩、好買的東西介紹給大家，看到大家高興的表情，我想不管幾次都看不膩的。

Joshua I will definitely join your **tours** after you become a tour guide!

等妳當上導遊，我一定要參加妳所帶的團！

必會單字一手抓

❶ tour guide n. 嚮導、導遊

The conscienceless tour guide takes the money and leaves the whole tour members high and dry.

那位黑心的導遊收了錢竟然將整團團員丟著不管。

❷ vision n. 美景、幻想、憧憬

Almost every girl all had this vision of marrying her Prince Charming when she was little.
每個女孩小時候的憧憬幾乎都是想嫁給白馬王子。

❸ tiny **adj.** 極小的
That little tiny almost invisible insect bites me.
那隻小到幾乎看不見的蟲子咬了我一口。

❹ ascribe **v.** 把…歸因（於）
The director ascribes the movie's box office hit to luck.
那位導演將電影的賣座歸功於幸運。

❺ indeed **adv.** （加強語氣）真正地、確實
Food in that restaurant is delicious indeed, but it's also very expensive.
那家餐廳的東西固然好吃，但是非常昂貴。

❻ mutually interested **adj.** 有利害關係的
They are two mutually interested relatives, so their testimony in court is not admissible.
他們倆人是有利害關係的親人，因此在法庭上為彼此作的證詞不被採信。

❼ backpacking **n.** 自助旅行
We went backpacking in Spain and had unforgettable memories.
去年我們去西班牙自助旅行並有很難忘的回憶。

❽ journey **n.** 旅程
A trip across the Sahara Desert is a very difficult journey.
橫越薩哈拉沙漠是一趟非常艱辛的旅程。

30 秒會話教室

A friend in need is a friend indeed. 患難見真情。need 在這裡是當作「困境」的意思，因此可以直譯為:困境中的朋友才是真正的朋友。

情境 70 用珍奶征服全世界

會話訓練班

即將臨盆的 Marjorie 除了擔心生產的事情以外，思考更多的是產後的計畫，因為她突然靈機一動，想要在美國賣台灣的珍珠奶茶……

About to **give birth**, Marjorie not only worry about things about the childbirth, she is also thinking more about the **postpartum** plan, because she suddenly flashes on an idea that she wants to sell Taiwanese **bubble** tea in the U. S....

Marjorie Dear, come over here. I have something to tell you.

老公，你快過來，我有事要跟你說。

Albert Honey, what's wrong? Are you going to labor?

親愛的妳怎麼了。要生了嗎？

Marjorie The due day is in the next week! I want to discuss with you about making money after the child is born.

預產期是下個禮拜啦！我是想跟你商量孩子出生以後，我也想要出去賺錢的事。

Albert Making money? Why don't you just stay home and take care of the child? I have the copyright income to support you and the child, you do not need to worry.

工作？妳就乖乖在家帶小孩就好啦，我有版稅的收入可以養妳們母子的，妳不需要著急。

Marjorie	But ... Your income is unstable as a writer, and you don't know how long and how much you can get from the royalties. You listen to my plan first! What do you think selling bubble tea in the U.S.?	可是……你當作家的收入不穩定，這次的版稅不知道可以抽多久、抽多少？你先聽聽看我的計畫嘛！你覺得在美國賣珍珠奶茶怎麼樣？
Albert	Bubble tea? Isn't the hand shaken drink last time we had when we went back to Taiwan to visit your family? The kind of drink you get obsessed? I'm having an **itch to** try it only by hearing it.	珍珠奶茶？不就是上次陪妳回台灣娘家喝的那種手搖飲料嗎？喝了會讓人上癮耶！光聽我就躍躍欲試了！
Marjorie	Oh, yeah, that's right! It'll certainly cause a great **sensation** in the U. S.! We can first use your royalties to open a shop. I don't expect to run it into a **chain**, as long as there is a stable income, and let me take care of the child at the same time, I'll be satisfied.	呵呵，沒錯吧！一定會在美國造成大轟動的！我們可以先用你的版稅開一家小店，我暫時不奢望能經營成連鎖店，只要能有個穩定的收入，並且讓我一邊兼顧帶小孩，我就心滿意足了。
Albert	This is indeed a highly feasible idea! Dear you can really see what others can't see! However, what about the most important ingredient-the **tapioca**?	這的確是個可行性很高的點子！老婆妳真是慧眼獨具！不過最重要的珍珠部分呢？

Marjorie Let me call my parents and ask them now. We just need to prepare some money and directly import it from the place of the origin. I think **source** is absolutely not a problem.

我現在就打電話回娘家問，只要準備一些錢，直接從產地進口，貨源絕對不是問題。

Albert I'm getting more and more excited about this discussion. It is so **ideal** that I can help in the store during the time I don't have to write, and can also drink some good bubble tea.

越討論我越興奮了，以後我不用寫作的時間，還可以去幫忙顧店，又可以喝到好喝的珍珠奶茶，實在是太理想了！

必會單字一手抓

❶ give birth 分娩

The health education teacher shows the students a video of women giving birth.

健康教育老師給學生們看女性分娩的影片。

❷ tapioca n. 樹薯粉、木薯澱粉

The peark of pearl milk tea is made from tapioca starch.

珍珠奶茶裡的「珍珠」是由木薯澱粉製成的。

❸ bubble n. 氣泡

When water boils, many small bubbles rise to the surface.

當水煮開後，水面會冒出許多小氣泡。

❹ obsess v. 迷住、使著迷
She is so obsessed with the new handsome colleague.
她被新來的帥哥同事給迷住了。

❺ sensation n. 轟動、激動
The rumors of the Doomsday once caused much sensation.
世界末日的傳言一度引起了一陣轟動。

❻ chain n. 連鎖店
That convenience store chain has more than thousands of stores in Taiwan.
那家便利超商在全台灣有超過上千家的連鎖店。

❼ source n. 根源、來源
According to the source, it is a high-level supervisor that the company is going to lay off.
公司要裁員的消息來源據說是一位高階主管。

❽ ideal adj. 理想的、完美的
Your suggestion is too ideal, completely without taking the reality into consideration.
你的建議太過理想了，完全沒有考慮到實際面。

❾ itch n. 渴望、慾望
He has an itch to speak to the girl he likes.
他渴望跟自己心儀的女孩說話。

❿ postpartum adj. 產後的
I've heard that many women will get postpartum depression.
聽說有許多女性都會得到產後憂鬱症。

30 秒會話教室

The basketball player caused a great sensation. 那位籃球員造成了極大的效應。This new movie is a blockbuster. 這部電影轟動一時。blockbuster 指的是轟動一時的事物。

好書報報-職場系列

國際化餐飲時代不可不學！
擁有這一本，即刻通往世界各地！

基礎應對 訂位帶位、包場、活動安排、菜色介紹...
前後場管理 服務生Must Know、擺設學問、食物管理...
人事管理 徵聘與訓練、福利升遷、管理者的職責...
狀況處理 客人不滿意、難纏的顧客、部落客評論...

120個餐廳工作情境
100%英語人士的對話用語
循序漸進勤做練習，職場英語一日千里！

作者：Mark Venekamp & Claire Chang
定價：新台幣369元
規格：328頁 / 18K / 雙色印刷 / MP3

這是一本以航空業為背景，
從職員角度出發的航空英語會話工具書。
從職員VS同事 & 職員VS客戶，
兩大角度，呈現100% 原汁原味職場情境！

特別規劃→
以Q&A的方式，英語實習role play
提供更多航空界專業知識的職場補給站
免稅品服務該留意甚麼？ 旅客出境的SOP！
迎賓服務的步驟與重點！違禁品相關規定?！
飛機健檢大作戰有哪些...

作者：Mark Venekamp & Claire Chang
定價：新台幣369元
規格：352頁 / 18K / 雙色印刷 / MP3

Learn Smart! 022

跟著偶像劇番外篇學英文會話

作　　者／伍羚芝
英　　譯／倍斯特編輯部、吳悠嘉
封面設計／高鍾琪
內頁構成／菩薩蠻有限公司

發 行 人／周瑞德
企劃編輯／倍斯特編輯部
印　　製／世和印製企業有限公司
初　　版／2013 年 12 月
定　　價／新台幣 299 元

出　　版／倍斯特出版事業有限公司
電　　話／（02）2351-2007
傳　　真／（02）2351-0887
地　　址／100 台北市中正區福州街1號10 樓之 2
E m a i l ／best.books.service@gmail.com

總 經 銷／商流文化事業有限公司
地　　址／235 新北市中和區中正路752號7樓
電　　話／（02）2228-8841
傳　　真／（02）2228-6939

國家圖書館出版品預行編目(CIP)資料

跟著偶像劇番外篇學英文會話 / 伍羚芝 ；
倍斯特編輯部, 吳悠嘉譯.
— 初版. — 臺北市： 倍斯特, 2013. 12
面； 公分
ISBN 978-986-89739-6-1(平裝)

1. 英語 2. 會話

805.188　　　102023112